Honor Among Thieves
Thieves
A Sam Jenkins Mystery

Wayne Zurl

Published by
Melange Books, LLC
White Bear Lake, MN 55110
www.satinromance.com

Honor Among Thieves ~ Copyright © 2017 by Wayne Zurl

ISBN: 978-1-68046-440-5

Cover Design by Lynsee Lauritsen

*To all the people who might visit Sam Jenkins if he was a real person,
and those no longer able.*

Chapter One

At 9 p.m., Kate and I sat on a loveseat in the living room watching a PBS special on Yellowstone National Park. Just as a small herd of bison began trudging through a soggy meadow in the Lamar River Valley, the phone rang. A county detective named Bo Stallins requested my presence in the morgue at Blount Memorial Hospital.

Twenty minutes later, I parked my unmarked Crown Victoria in one of the police spots near the emergency room entrance. A chill November breeze blew down my neck and caused my open jacket to flutter. As I approached the building, double sliding doors parted like the Red Sea, and I found Stallins leaning against a wall next to the triage nurse's station. The tall man flexed his shoulders and pushed off the tile.

"Hey, Sam, you doin' aw right today?"

"You interrupted an important incident I was handling, but I'll live."

"Shoot, you's probably jest watchin' TV."

"So smart. No wonder you're a detective. What's up?"

He handed me a wrinkled 3x5 card with *Sam Jenkins Prospect Police* and the office phone number written on the face.

"Hey, that's me. What do I win?"

"A thank-you if ya can gimme a name for the dead guy who had this in his pants pocket. Let's take a look."

Not exactly the answer I wanted to hear.

We walked through institutional green hospital halls, took an elevator to the lowest level and adjourned to a dimly lit corner of the morgue. The unmistakable shape of a fairly large body lay on a stainless steel gurney under a sage green sheet.

Stallins and I stood by as a young attendant with a crew cut and long sideburns lifted the sheet to show me a face attached to the body.

1

"Know him?" Bo asked as he unzipped his black leather jacket. An oval Sheriff's Department badge hung on his belt just forward of a Glock .40 caliber pistol.

I took a quick look and nodded. "I'll be damned. Carly Nickels. He's a long way from home. Hasn't aged well."

"Nichols, ya say?" Bo asked. "N-I-C-H-O-L-S?" He spelled it out.

"Not Nichols, Nickles. Like dimes and quarters."

He looked confused. The morgue attendant was busy picking at a hangnail on his left thumb and paid no attention.

"His name's Carlo DeCenzo. They called him Carly Nickels because his old man owned a vending machine company. Carly was the bag man. He collected coins from the machines and restocked them. And he probably did a few not so legitimate things."

"Uh-huh," Bo said. "How long ya known him?"

"I met him a long time ago. It's been twenty-five, thirty years. He was just out of high school when a uniform cop collared him for assault. He almost killed another kid who tried to get fresh with his girlfriend."

"When you worked in New York?"

"Sure. The DeCenzos lived in a community called Mastic Beach. I was the squad dick who handled the arrest."

"He do time for the assault?"

"No, I thought Carlo was justified in using force to terminate the sexual abuse and cut him loose. I told the victim to take it to civil court if he thought the force was excessive. Carlo didn't look like an angel, but the complainant was a shitbag."

Bo raised his eyebrows.

"Witnesses confirmed the girl's story and said Carlo did what he had to do."

Bo still looked a little skeptical.

"It was that kind of neighborhood. And I doubted any witness would want to get on the wrong side of Carlo's old man, Alphonse DeCenzo. He was a *family* man if you know what I'm saying." I used my index finger to push my nose to the side.

Bo looked confused again. Stallins was in his mid-forties and a hair over six-foot. I'd known him for almost four years and had watched his hair turn gray from the job.

2

"Bent noses? Wise guys?" I said. "Organized crime family?"

He nodded. "Don't get much o' that here in Tennessee."

"Yeah. Makes our jobs easier." I took the end of the sheet and pulled it down to Carly's waist. Just below the intersection of autopsy stitches that formed a Y and closed up Carlo's chest cavity, someone had fired two shots into his ten-ring. They looked about nine-millimeter size.

"Ouch." I said. "Now, I suppose you'd like to know who did that?"

"That is why we're standin' here."

"Who found him?"

"Airport police at McGhee-Tyson. In the covered parking structure, second floor. I checked the airlines. He got in on a flight from Islip-MacArthur on Long Island and came in by way o' Charlotte 'round 5:45 tonight. Never picked up his rental car and never checked inta the Country Inn in Alcoa where he had a reservation."

"Safe to assume someone he knew met him?"

"Be my guess. But mebbe a gun in his ribs would make him leave the terminal with a stranger. You think of anything better?"

I shrugged. "If no one witnessed a struggle, I haven't got a clue." I did a little quick math. "Haven't thought about him, much less seen him in eighteen years. Why he's here looking for me is as much a mystery as who kidnapped the Lindberg baby. I remember him, but knew his old man much better."

Turning to the morgue attendant, Bo said, "Thanks, Virgil. We're done here."

The young man nodded, took a bite of cuticle and covered the body.

Bo and I rode the elevator up two floors and walked back to the hospital lobby.

"I got me a feelin'," he said, "there's one o' them New York war stories under yer hat. How's about we get us a cup o' coffee and you tell me what ya know?"

"Sure, but I don't wear a hat. And who drinks hospital coffee? Let's go to Howell's. I'll buy you a beer, and we can talk like civilized gentlemen."

"Works fer me."

A Wednesday night in Prospect, Tennessee is about as busy as Christmas in Tel Aviv. We found only three cars in the parking lot at the pub and four patrons sitting at tables inside. I ordered a pint of black and tan and got Bo a Budweiser. We sat at a small round table near the dart board.

"Okay, young feller," I said, "sit back and listen to something that sounds like the plot of a Martin Scorsese movie."

Bo took a big sip of his Bud, stretched out his long legs and got comfortable.

"Carlo's father is Alphonse 'The Torch' DeCenzo, former contract arsonist and trusted soldier in the Musucci family of New York and New Jersey."

That captured Bo's attention.

"The Torch? Carly Nickels? People really get names like that?"

"Sure. Charlie the Waxer, Tony Big Ears, Louie the Fat Man—who, by the way, was only about a hundred and forty soaking wet. Yeah, everybody gets a nickname. It's part of the culture."

"And this arsonist was a friend o' yours?"

"Not a friend—a cordial acquaintance. He was out of the arson business when we met. Alphonse became a made man in the Musucci organization and got a vending machine territory on Long Island for services rendered." I shrugged. "A step in the right direction, you might say—unless he laundered money through the all-cash machine business."

Bo shifted in his chair and took another long pull on the Bud. "Back to my original question. What's this Carly Nickels got ta do with you?"

"I'm getting there. I doubt *he* has anything to do with me, but his father may."

Bo drank more beer. Two customers picked up their check, called out a good-bye to Reggie, the barman and headed out into the dining room to the cash register.

I downed a bit of black and tan and continued.

"Two local idiots burglarized Alphonse's home, and I caught the squeal. One of the things taken was a carved shell cameo that once belonged to his wife's grandmother. Not a terribly expensive item, worth maybe three hundred and change, but one of the things you don't do, is screw with a goombah's family. Understand?"

"Not really, but I can see yer point."

"Okay. So, I felt sorry for Marie, Al's wife."

4

Another one of the bar patrons picked up and left, and I looked at my watch.

"To get to the bottom of my investigation, I tossed an informant out the window and got a name. And I recovered the brooch, made two collars and after that, The Torch said he'd be eternally grateful."

"Y'all threw somebody out a window ta get information?"

I nodded. "He was a sleazy little paid snitch who was lying to protect a friend. We had to correct a simple quality control problem. And besides, it was split-level, probably no more than ten or twelve feet off the ground. No big deal. He landed in a bush."

"Lord have mercy."

"Anyway, guys like Alphonse have this thing about debts and honor. He said he owed me one, and he knew money or something material was out of the question. Over the years, Alphonse has handed me a few tidbits of info on a few other mooks I should know about. I always thought he was just sticking it to the competition, but I didn't look a gift-horse in the mouth. So, I'm guessing he sent Carly here to tell me something. And someone shot him before he could deliver."

"Any idea what he wanted ta tell ya?"

"No, but I guess I'd better find out."

Chapter Two

The next morning, I dialed a 631 area code and the direct line to the polygraph section of my old job in New York. A young-sounding female detective answered.

"Hi," I said. "My name's Sam Jenkins. I retired from the job up there a long time ago. I'm looking for Vinnie Falcone. Is he working today?"

"You're Sam Jenkins?" She sounded surprised.

I borrowed a line from Hercule Poirot. "There is but one, and I am he."

"Wow, I've heard stories about Lieutenant Sam Jenkins. This is awesome. Vinnie talks about you and the guys in your section all the time."

"Vinnie and I worked together before he got into the lie detector business."

"Yeah, I know. I hear you guys were amazing. Things like you did don't happen anymore. Like, I guess they can't. Yeah, awesome."

"I'm sorry...I didn't catch your name."

"Detective Bedford. Sylvia Bedford."

"When did you get hired, Sylvia?"

"January of 2002, during that big push right after 9/11. Been on almost nine years now."

"2002? God, I feel old. I was retired ten years then."

"Wow, that's like, surreal. You're a police chief now, right?" She didn't wait for an answer. "Somewhere down south?"

"Yeah, Prospect, Tennessee. That's why I'm calling. I need an official favor. Something Vinnie can do for me."

"Oh, awesome. But Vinnie's not here. He comes in tomorrow for his first five-to-one."

"Rats." Complications disturb me, and I needed some information pronto. "Oh, well, I guess another day won't matter. Would you ask Vinnie to call me? He's got my work and home numbers."

"Yeah, sure, Loo, I'll tell him. But, hey, is there anything I can do for you? You need a records check or something?"

"Actually, you could do something for me and make Vinnie's life easier."

"Yeah, sure, name it."

"This is kind of sensitive, so I'd like you to keep it in house. In other words, don't call the DA's Rackets Bureau. I don't want them involved."

"Sure. Okay. I understand," she said.

"See if you can get me current addresses and phone numbers for two people—Alphonse DeCenzo and Gino Musucci, a pair of old-time wise guys."

"Oh, yeah, awesome. I can do that. My boyfriend's father is a sergeant down in Criminal Intelligence."

"What's his name?"

"Pat Herlihy."

"Good God. Pat's still around? He must have more than forty years in now."

"Yeah. I know. He's been here, like, forever."

"Okay, tell Pat it's for me, and it's important. And tell Vinnie to call soon. I miss him."

I gave Sylvia my phone numbers.

"I will," she said. "And it's been amazing meeting you."

"Yeah, Sylvia. Nice talking with you. It's been...*awesome*."

* * * *

I thought I'd have to wait for Vinnie Falcone to track down my pair of aging goombahs before I'd get something remotely like a clue to why Carly DeCenzo had come looking for me. But since my reputation lingered after me, perhaps young Sylvia Bedford would close that gap sooner than I thought.

Then at one o'clock, PO Joey Gillespie, our desk officer, buzzed my phone, and the gap began slamming shut.

"Boss, I got a Mr. Musucci and a Mr. Vito here lookin' ta see ya."

7

In the background, I heard, "No, kid, not Mr. Vito, just Vito. Tell him it's Gino…Gino Musucci. He knows who I am."

I blinked a few times in surprise. "Either one of those gentlemen look like he has a machine gun under his coat?"

I heard Joey swallow. "Do what?"

"Never mind. Send them in."

For decades, Gino Musucci ran a highly successful criminal enterprise from his home and a particular 'social club' in Hoboken, New Jersey. By now, he'd be in his mid-seventies. We never held any animosity toward each other, but it was his son, a dipshit named Anthony, with whom I had a few problems. Anthony ran a franchise of the family business and a restaurant on Long Island, and like many second-generation hoods who watched *The Godfather* as a training film, Anthony decided to call himself Sonny like Don Corleone's offspring. Because he had a pumpkin-sized head, everyone else called him Moonface. Sonny and I didn't like each other.

I always remembered Gino as a polished guy, the perfect gentleman— for a hardcore thug, that is. And he always entered a room like he owned it. My office was no different.

The elder Musucci looked sharp. He had stayed slim, spent at least a hundred dollars on his haircuts, and the average man-on-the-street would have needed a twenty-year mortgage to afford Gino's gray silk suit. Vito was a large specimen, about thirty-something years old with an olive complexion and dark wavy hair, combed straight back. He appeared similar to a slightly overweight grizzly bear wearing a black turtleneck and navy blue blazer.

I stood as Gino walked up to my desk.

"Sam Jenkins, how the hell are ya?" he said. "Still lookin' good. You stayed in shape. A little more gray on top, but you haven't changed."

I couldn't help smiling. "Hello, Gino. It's been a long time. You're looking good yourself."

Without invitation, he sat in one of the guest chairs in front of my desk. Vito remained standing. I dropped into my big swivel chair.

"Yeah, I feel good," he said and looked around my office. "Got yourself a nice gig here. I hear you're happy livin' in the country."

"You hear right. The scenery is breathtaking. The weather's nice, and we've even got a good Italian restaurant nearby."

"I know, I know. I've been talkin' with Nicky. He says hello, by the way. Wants ta know how come you haven't been in lately."

"Why am I not surprised?"

Gino shrugged when I acknowledged Nick Cutrone, owner of The Villa Napoli, an upscale restaurant in nearby Maryville.

Still wondering why the capo of a northeast crime family had wandered into my office only days after a low-level mutt like Carly Nickels got whacked a few miles from beautiful downtown Prospect, I decided to stop the foreplay.

"You came down here to see Cutrone and decided to stop in and say hello for old time's sake?"

"Not exactly."

"I can hardly wait to hear why. We weren't exactly fraternity brothers." He smiled and was about to speak when I added, "Before you explain, introduce your associate."

"You don't know Vito?"

"Vito looks too young. I haven't worked in New York for eighteen years." I moved my eyes to the big man. "How's it goin'?"

He nodded and shifted his weight from one foot to the other, moving his body an inch or two. Vito's blazer appeared expensive, although the wide butt of a high-capacity semiautomatic still made a slight bulge in the well-cut garment.

"You might remember Vito's uncle, Hank DeMaio. He lived out there in your area."

"Sure, I remember Hank. He owned that giant Newfoundland dog. That thing was almost as big as a hippo."

The corner of Vito's mouth raised a sixteenth of an inch. His version of a smile.

"You imagine livin' with that mutt shedding all over the house?" Gino waved a hand dismissively. "Forgetaboutit."

Always the consummate host, I waited a moment and asked, "Would either of you like coffee?"

Gino answered for both. "No thanks. We had lunch at Nicky's place not too long ago. I'm full."

I dipped my head an inch to acknowledge his answer and figured he didn't care if Vito was thirsty or not. "So, to what do I owe the pleasure of your company?"

Gino ran a hand over the side of his gray hair that needed no attention. "I'm here as a courtesy. You know what I'm sayin'?"

Obviously, I had no idea what he was talking about, and apparently, my expression indicated as much.

"Course ya don't. I asked Nicky not to say nothin', and Nicky's a good boy. I stopped in to talk business with ya."

"Business?" I shook my head. "I'm waiting with bated breath, and it's your dime."

Gino laughed. Vito maintained his impression of the sphinx.

"You're hot shit, ya know?" he said. "Always were. Look, let me get ta the point. I'm retirin' from my operation and gettin' outta Jersey. I want a nice quiet place to live in my old age."

My eyes clicked open an extra inch. "In Prospect?"

Chapter Three

Gino shifted abruptly in the chair. "Hey, don't get excited. I said I'm retirin', not just relocatin'. Know what I'm sayin'?"

"I hear you, Gino, but can I believe my ears?"

"Look, man, I'm bein' honest here. I wanna retire. My wife wants me ta retire. My son and the people who want ta step into my shoes want me ta retire. There's handwritin' on the wall. You know what I'm sayin'? I do not want to end up floatin' in the Hudson because my kid and one or two other *gavoons* want my job. Jesus, you retired. Why can't I? Am I right?"

I shook my head in mild disbelief. "And you picked Prospect, Tennessee out of all the places in the world?"

"'Ey, Blount County is on a list of the ten best places to live when you retire. I think Florida sucks. Where the hell should I go? My father's village in Naples?"

"I'll bet the food is good there."

Gino smiled. "Like I said, you're hot shit. Anyways, I'm here. Nicky said I'd love the neighborhood. He's right. I bought ten acres with nice mountain views and rented a place while I have a house built. You okay with that?"

I nodded slowly. "Gino, I've always known you to be a standup guy. You have not committed a crime here, and if the Feds want you, you're their problem. I have no reason to think you're lying to me. So, yeah, I'm okay with that." I looked at Gino's bodyguard. "Vito, can I count on you to be sure he behaves himself?"

Vito's upper lip raised three-sixteenths of an inch. I guess he was uncontrollably amused.

"Now, I've got a question for you." I opened the bottom draw of my desk and took out a bottle of Glenfiddich. "This may take a while, and

11

since you don't want coffee, can I give you a scotch?"

Gino eyed the single-malt and responded first. "You drink good stuff. I won't say no."

"Vito?"

His mouth turned down, and he shook his head imperceptivity. I brought two glasses out of the draw. "Ice? Water?"

Gino said, "If ya got no soda, a little water and a lot o' ice."

I stepped over to the mini 'frig on the side of the room, fixed two drinks and returned to my desk.

I covered the basics about Carlo DeCenzo's death.

"That's a damn shame," Gino said. "Carly was a nice kid. Shit, he's not a kid anymore."

He sipped the whisky and shook his head. I waited.

"He wasn't the brightest bulb on the string of Christmas lights, but he always did what he was told. I got no idea who'd kill 'im."

"Where's Alphonse?" I asked.

"Florida, last I heard. Delray Beach, Boca…some fuckin' place. He quit his business couple years ago. Carly took over the route, but I didn't keep track o' Alphonse."

"Yeah?" Hard to believe.

Gino nodded and took another sip.

We spoke for another fifteen minutes. Gino was always entertaining, but I learned nothing to further my investigation.

He stood to leave. "It's been good seein' ya."

I nodded. "Thanks for the visit."

He put his hand in a front pants pocket and jingled some change. "'Ey, lemme buy you lunch sometime, okay?

I shrugged.

"Come on. No strings attached. I know how you operate. We'll go to Nicky's place. I'll have his kid Tommy make somethin' special."

I nodded. "Okay."

"You like scungil'?"

"Yeah. Fra diavilo."

"No kiddin'? Me too. Good. It's done. That and a little fried calimar' with marinara."

"Deal. I'll get the wine," I said.

"Yeah, good, it's settled, then." I stood up, and we shook hands. "I'll call ya."

I smiled. "Okay, and Gino—if you're not happy with any of your building contractors, talk to them. Don't break their thumbs."

He threw his head back and laughed. "Hot shit! You always could make me laugh."

Gino did an about face and started to walk out. Vito winked and began turning to follow his boss.

"Nice talking to you, Vito."

Chapter Four

Should I believe in coincidence? Hoping to get a leg up on a homicide investigation for another jurisdiction, I started looking for two old gangsters I hadn't seen in over eighteen years. And in less than twenty-four hours, one of them walked into my office. Why?

Gino Musucci claimed to know nothing about the death of Carlo DeCenzo. Without current information on the whereabouts of Alphonse the Torch, I had few alternatives to pursue and help Bo Stallins. Since I couldn't find an Alphonse or Marie DeCenzo listed in the Florida White Pages and nothing under domestic or commercial arsonist in the Yellow Book, I waited patiently for Pat Herlihy's help.

When stymied, I usually stand at our back door and gaze into the parking lot looking for inspiration. On an unseasonably warm, sixty degree, clear and dry day, it was the perfect time to put the top down on my 1967 Austin-Healey and take a drive into the mountains. But I stood at the back door looking toward Hardees where the cars wrapped around the building, the drivers waiting to place an order at the drive-in window and boost their sagging cholesterol levels.

Then a beige VW beetle with a cinnamon-brown cabriolet top pulled into one of the spots marked for police vehicles only. My first impulse was mild annoyance—until I saw the driver.

Former Sergeant Bettye Lambert got out of the car and slammed the door. She slung a purse strap over her shoulder and headed toward the back door of the PD. At the top step, she smiled and walked through the open door I held for her.

"Hey, kiddo," I said, "Damn, but you're looking good."

"Hey yourself, darlin'." She stood on her toes and kissed me on the cheek.

Sixty-six days earlier, Bettye reluctantly resigned from the department. Only days before that, she and her son had been taken hostage by an abhorrent madman who threatened to kill them just to annoy me. That was the second incident since I signed on as chief where her life had been in jeopardy. After this one, her husband asked her to quit. But I didn't accept her resignation. Instead, I put her on ten days of accrued vacation and a sixty-day leave of absence so she could take time to consider her decision.

"Nice wheels," I said. "When did you get that?"

She smiled, took the sunglasses she'd been holding and placed them in her blonde hair, a few inches above her forehead. "Three weeks ago. Like it?"

"You bet. I had a VW convertible once—long ago."

"I know. A '58."

"I told you?"

She nodded.

"And you remembered?"

"'Course I remembered."

Bettye Lambert represented the most perfectly proportioned, forty-six year old cop I'd ever met. From her I learned that a woman five-foot-six in flat shoes came up to my nose, and if I ever wanted to breech my rule of being the perfect supervisor, I would have kissed her on the forehead.

She was wearing a gray, long sleeved Pellissippi State T-shirt tucked into snug blue jeans. Her recently cut natural blonde hair hung just above shoulder length. The brown leather bag hanging on her left shoulder looked like she bought it in a police supply store. I assumed she was carrying her snub-nose revolver in a secret compartment.

"Have you changed the code for the back door yet?" she asked.

"Then you wouldn't know how to get in?"

She tilted her head. "I don't work here anymore."

I shrugged. "You do for four more days."

She fluttered her eyelashes a few times. I think she knows it gets my testosterone flowing. "That's what I want to talk to you about."

I smiled. "Follow me."

We sat in the two saddle leather tan guest chairs in front of my desk facing each other. She didn't want the coffee I offered, and neither did I.

15

"Can I have my job back," she asked, without a hint of shyness.

I crossed my legs, right over left. "I thought Donnie wanted you to terminate your po-leece career."

"I think we're past that."

"Did he say so?"

"I guess."

That wasn't very convincing. "You guess?"

In the lobby, the radio squawked. Officer Bobby John Crockett in unit 507 called in a patrol pickup of an altercation stemming from a parking lot fender bender. Joey Gillespie acknowledged the call and dispatched Junior Huskey to assist. Bettye listened to the transmissions before she continued.

"He said okay. Didn't sound one-hundred-percent happy, but I think everything will be fine."

"He may be okay with you doing the job, but the last I heard, he told you to stay clear of me. He thought I was trouble."

"I think we're past that, too. He knows you saved my life and our son's, and he isn't sure someone else could have done that."

I nodded. "You think this is the right thing to do?"

She took a long moment to respond. "I am not a housewife, Sam Jenkins. I miss the job." She paused again. "Oh, hell, Sammy. I miss you."

I tried to keep a straight face, but couldn't quite pull it off. "I've missed you, too, Betts. The occasional phone call just didn't do it. Losing a partner was traumatic for a guy my age."

She blinked and smiled like a little girl. "So, boss, whaddaya say?"

I frowned, shook my head and tried to appear serious. "Jeez, I don't know. This is a big decision."

She switched her little girl look into one of the sexiest women on the planet and added an extra dose of country to her voice. "Darlin' they's a big plate o' my ol'-fashioned peenut-buttah cookies in it fer ya."

I uncrossed my legs, sat forward and returned the smile. "I may be a tough guy, Goldie Locks, but I'm only a hundred and eighty pounds of Silly Putty in your hands. Welcome back."

She sat forward, almost on the very edge of the chair and slapped my knees. "Have I ever told ya, darlin', how much I love ya?"

"You just did. How about I tell you I love the new haircut. Shorter is very classy. Makes you look sophisticated and younger."

"Well, thank you, sugar. You always know the right things to say."

If only.

"I'm the boss. I know everything."

She laughed. "Am I back on the duty roster?"

"I'll put you there. Take your last four days leave to iron your uniforms."

Bettye stood, slung the purse back on her shoulder and bent down to kiss my forehead. "See ya Monday, Sammy."

* * * *

I used exactly two sentences getting Mayor Ronnie Shields to agree to rehire Bettye.

"That makes sense, don't it, Sam?" he said. "Takin' Bettye back saves us from payin' to train a new officer."

I knew he meant well, but I didn't care for how he phrased that, and I didn't try to mask my lousy attitude. "Saving money and time wasn't paramount in my mind, Ronnie. Bettye represents a lot more than just a body in uniform."

He sensed my annoyance and tried his best to placate me. "I know…I know, Sam. Bettye is a good woman. Always has been. I jest meant—"

I didn't let him finish. "She can run this department as well as I can. You shouldn't forget that. She's worth more than what we pay her."

Ronnie never likes to argue and quickly slips into his politician's mode by grinning and casting a light note into the conversation. "Well, good than. I'm glad she's back. Touch base with payroll, and they'll fix ya right up."

He probably thought I'd ask him to give Bettye a raise.

I nodded and assumed our business was finished. As I pushed myself out of his guest chair, Ronnie broached a new subject.

"Sam, I got a call from my cousin Albert, the building contractor. Says an older feller name o' *Gee-no Ma-soo-chee* is lookin' to build a big home in Prospect. The man asked him what kind o' deal he could get if he paid cash money."

I rolled my eyes and sat down.

"Now, Sam, what kinda man's got cash, not a check, fer a house that's gonna cost seven, eight hunnert thousand dollars?"

17

I nodded. "I know Gino Musucci. He's a New Jersey gangster. He stopped in to talk with me."

Ronnie looked as if I said Johnny Cash was really alive and well and building a music hall in Prospect.

"Musucci says he's retiring from his old life and wants to settle in a quiet place. He says he's afraid that if he stays in business much longer, his son or one of his lieutenants will buy him a one-way ticket to swim with the fishes."

"Swim with the fishes?" He gasped, so I assumed that shocked him. "Ya mean git killed? By his own son?"

"Or some other hood who wants to be boss. Not an unheard-of occurrence. Gino is a realist. I think he's telling the truth. I doubt he'll give us any trouble while he lives here."

"Lord have mercy, Sam. The man's in the Mafia? Ain't there something we can do?"

I shook my head and patiently explained the facts of life to Ronnie. "Not a hell of a lot. Gino's a known criminal, but he isn't wanted for any particular past crime, and he hasn't committed an offense here. Buying a house for cash is unusual, but not illegal."

"Why is he comin' here? Cain't you do somethin'?"

"Like what?"

"Like...I don't know. You used to deal with these people."

"Gino is what we cops and his cronies called a standup guy. He's given me his word he's only here to live a quiet life. An oath is important to guys like Gino. I tend to believe him. If he breaks the law, I'll arrest him and at least cost him money in legal fees. So far, he's only building a house."

Ronnie shook his head in frustration. "Maybe we can put pressure on him...make him uncomfortable."

I shook my head. "Like break his ass with building code violations?"

The mayor nodded vigorously. "That's possible."

"He won't try to cut corners. Gino likes quality. He drives a new Mercedes, not a used Chevy. If the building inspector throws chicken-shit violations at him, he'll call in a platoon of lawyers that would eat City Attorney J. Newcomb Bixby and his team of paralegals alive. Ronnie, the man's got more cash in his glove box than you've got in the city's operating fund."

Ronnie used his right hand to cover his eyes for a moment. "Prospect is not a place for his kind."

"Gimme a break. Prospect is not a place inhabited by people awaiting canonization. Leave him alone until he does something wrong."

Ronnie almost ran a hand through his fiber-glassed hair but stopped before a strand broke free. He settled for again gasping, "Lord have mercy."

Chapter Five

Detective Sergeant Pat Herlihy called bright and early the next morning—with good news and bad news. But first, I told him about finding Gino Musucci.

"Jesus," he said. "Gino's moving to Tennessee? A Neapolitan hillbilly. What's next?"

"That's one accounted for. How about his old goombah?"

"We've had tabs on Alphonse for a few years," he said. "Ever since he bought a place in Jupiter Hills, a big gated community Burt Reynolds built years ago."

That statement surprised me. "That's the place where Jimmy Baxter works as chief of security."

"That's the one. Jimmy was one of your guys, right?"

"Yeah, for about four years."

"He called us with a heads-up."

"Jimmy's a good man."

"Nice he still thinks of us."

"Uh-huh."

"Reason I didn't call sooner," Pat said, "We started getting news about Mr. DeCenzo day before yesterday. Mind if I ask why you're tracking him down?"

I told him the story of the large body lying in the Blount County morgue.

"Interesting," he said. "We picked up an alarm from the Martin County Sheriff. Alphonse was found murdered near Hobe Sound."

"Who has a hard-on for the DeCenzo family?"

"I'd like to know."

"How murdered?" I asked.

"I spoke to a dick we know down there. Looks like a professional job.

At least two shooters. One blew out the passenger's window with number four buckshot. The other put two nine mils in Alphonse's head. The car ended up in a swampy drainage ditch on a lonely stretch of US 1 between a national and state park."

"You're right," I said.

"What?"

"That's interesting. He still driving a shiny black Lincoln?"

Pat chuckled. "Ah, glad you asked. How about a funky yellow '89 Sunfire?"

"You're kidding."

"I thought that would get a rise."

"Alphonse DeCenzo wouldn't be caught dead—" I stopped myself. "Bad choice of words. He never drove anything but a Lincoln in his life. New one every three years."

"Exactly. This Martin County dick, a guy named Elvis Rafferty, said Alphonse picked up that little Pontiac from a used car dealer in Stewart the day before he died. Paid cash. His MK-S was sitting at home, in a locked garage when he bought the farm."

"Elvis Rafferty?"

"You can't make this stuff up."

* * * *

I called Jimmy Baxter.

"Hey, Sambo. What's goin' on?"

I explained.

"Yeah, I saw that in the paper and on TV. Some shit, huh? You knew him pretty good, didn't you?"

"Yeah, for a long time."

Then I asked Jimmy to do me a professional favor.

"Sure, boss," he said, "I'll go and see Marie, offer my condolences on two counts and ask if she knows anything. In case she asks, when do you think your locals will release Carlo's body?"

"Beats me. Tell her I'll call you as soon as the Blount County dick tells me. He'll appreciate the help finding a next-of-kin for Carlo."

"Okay, I'll call with what I find out. Cool, huh? We're working together again."

21

"Yeah, Jimmy. Just like the old days. Thanks for your help."

* * * *

Bo Stallins called at 11:30 and ruined my lunch.

"Sam, I want ya ta unnerstand, this ain't me."

I waited for a punch line.

"The sheriff called, told me ta drop this Carlo DeCenzo thing on Internal Affairs."

"What?"

"He said 'cause your name was found on the victim, he wanted IA to investigate ya."

Chapter Six

Tennessee isn't New York. At Prospect PD, I had no Superior Officer's Association delegate to consult with. No bargaining unit to look out for me. No legal fund paid for through my union to pick up an attorney's fee.

After hanging up on Bo Stallins, I called Joe Costello, the best lawyer around. With a quick explanation, he bit the hook. I'd speak with the sheriff's IA investigator on a limited basis. If I didn't like what he said, I'd lawyer up. If the criminals can do it, so could I.

* * * *

The Blount County Justice Center sits on US 321 in front of the ugliest jail in the world and across the highway from Blount Memorial Hospital. The Internal Affairs Bureau is on the second floor of the Justice Center.

One receptionist handled the entire administrative division. She buzzed a Captain Burchfield and sent me heading in his direction. I found the windowless ten-by-ten office with an appropriately marked door and knocked on the jamb. A young man with a blond crew cut and wispy mustache sat behind a typical gray metal desk. A matching armchair stood in front of the desk and a battered side chair on the left flank. Captain Burchfield didn't look old enough to legally own a handgun. Not a good start.

The blond looked up from a report he wanted me to believe he was casually reading and introduced himself.

"Captain Burchfield. Have a seat."

No first name and he didn't offer to shake hands. Strike two. He pointed to the armless side chair close to him. I took the one in front of his desk and pushed it back a foot. The name plate sitting on the front edge of the desk said Rodney Burchfield, Jr. He got right down to business.

"A card with your name and phone number was found on the dead body of one Carlo DeCenzo."

He made it sound like five names: Car-lo De-Cen-Zo. And he didn't use the Italian pronunciation of *DeChenzo*.

"I know that," I said.

"Why?"

"Beats the hell outta me." *And grow a proper mustache, sonny.*

"You expect me to believe that?"

He wore a blue and white striped short-sleeve shirt and a dark blue tie with white polka dots. The four-in-hand knot sat off center to the right of a collar an inch or two larger than Rodney's neck. I assumed that his mother hadn't checked his appearance that morning when she sent him off to work.

Okay, that's it, I thought. "Has anyone ever told you, Rodney, you've got a lousy bedside manner?"

He scowled and sat back in his chair. I crossed my legs and settled in for a battle of words.

"What's that supposed ta mean?" He sounded offended.

"You ain't seen nuthin' yet, sport."

When I get annoyed, my Nu Yawk accent really shines.

"I'm lookin' for some he'p here…a little professional courtesy," he said.

"Yeah, right. And all I want for Christmas is my two front teeth."

"Lord have mercy, man. You've got to talk to me."

"You obviously have no idea how to interview a subject or suspect or potential witness. As far as detectives go, you remind me of something we used to say back in New York."

He scowled again, perhaps trying to look mean and formidable. "What's that?"

"You couldn't find a Jew in the Bronx."

I doubted he knew where the Bronx was, and there was only a slight chance he'd ever met someone of the Jewish persuasion, but his tiny faded blue eyes bugged out a little.

"I wanna know about your involvement with this."

"I have no involvement with it. Have you spoken to Detective Stallins?"

"I'll ask the questions here."

"I like Bo Stallins. He's a good cop. I'm attempting to assist him with his investigation. You have offended me. You can kiss my ass."

He remained silent for a long moment. Burchfield was too young and too small to look tough or menacing. He appeared annoyed and petulant.

"De-Cen-zo was killed with two nine millimeter rounds fired from a Glock. You own a Glock 19."

"So do half the cops in the world and the entire Austrian Army."

His nose twitched, and he did some stupid thing with his mouth trying to look angrier.

"I want to test fire your gun. See if I can get a ballistics match to the bullets that killed De-Cen-zo."

I shook my head. "Rodney Junior, you are such an asshole. Why didn't you just ask?"

He looked surprised and annoyed, but didn't object to being called names. So, I gave him a lesson in good police work.

"Let me tell you something about a successful murder, son. If I wanted to snuff Carly Nickels, and I have no reason to do that, I wouldn't use my registered gun. I also wouldn't use an automatic and run the risk of the ejected shell going missing, perhaps later to be found by a sharp evidence technician. But that's only me. I'd use a revolver so there'd be no brass to pick up, understand? I'd be a smart killer, 'cause I've been around—lots."

I heard my voice getting louder and angrier.

"I'd buy an unregistered revolver out of someone's trunk at a local gun show or flea market. For cash. Wrinkled twenties. No questions. No paper. And I'd use something bigger than a .38 or nine mil. Carly was a big guy. I wouldn't want to get within arm's length, but I'd want to punch his ticket with only one shot. I'd use what? Personal preference, a .41 magnum loaded with Winchester hollow points. So, as far as I'm concerned, your theory of me as your killer stinks."

He made a face, frowning and doing the lip thing again, looking even more petulant. I considered him as popular as amoebic dysentery.

"Rodney," I continued, "being an imbecile, you probably never reasoned it out yourself, but your theory of a cop being the shooter has merit. Know why?"

He switched his look from annoyed and offended to clueless. I didn't give him a chance to make an inane comment.

"Of course you don't. You're not much of a cop. Okay, let's look at assassinations by mob professionals. Generally, the hit man, sorry, I'm being politically incorrect, hit person, probably knows the victim or poses no threat and gets up close and personal without a hassle. Many good pros use a .22 caliber weapon. It's often small and concealable, has a relatively low report and no recoil, and one behind the ear will do in the biggest guy immediately or at least render him incapacitated until he dies. A couple of nine millimeters in the heart from further than point blank range shows a familiarity with the weapon and use of a probable service gun. It's not a sure thing, but I'd keep an open mind on that one."

"You gonna surrender your gun?"

That wasn't the response to my lecture I expected.

"You got a court order for that or a warrant to search my home or work place?"

He dropped his eyes and hesitated. *Bad move. Never let them see you sweat.*

He sucked on his bottom lip for a few seconds. "No."

"Remember what I said about kissing my ass?"

He said nothing.

"You gonna arrest me?" I asked.

"No."

"Okay, tell ya what, Rodney. I won't give you my gun because I like you as much as a dead skunk. I don't want you treating me like a defendant and scratching your initials on the slide or replacing the barrel for some ungodly reason. I say that because I believe your investigation of me is suspicious. There is not one fact that points to me as a possible shooter. Grab a law book and look up *probable cause to believe*. I won't ask who put you up to this because you'd only lie."

Rodney wrinkled his eyebrows. "You are one insolent sum'bich."

"Yes, I can be, and you are getting dangerously close to losing a few teeth. But I'll tell you what. Since I rarely carry my Glock, I'll pick it up at home and hand-deliver it to the TBI lab in Knoxville. When they finish their test, I'll have them send a report to Detective Stallins. Like that idea?"

He shifted in his seat like he wanted to pass gas. "When?"

"When I get damn good and ready."

I stood abruptly.

"You have ta—"

"Shut up, you little piss ant. I do not work for you."

I took a step to the edge of his desk and leaned over. "I've known your type all my life. You look for a job in the rat squad because you're not smart enough to catch criminals. That's great. Use your talents to follow patrol cops and catch them taking a free cup o' coffee."

He leaned back to give us more space. "There's no reason—"

"I said shut up. The next time you want to speak to me, call my attorney, Joseph Costello. He's in the Yellow Pages."

"Your contract says you have to give me a statement."

"You're right. I'll send you one in the mail. Be happy about that because if I ever see you again, I'll slap the shit out of you and toss your scrawny ass out the window."

"Don't threaten me."

"Screw you. That wasn't a threat. It was a promise. Here's another one. I'm going to learn who recruited you for this witch hunt and make everything blow up in your faces. Next time you're at the water cooler, sonny boy, ask what happened to the last IA captain who falsely accused me and my cops of something." I turned and left.

In the hallway, Bo Stallins stood talking with another detective. He stopped abruptly and spoke to me. "Sam, I jest wanna say—"

"Save it, Bo. I have no problem with you. Little Rodney and I just had a friendly chat. Now, I'm heading to Howell's for lunch and a couple beers. Wanna come?"

* * * *

After lunch, I returned to the PD and thought about just letting my head explode. It would have made the next few days much simpler.

I had no information that would lead me to the killer of Carly Nickels. It was becoming apparent that if I wanted to shove the internal investigation where the sun didn't shine on Rodney Junior, I'd have to lead Bo Stallins to the killer or lock him up myself. But for all I knew, the gunslinger wasn't even in Tennessee any longer. And my entire investigation depended on other people. Two pints of Bass ale did nothing to smooth me over, and I had no interest in doing anything for the remaining couple hours at work except gobble up a half dozen Advil and attempt to exorcize the tension headache caused by Captain Rodney Burchfield, boy wonder.

While Joey Gillespie took lunch, I picked up the phones, growled at the callers and dispatched cars to motor vehicle accidents, first aid cases and a real heavy—verify the return of a stolen bicycle. I waited impatiently for a cat-in-the-tree call. I really needed Bettye back at work.

Joey returned to the office at 2 p.m. I traipsed back into my room to plot how I'd kill my new nemesis, Rodney Burchfield Jr.

At 2:20, my phone rang.

Joey said, "Boss, a Miss Foster is... Uh, ma'am, please don't—"

I dropped the phone onto the cradle and stood up. A moment later...

"Hello, Sam."

My eyes popped open like a 'possum caught in the headlights of a speeding car. "Dixie."

She stood framed by my doorway, purse strap over her shoulder, right hand on her hip. After all the years, she still looked lovely. A face that would make Helen of Troy jealous, red hair to her shoulders, a knee-length green dress above tan suede boots, and a seductive smile I first saw in 1972.

"Good to see you, tough guy."

In the front office, the radio squelched. Joey sent Officer Billy Puckett to handle a report of criminal mischief at the Prospect Middle School.

I stepped from behind my desk feeling awkward. What do you say to the woman for whom you almost left your wife?

Chapter Seven

"Good to see you, too," was the best I could come up with.

I stood there like a kid on a first date, afraid to make a move.

She just kept smiling, and my knees were turning to rubber.

"It's been eighteen years." She sounded a little impatient. "You think I could get a hug?"

I blinked a few times. "Yeah, sure." The suave, clever remarks weren't exactly rolling off my tongue.

I put my arms around her, and she reciprocated.

"I've missed you, Sam."

"Me, too. I think about you a lot."

She put her hand on my neck, ran her fingers up through the back of my hair and planted a long kiss on my lips.

The last time I saw Dixie Foster, we closed up the restaurant where they held my retirement dinner. I did some quick thinking and remembered that she had turned sixty last April. She looked much younger.

She finished kissing me, and after coming up for air, I said. "April 10th, 1992."

We let go of each other, and Dixie grasped my two hands. "I remember."

"At two in the morning, they invited us to leave the barroom at The Harbor House. We were the last people there."

"We were always the last two to leave a party," she said.

"Bad habits."

Her gray-green eyes twinkled. "You were never as bad as I wanted you to be."

I almost choked on my Adam's apple.

"So, uh, tell me how you ended up in Prospect," I asked.

Her smile intensified. "You just changed the subject."

"Yeah?"

"Chicken."

I chuckled. "You bet."

I turned two guest chairs to face each other.

"Sit down," I said.

We did, and I asked for an answer to my last question.

"Came to see you. Eighteen years is too long."

"I've missed you."

"You've already said that."

"Yeah?" *Sam Jenkins middle-aged nitwit.*

She nodded. "You remember my mom came from Memphis." It wasn't a question.

I nodded. "How's she doing?"

She hesitated for a heartbeat. "Passed away two years ago."

I touched her hand. "I'm sorry."

Dixie shrugged. "Thanks. She had so many problems."

After a long moment, she continued. "About six years ago, my aunt Faith moved from Memphis to a retirement community in Crossville. Last month, she checked into a nursing home. Now that Mom and Dad are gone, she's all I've got left. I wanted to see her before—"

"And you stopped along the way."

"Yes. I mustered up the courage."

"A wise man would say this isn't good for either one of us...but I'm glad you did."

"Yes." She paused for another brief moment. "I saw Vinnie Falcone at the Detective's Association picnic. He told me about doing polygraph work for you and all about your big case."

"Vinnie was a big help. You still at the DA's office?"

"Still there. I got promoted. I'm his administrative assistant now."

"I'm impressed. You're making as much as a cop."

"The money's nice, but expenses on the Island are out of sight."

"So I hear."

"Vinnie said John Gallagher works for you."

"Right. He should be coming in soon. He's on the road doing a background investigation for a civilian employee."

"Still the same old John?"

"Impossible to change him."

Dixie paused and looked like she wanted to say something, but didn't know how.

I offered a gentle prompt. "What?"

"Sam, I didn't come alone."

"Oh?"

She hesitated. "Greg wanted to come."

There could be only one Greg she might be shy about mentioning.

"Greg Buggarelli?"

She nodded. I did nothing to hide my displeasure.

"He wanted to see you."

I made a face. "Lucky me."

She gave me a look dripping with disappointment. "Oh, Sam." She shook her head. "Are you still holding a grudge?"

I didn't answer. Dixie let out a sigh.

I snorted. "He always had the hots for you. Are you two together now?"

"No." She shook her head. "Greg is still married."

"Explain."

"Do I have to?" She frowned, and a look of impatience changed her face.

"Up to you."

She shook her head in frustration. "He's along for the ride. He really wanted to see you."

Big deal.

"Where is he now?"

"I didn't think we should come in here together right away. He's putting gas in my car and checking into the motel."

"The motel?"

She clenched her teeth. "We have separate rooms."

"Uh-huh."

"Damn it, Sam, I don't sleep around. Never did."

"I remember."

I'm not a certified expert on body language, but it looked like Dixie was getting mad at me.

"I can't count how many opportunities *you* missed," she said. "I don't sleep with married men, but you were different. I would have made an exception."

"Please don't, Dix."

She looked like she wanted to hit me. "Sam, when I kissed you good-bye all those years ago, I never took a minute to explain something."

"You don't owe me any explanations."

Her face showed more stress and frustration than I anticipated. "You are such a fool. I need to say this for me."

I shrugged. "Sure."

"I broke the rules of fair play, Sam. When you and Kate were having problems, I tried to take you from her."

I closed my eyes and remembered those days.

"That's not something you have to apologize for," I said. "No one made me say I love you."

She sat forward and put her hands on my knees. "I know. And I've never forgotten that."

"But you were the smart one. You never said that to me."

She sat back quickly. "Oh, for God's sake. You'd have to be blind not to see I loved you."

"Maybe I would have liked to hear it."

Did I just sound like a little boy?

"Sam, you idiot. Why wouldn't I fall in love with you? When we worked in the squad, you treated me like a princess. If I typed a big case for you, you bought me flowers, took me to lunch, or—" She stopped, her shoulders dropped, and she looked exhausted.

"I just thought you deserved something nice," I said. "All you did was extra work. You had a whole squad of guys to deal with, and you helped me a lot."

She smiled. "Because your handwriting looks like Chinese and you spell like a foreigner?"

I felt an old familiar embarrassment come over me. "Yeah, I guess. You were a good secretary."

"Oh, Sam." She shook her head. "How many years did we spend going to lunches, Association picnics and who knows what else?"

"I know. Even after Kate and I ironed out the problems. I shouldn't have. I didn't want to lead you on."

She slapped my leg. "Nonsense. I didn't discourage you. If you had asked me to make love to you, I would have had my clothes off before you could say—" Dixie smiled and shook her head. "I'll open the wine."

"And if I did, what would you have thought?"

"Sam, sweetheart, I didn't say it with words, but I invited you."

"If I cheated on my wife, maybe even left her for you, how could you ever trust me not to cheat on you?"

Moments went by, and she didn't answer.

"Well?" I said. "Falling in love happens. It's involuntary, like catching a cold. My fault for being susceptible. I should have taken more vitamins. And your fault for being beautiful and treating me so nicely when I had a problem. Somehow, I don't see those actions as sinful."

"Oh, my sweet Sam." She leaned forward and touched my cheek. "I shouldn't have come."

I took a turn shaking my head. "Don't be silly. I'm happy to see you." Then my evil twin took over and couldn't keep his mouth shut. "Maybe you shouldn't have brought Greg."

Dixie sighed. "Sam, You two used to be good friends. Now it sounds like you'd like to cut out his heart."

Ya think, Dixie?

"He offended me," I said. "Greg should have known better, and he's never apologized. Screw him."

"Tell me again why you're offended." She sounded like a mother trying to iron out her little boy's problem.

"You know damn well what he did. He called me into Internal Affairs and accused me of trying to shake you down for sex."

"Sam, my love…he made a mistake. He got his signals crossed and thought he was looking out for me. Please forgive him."

"Nuts! He should have asked you first. He knew me. I don't do things like that."

"I know that, but he received bad information and *didn't* call me first. He let his imagination run away with him. Greg knows he was wrong. I told him, and there's no reason to rehash the whole thing. It was a big misunderstanding. Please, Sam, for me?"

"Dixie, that's not fair. You know I'd gallop into hell for you. What about him?"

"You want an apology?"

I shrugged.

"Sam, they make movies about the kind of things you've done with your life. You're acting like a child."

I saw her point and laughed silently. "Am not."

She laughed. "See why I love you? Underneath that big handsome guy is nothing but a silly little boy."

"There, you said it. Now I'm happy."

"Is that all you needed?"

I shrugged, and the silly little boy answered. "I don't know."

She shook her head and looked like she wanted to smack me. "How did I thank you after you'd take me out for a lunch?"

"You said thanks and gave me a kiss."

"I didn't just kiss you, stupid. I threw my arms around you and stuck my tongue half way down your throat. Didn't that say love?"

"Since you put it that way."

"I've never stopped wanting you, Sam. And I never found anyone else."

That sounded bad. My smile faded. "I'm sorry."

Hers didn't. "Me, too."

I've felt mixed emotions in my life, but this was like watching my mother-in-law drive over a cliff in my new Maseratti.

Finally, I chuckled. "Dix, I'm really glad to see you…but you make me feel like crap."

She laughed again. Her full lips parted, and the little smile lines at the corners of her eyes added to her beauty. "Don't," she said, "we're too old. I should have come sooner."

"Yeah, well—"

"Hey, I've been here all this time and you haven't given me a chance to say how good you look."

"Thanks," I said.

"Without the gray hair, you'd look forty."

My turn to smile again. "You're crazy. You're the good-looking one."

"And you never stopped telling me that."

That made me feel sad. I took a deep breath. "I've wanted to send you birthday cards, tell you things, but…I didn't think it would be good for anyone. Sorry."

"You're right. It wouldn't have allowed us to get on with our lives. But I always thought about you."

"I know the feeling—every time I use the gold pen you gave me when I made sergeant."

"You still have it?"

"Guard it with my life."

"You were always easy to please."

"From the first day we met."

I saw a truckload of nostalgia in her smile. "I first saw you when I was a kid working at the academy. Recruit Jenkins came marching into the office, looking for something. Love at first sight. Then years later, when we worked at the squad, and after that, at main office, you were always my hero."

Suddenly, my eyes were in danger of leaking. "Dixie, I don't know what to say."

"I know. Let's stop, okay?"

I tried to relax and only sagged in my chair. "Okay. Tell me what you've got planned."

Chapter Eight

Dixie didn't get a chance to answer before Joey Gillespie knocked on the jamb of my door.

"Boss, there's a gennelman here ta see ya."

Former Detective Sergeant Greg Buggarelli stepped around Joey and into my room all smiles. Dixie and I stood, and Joey retreated to the desk.

"Sam, how are ya?" Greg always acted like a politician: big smiles, white teeth and lotsa bullshit.

He thrust out his hand and, as I extended mine, grabbed my shoulder and gave it a friendly squeeze.

"Greg," I said. "It's been a long time."

I didn't scowl, but don't remember beaming.

He had aged. His dark wavy hair had thinned on top and grayed at the sides. His waist had thickened, and his face had softened, but he was still a good-looking guy—if you like the swarthy Mediterranean type.

"Yeah, it has," he said. "I'm sorry you never got a chance to answer my letter."

Did he sprinkle a little subtle sarcasm on that statement?

I tried to act shocked. "Your letter? Never received it. Must have gotten lost in the mail." I crossed my fingers, so it wasn't really a lie. "When did you send it?"

"Years ago. Right after you left New York. Ginny in Personnel gave me your new address."

"That's a shame."

I'm sure Dixie didn't believe a word I said, and I didn't care if Greg did.

"Dixie tell you that after I retired, I took a per diem job as an investigator in the DA's office?" He sounded proud of himself. "In the

36

Rackets Bureau."

"No, not yet. We were still talking about what she's done in the last eighteen years."

Dixie added. "I was just about to ask Sam about his new job."

Greg nodded and took a quick look around my office. "Yeah, nice setup ya got here. Like being the chief in a *little* department?"

I thought he put too much emphasis on *little*, but maybe that was just me.

I smiled. "Certainly do. Couldn't be happier. I run the entire show, and they pay me a ridiculous amount of money." *So there.*

Then Dixie stepped in before her boys got carried away. "Tomorrow I'm driving to Crossville, so I expect you two can do all your catching up then. But, Sam, I'd like to hear how you got this job."

We sat in a circle, drinking coffee and talking for almost thirty minutes before John Gallagher arrived. He waddled into my room in his usual intrusive manner.

"Hi, Boss," he said. "I see you got company. Don't mind me. Just gettin' a cup o' coffee." It took him a few seconds to recognize my guests. "Oh hi, Dixie. Hi, Sarge. Long time no see. What are you two doin' here?" John sounded like he had seen them only last week. I wanted to smack him.

John monopolized the conversation for more than his share of time, and then Sergeant Stan Rose paid us a visit. The introductions took up a little more time.

At four o'clock, Dixie and Greg invited me to dinner.

"I'd love to, but I've got other plans. Kate is getting an award at the library tonight, and I'd like to see her receive the certificate."

"Gentlemen," Dixie said, "Tomorrow I'm leaving early and won't be back until late, but how about the next day? Can we get together?"

"I'll show you around," I said. "Maybe take a tour of the national park. We can talk and look at the scenery."

"I'd like that," Dixie said.

Greg agreed and asked a question, "Got a few minutes for me tomorrow, Sam?"

I had an idea what he wanted and would have loved to avoid it, but, schlep that I am, I agreed. "I've got to take something to the TBI lab in Knoxville in the morning. Want to ride along? We can go and grab some lunch before I help a county dick with an investigation."

"Sounds good," he said. "Can you pick me up in room 118 at the Foothills View Motel?"

"Nine-thirty?"

"I'll be ready. And will you steer me to a place I can rent a car while Dixie's away for the day?"

"John can take care of that for you and have it here for when we get back. Tell him what you're looking for."

"Just something small to get around in."

"Where will you be going?"

"I don't want to monopolize your entire day. I'll just take a drive around and see you when Dixie gets back."

"Sure. Will you handle that, John?"

"I'll make a few calls, Sarge," John said, "and get you a good deal."

After Dixie and Greg left, John and Stanley hung around to annoy me.

"Good-looking woman," Stan said.

I nodded. "She is."

"You shoulda seen her twenty or thirty years ago. Right, Boss?" John didn't allow me to respond, so I nodded while he kept rolling along. "Last I remember, she was the deputy commissioner's secretary," Gallagher said. "And she used to be sweet on the Boss back then. Right, Boss?"

John looks like an overweight leprechaun when he tries to be humorous. I showed him something between a smile and a sneer.

"And the Boss liked her, too."

"Hey, John, you have a death wish or something?"

Stanley waited patiently with a monster grin spanning his face.

"You know, Sarge, a lot of girls at headquarters liked the Boss back then. He was good-looking, and because he never had any kids, they knew he always had money. But he never treated them as nice as Dixie. Right, Boss?'

"What part of *I might shoot your ass* don't you understand, you Irish nincompoop?"

"See how sensitive he gets, Sarge? It must be true."

Then Stanley took a turn. "Besides your wife, just how many women have you been in love with?"

"Just another dump on Sam day at Prospect PD? Now I know why so many civilians hate cops. You guys are a real comfort."

"Boss, you can't mean that," John barely kept from doubling over laughing.

"I'm glad Bettye's coming back. She doesn't harass me like you two goons."

They left my office snickering, and I had a half hour before I'd go home.

I sat behind my desk and thought how I wasn't looking forward to hearing Greg Buggarelli's rationalizations in the morning. But I might accept an apology. Maybe.

Chapter Nine

I walked into the PD at quarter to nine the next morning and headed directly to my office. Over my shoulder, I said, "Hey, Joey, how's it going?" but didn't wait for a response.

Before I hung my jacket, Officer Gillespie rang my phone. Moments later, I met Alvie Greenblatt who had been waiting in the lobby since eight o'clock. He was a slight man, no more than five-and-a-half feet tall with thinning red hair and horn-rimmed glasses. Alvie made Woody Allen look like a lumberjack. He wore a wrinkled black three-button suit and narrow purple tie—straight out of the 1960s. Alvie Greenblatt looked as out of fashion as a handlebar mustache.

He stood in front of my desk fidgeting and wringing his fingers like a Jewish version of Lady Macbeth.

"Are you Sam Jenkins?" he asked. "Formerly of *Long-guy-land*?" He spoke like Woody Allen, not Mrs. Macbeth.

After he quit strangling his fingers, he pulled a business card out of his jacket pocket and managed to smile with a pair of twitching lips. He waited for my response.

Alvie didn't seem like a bad guy, but I thought he may have wanted to serve a subpoena. Since I've never worried about a paternity suit, I figured, 'What the hell?'

"I am he." I offered that with an almost imperceptible bow.

He relaxed and grinned at his victory. "Ah, I thought so. You sound like Nu Yawk."

"You, too. Brooklyn?"

His eyes widened. "How did you know?"

"Good ears. Brighton Beach?"

He spread his hands to the side, perhaps in awe. "My God, you're

40

good. I'm amazed." He pushed his glasses up with the middle finger of his right hand.

Alvie spoke with more hand gestures than someone relaying a conversation in sign language.

"What did you want, Mr. Greenblatt?"

"Here." He handed me the business card. "I represent these people and have something for you."

I read the card. "Sheinbaum, McCluskey, and Clancy?" An unlikely trio. "What kind of law do they practice?"

"Eh." He shrugged. "A general practice. In Stewart, Florida."

"I see. What do they want with me? Are you an attorney?"

"I'm a private investigator. Licensed and bonded, I'll have you know. I've brought a document for you."

"A document? You've just lost me. I don't know anyone from Stewart."

"We believe you were acquainted with one Alphonse DeCenzo."

"Hmmm. Alphonse the Torch."

"Heh, heh, heh." He said that; he didn't laugh. "That's very colorful. I never met the man, but Mr. McCluskey represents...Uh, did represent Mr. DeCenzo who left an envelope he wanted delivered to you if anything *happened* to him."

Wasn't this interesting?

"I understand he died recently," I said. "When was this envelope given to your employer?"

"Ah, an important question. Two days before your Mr. DeCenzo was... Uh, died."

I raised my eyebrows. "Aha."

"Yes, aha. Interesting?"

"Very."

Alvie may have appeared simple and grinned like a court jester, but looks can be deceiving. That little operator had shrewd eyes and the quick fingers of a pickpocket.

"Do you want the envelope?"

"No."

"Whaattt?" Alvie looked shocked.

"Of course I want it."

"Oh. Heh, heh. You're funny. Very good. You got me there."

The odd little bird deftly extracted a sealed, legal-sized envelope from his inside jacket pocket and handed it across my desk.

"What does it say?" I asked.

Alvie shrugged. "I haven't read it. Not my business."

I nodded. "Do you need me to sign for it?"

He nodded. "Ah. I almost forgot. Yes. Thank you. You're a gentleman. And I say that with all sincerity."

He plucked a well-worn receipt book, roughly the size of a thick dollar bill, from his side pocket and began patting himself down for a pen. I took one from my shirt pocket and handed it across the desk.

"May I sit?" he asked, already half way toward the seat of one of my guest chairs.

"Please."

He finished filling in the blanks on the small page, hopped up and handed the pen and book to me. I read, signed, pocketed the pen and returned the book to Alvie who in turn ripped out the yellow second copy and handed it back.

"For your records," he said. "Always good to know what you signed. And see?" He pointed to a spot on his copy of the receipt. "My initials in the corner."

I smiled at his efficiency.

"Did you drive up from Stewart?"

"I flew," he said, as if I should have known. "You have a nice airport here. In a motel off Alcoa Highway I stayed last night. I get points. Frequent guest. I travel a lot. A rental car I'm using. It's not much, but you weren't far away."

Too much information, Alvie.

"Is your Mr. McCluskey handling DeCenzo's estate?"

"He is, but you're not named in the will."

"I didn't think so."

"Ah." He started messing with his fingers again.

"If I have questions about this document, may I use the number on your card to call Mr. McCluskey?"

"Uh, yes and no."

I tilted my head at that one.

"I mean, yes, you may call," he said, "but Mr. McCluskey didn't prepare or notarize the document. He only held the sealed envelope per Mr. DeCenzo's instructions."

"Okay. Thank you then."

"Ah, yes. Thank you very much." He stretched out the last word like a rubber band.

Alvie Greenblatt extended a hand across my desk. I shook it. It felt as clammy as a dead squid.

He repeated himself. "Thank you very muchhh."

He didn't move.

I smiled. "Have a safe trip."

Still no movement. *Was he waiting for a tip?*

"Nice meeting you," he said. "Nu Yawk? Ha. Small world."

I grinned. He shrugged.

Alvie turned and left. Joey Gillespie forwarded a call to my phone. Earl Biggins, the city mechanic, reminded me that I was again late with my monthly vehicle reports. We chatted for a few moments. I hung up and checked my watch. 9:25. I pocketed the envelope Alvie Greenblatt had given me and left to pick up Greg Buggarelli.

Chapter Ten

The weather remained perfect—clear blue sky, liberally smattered with high altitude cumulus clouds that looked like giant raw cotton balls— a cool fifty-five degrees with no breeze—exactly right for wearing a sport jacket.

I accelerated up the sloping strip of blacktop leading to the Foothills View Motel with the twin exhausts of the Crown Victoria gurgling like the pipes in an old Brooklyn apartment. I parked in one of the vacant spots near room 118 and beeped the horn.

After two minutes, still no Greg. I gave the horn another tap, took Alvie Greenblatt's envelope from my inside jacket pocket and used my pocket knife to slice it open.

The single sheet of high quality bond paper held a simple message.

You've always been a standup guy, and I'm guessing this will be the last time I can do something to repay the kindness you showed me and my wife years ago.

They told me my son died on his way to see you. Catch the bastard who did that. For Marie.

Someone wants you dead. I wish I could give you more information, but all I've heard is look at your friends as well as your enemies.

Alphonse

It might have been my imagination, but I thought the temperature just dropped a little as a cold chill worked its way up my spine. I thought: *Like I need this at my age.*

I stuck the letter back into my pocket and realized that Greg still wasn't out.

I slammed the car door with more force than necessary, stepped quickly to the door of number 118 and pounded three times.

No answer. But a sliver of light showed between the closed drapes on the front window, half of which had been pushed open to the side. I put my face near the screen and yelled, "Let's shake it up, Greg."

Still no response, so I slammed my fist against the door again, making a lot of noise in case he was in the bathroom.

A man on the balcony directly above called out, "Is there a problem down there?"

I stepped off the concrete strip and looked up to find him hanging over the railing. After showing him my badge I said, "I'm looking for someone. Sorry to bother you."

He nodded and withdrew. I knocked a third time. Having no luck, I walked to the office and found manager Clay Plemmons behind the reception counter.

"Mornin', Chief," he said. "You doin' aw right today?"

"So far, Clay, no. I need a little help. Ring Mr. Buggarelli in 118 for me."

He did and after a very long moment, shrugged. "No answer."

"Got something that will get me into that room?"

"Sure. Hang on." He placed a key card into a small machine, tapped in a few numbers and then handed me the coded card.

Before opening the door to 118, I knocked again. But still no results, so I swiped the card, pushed the door open and peeked inside. I didn't need to announce myself because it was evident Greg was in no position to answer the door. I found him lying on the floor next to the bed looking as dead as yesterday's news. But I checked for a pulse anyway. His neck felt cold, which was no surprise because the room was about the same temperature as outside. I assumed that the window had been open all night.

I threw open the drapes to put more light on the subject. Greg was wearing the same outfit I had seen him in yesterday. That, his temperature, rigor mortis, and the noticeable lividity told me that he probably died sometime last night. A patch of dried blood within the hairline of his temple kept me from assuming he may have died of natural causes. The wound suggested a hard but blunt object sent him across the River Styx.

45

I called the PD and asked John Gallagher to arrange for a crime scene unit and the medical examiner to respond and to haul his Irish ass to the motel post haste.

I closed off the room and went back to the office to ask Clay Plemmons about Dixie Foster.

"She's in 116," he said.

"Ring the room."

No answer.

"I got here at eight, and her car was gone," he said.

"What was she driving?"

"Oh, a medium-sized white something. Lemme check her registration."

I waited while he dug out the form.

"Yessir. White '07 Lexus IS 350. New York tags. That he'p ya?"

Fast car, I thought. Dixie always had a heavy foot.

"Maybe. Did you see her driving away?"

"Nosir. Like I said, gone when I got here."

"Let's open 116," I said.

Clay accompanied me and used his pass card to unlock the door to Dixie's room. My stomach turned over as I eased the door open.

"Dixie?" I called. "Dixie, it's Sam."

No answer. The bed clothes had been tidied up, but remained unmade. An open suitcase sat on a low counter next to the television. A couple articles of clothing hung in the closet and a cosmetic bag sat on the bathroom vanity.

Clay Plemmons and I locked up Dixie's room. He returned to the office, and I walked up to the second floor, intending to interview the nosey guest in room 218. From the north, a police siren wailed, probably clearing any traffic around the town square as he headed toward the motel.

I banged on the door of 218.

"Who is it?" came from a female voice.

"Police officer." I held my badge in front of the peephole for her to see.

The door opened as far as the security bar would allow. I saw an eye, the right side of a face and some short, curly blonde hair.

"Do you have any photo ID?" she asked.

"Who is it, Marion?" a male voice called from somewhere within the room.

She raised her voice. "He says he's the police."

"Don't open that door!" Marion's male counterpart said. "Might be the guy I saw before. I don't trust him."

Another shout. "I asked for photo ID, Harry."

"I said don't open that door!"

Someone in Maryville might have heard Harry's instructions.

"I heard you!" she screamed.

"Ma'am, here's my ID card." I held *it* up for her to see.

"Give it here."

"No ma'am. You can see it. You can't have it."

From inside, "Don't open that door, Marion!"

"All right, Harry. All right. I hear you."

"Marion," I said, "I'm the police chief. Please look at my ID. If you don't believe me, call the desk and ask Mr. Plemmons. He knows me."

"You can't be too careful, you know."

In the background, two sirens were now disturbing the tranquility of Prospect's early morning.

"Yes, ma'am, I understand. Do you hear the sirens? Two uniformed police officers are coming here. I'm a police officer, and I need to speak to you and Harry. Something happened downstairs."

"I don't know," she said. "I need time to think."

She sounded distraught.

I shook my head. "Oh, Christ almighty. Is your husband there?"

"You're pressuring me. Stop. He's on the toilet."

I sighed. "I'm sorry, Marion. There's a dead man in the room below yours. Please, I need to speak with you and Harry."

She turned away. "Harry, he says there's a dead man."

"A what? Where? Wait a minute! Do nothing."

The sound of a toilet flushing filled the motel room. A moment later, "What's going on here, Marion?"

"Harry?" I said. "My name is Sam Jenkins. I'm a police officer. Please look at my ID."

"How do you know my name?" he asked.

I let out a burst of air and slapped my hands against my thighs. "Your

47

wife told me. Look at my ID, please."

"Marion, you gave him my name? Did you give him my social security number? Are you crazy?"

"Don't yell, Harry," she said.

PO Will Sparks walked up next to me. "Hey, boss, whatcha got?"

"Oh, thank God, Harry," Marion said. "Look, a policeman."

Harry pushed Marion out of the way. "Officer, do you know this man?"

Will said, "Yessir, he's the po-leece chief."

"All right, wait," Harry said.

The door slammed shut, the security bar slapped against the hollow metal door, and then it opened almost a foot. Harry stood there with Marion behind him.

After ten minutes of discussion, I learned that Harry and Marion Dektor saw, heard and knew nothing...specifically about the death of Greg Buggarelli. I suspected my notion was even more far-reaching.

I returned to room 118 to find not only John Gallagher but crime scene investigators Jackie Shuman and David Sparks, Will's cousin.

As the evidence technicians puttered around the room with almost silent efficiency, John said, "Some shit, huh, Boss? Greg's still got his watch, wallet and a small nine millimeter in an ankle holster. Not a robbery. Who'd want to croak him down here?"

"Greg had a talent for pissing off people, but I don't think he knows anyone down here." I handed John the letter delivered by Alvie Greenblatt, PI. "I'll bet this has something to do with it."

John began reading.

"Remember Alphonse DeCenzo?" I asked.

He looked up at me. "Sure. Wise guy they called The Torch."

"He got whacked down in Florida, coincidentally only two days after his son Carlo was found dead by airport cops. As you know, Bo Stallins has that case. A PI from Stewart delivered that letter this morning."

John frowned and finished reading. "Holy shit. And he says someone's got a contract on you?"

"Looks that way."

"What's Carly been doin' lately?" John asked.

"He took over running A&M Vending from his old man."

"Think he's doin' more than tending the machines?"

"What do you think? Probably pushing untaxed cigarettes and laundering money for someone."

"Two connected murders and Gino decides to relocate to Prospect? What did we always say about coincidence, Boss?"

"Exactly. Is Gino involved, or is he running for his life?"

"Good question. Any ideas?"

"Not yet," I said. "I'll start by asking Gino Musucci."

"And what about him?" He pointed at Greg Buggarelli's body.

"I don't know. He's cold. Been here for hours. We'll know better when the ME gets a temperature from his liver."

John nodded. He knew the drill. "Dixie okay?"

"Don't know that either. Clay Plemmons says she left before eight this morning—or at least her car was gone."

"You call her?"

I could have kicked myself in the head. "I never asked for her cell number. Said she was going to visit her aunt in Crossville."

"Got an address?"

"No, John," I snapped. "I don't have an address. Some nursing home."

"Okay, Boss. Want me to call around."

I shrugged in frustration. "Yeah. Ask Crossville PD for some help if you need it."

John nodded.

"You find anything here while I was upstairs?"

"Not much," he said. "I figured the ETs would sweep the place clean. Greg didn't even unpack."

"Okay. Go back to the barn, and see if you can find Dixie. Her spinster aunt's name is Faith Garvey."

"Right, Boss. I'm on it."

Chapter Eleven

After canvassing all the motel guests present, I obtained a list of people who checked out prior to my arrival and left cards requesting a call from anyone that was out for the day, but booked in for additional time at the Foothills View. All that still allowed me to leave before the evidence technicians and the medical examiner completed their work.

I arrived back at Prospect PD a little after noon. John Gallagher was waiting for me.

"I told Joey to take an early lunch, Boss. Figured you'd want to hear how I made out."

"Good. Did you locate Dixie's aunt?"

He smiled like the village idiot. "Boss, I'm hurt. You think I couldn't find an old lady who wasn't hiding from us?"

"What was I thinking, John? Did you speak to Dixie?"

"No, she signed the aunt out of the old folk's home for the day. Said they were going to the outlet mall in Crossville and then to lunch. I asked a woman there to get Dixie to call when she gets back."

"Good job. Sounds like Dixie is okay. Let me give her the news about Greg when she calls."

"You got it, Boss. Hey, were those two…you know, uh, were they—?

I raised my eyebrows and shrugged. "I asked. She said no. Said when she told Greg about heading down here, he asked to tag along. Said he wanted to see me. As we saw, they had two motel rooms. I believed her."

"He always seemed to have the hots for Dixie, didn't he, Boss?"

"Lot of guys did. He's known her since he worked at the squad with us. I guess after a while, he wasn't going to leave his wife, and she didn't go out with married men, so he cooled off. Who knows what he thought.

Greg was an odd guy at times."

"Yeah." John shrugged. "Well, anyways, what else you need?"

"Call the Rackets Bureau, and tell Greg's supervisor what happened. They'll have to notify his wife. And see if they know of anything he was working on that would tie into this."

"Will do. Wanna get something delivered for lunch?"

"Sure. Chinese?"

"Sounds good," he said. "Want me to call?"

"Yeah. I've got to go up to the building department and get an address for Gino Musucci from his building permit application. Then, I'll tell his Excellency about the murder in his sleepy little city."

"Okay, Boss. What are you eatin'?"

I thought for a moment. "Home-style tofu and vegetables with steamed rice. And tell old man Lum to make it spicy. He knows how I like it."

John wrote down my instructions. "Got it. I think I'll have my favorite, *moo goo foo goo*."

I hadn't heard that one before. "That sounds disgusting. What is it...some kind of Cantonese slime?"

"No, Boss. I thought you'd know. Chicken and vegetables in a white sauce. Very nice."

"Oh. Is it anything like moo goo gai pan?"

"I don't know. Have I ever had that?"

I shook my head. "How should I know, John?"

When I returned from my trip to the building inspector's office and after spending a few minutes with the mayor, I found a brown paper bag with the *moo goo foo goo* and tofu on John's desk. He was on the phone.

"Uh-huh," he said. "Uh-huh. Uh-huh. Yeah, he just walked in. Hang on, I'll transfer the call."

I did my DeNiro impersonation for John. "You talkin' ta me?"

"Yeah, Boss. Steven Holmes, Chief Investigator at the Rackets Bureau. I'll switch it to your phone."

I picked up in my office, dispensed with the introductions and got down to business.

"Your detective didn't offer many details," Holmes said. "What do

51

you know so far?"

"A broad time of death and the obvious head wound. It wasn't a robbery. That's about it so far."

"And you're sure it's a homicide? Could he have just fallen?"

Taking a little offense at that, I swallowed a nastier comment. "Even Greg wouldn't hit himself on the head multiple times."

He didn't reply immediately. Perhaps he was thinking, or perhaps I had offended him. "Did he discuss anything with you?"

"We had a general conversation yesterday afternoon. Just the usual stuff you say when you haven't seen someone in almost twenty years. I intended to pick him up this morning."

Another long moment of silence. "I sent Greg to Tennessee to speak with you. He didn't give you a message?"

"What kind of message?"

"Something very personal. Information we picked up on a wiretap."

I was beginning to get impatient. "How about we get specific, Mr. Holmes? Greg didn't discuss business with me. Neither did the DA's personal assistant, Dixie Foster. I spent more time speaking with her. Greg just stopped in to say hello and make sketchy plans to get together today and over the weekend. Was Dixie involved in this business?" I showed a little attitude in my questions.

"Dixie is *not* part of this. When we discussed this information at a team meeting, Greg volunteered to make the run because of your past association."

"Greg is dead, and I've got you on the phone. Give me the message directly."

He sighed. "We overheard a conversation where you were mentioned. First, I should tell you that the connection was bad, and because of the location of the call, there was a lot of background noise, so we couldn't positively ID the callers. But the gist was that someone wants you dead."

"Where were the phones you tapped?"

"The landline was at the Canaan Lake Club. Unfortunately, the call was made from the kitchen extension, and the background noise was considerable. The other party was on an untraceable prepaid cell phone. And you know how those people almost talk in code."

"Yeah. So your assumption is sketchy."

"We're pretty certain."

"Does Sonny Musucci still own that restaurant?"

"He does."

"That's interesting, Mr. Holmes, but I'm afraid your information is a half day late, and Greg Buggarelli is now more than a dollar short. Sit back, relax and I'll tell you about several things that've happened over the last few days."

I explained almost everything that happened from Carly Nickels' dead body to our most recent corpse, retired sergeant and now contract DA's investigator, Greg Buggarelli.

"I've got to admit," Holmes said, "we hadn't heard about a few of those things."

"Now that you're up to speed, why do you think someone wants to kill me after all this time? I've been out of New York for eighteen years."

"We were under the impression it has to do with more recent events."

"Like what?"

"You would know better than I."

That was a big help.

"Okay, tell me why Buggarelli had to make a personal visit. Why couldn't someone have just telephoned?"

"The visit had two purposes. We also wanted him to pick your brain. With Gino Musucci retiring, his relocation to Tennessee was news to us. His son, Anthony, is next in line to take over the family business. That means the operations center moves from Jersey to the Island—our area."

"Aha."

"And since you had extensive history with Anthony, we wanted to recover some old bases and dig up the past to see if you had anything in your head not already on paper."

"Was Buggarelli in charge of the investigation?"

"No. Now I'd like you to talk with Dave Barry. He's our lead investigator on this."

"Any relation to the late Detective Dave Barry from my old job who worked at Rackets years ago?"

"His son."

"How about that? Old Dave was a good man. I worked with him in the 5th Squad and did lots with Dave and his partner Jack Lynch when they worked in Rackets back in the '70s and '80s."

"We know. And young Dave is an excellent man himself."

"Okay. Will we be doing this on the phone or in person?"

"In person. But the circumstances are quite different. He'll fly down. And I think taking a motel outside of Prospect might be a good idea."

Chapter Twelve

At 1:45, Dixie called Prospect PD from the nursing home in Crossville. Joey Gillespie transferred the call to John. John knew I wanted to break the news to Dixie, and he switched the call to my phone.

"I get less of a hassle calling a deputy director at the FBI," she said. "Messages to call immediately and neither your PO nor John would tell me anything. What's going on, Sam?"

I sat straight in my swivel chair and prepared to deliver the message. "Some bad news, Dix. It's about Greg."

Immediately, she shot me a question. "Was he in an accident?"

"It was no accident. And it's very bad news. Greg's dead."

She gasped before speaking. "What? How? What happened?"

"I found him in his motel room."

"That's ridiculous. I saw him early last night."

"It's real, Dixie. Someone killed him."

"My God. Who? Was it robbery?"

"No. He had all his property with him. I'm sorry."

"I can't believe this. Who? Why?" Dixie sounded beyond upset.

John Gallagher stepped into the doorway to my office and listened to our conversation.

"That's what I have to find out."

"Have you told his wife?"

"John and I spoke to people at the DA's office. They're going to take care of that."

"This is unbelievable. He didn't know anyone down here."

"That's what I said. You were in the car with him for more than twelve hours. Did he say anything that might help me?"

She took a long moment to answer. "I'll have to think about that, but right off, I doubt it. He mostly spoke about his kids and grandchildren.

Then about the place he bought in Florida. About the mortgage, the taxes, the area. Just general things about that. Small talk. You know Greg. He could spend hours talking about nothing."

"Okay, but please think about it, and we'll talk later. Now…how about you? Is there any reason why someone would be looking to harm you?"

"Me? Why? You think—?"

I interrupted before she could finish. "I don't know. Have you broken up with anyone recently? Could an old friend have gotten jealous of you travelling with Greg? Perhaps someone killed him for being with you and now may contact you to make up or…I've got to say this, or to make you pay?"

"Oh, God, that's a gruesome, thought. No, I can't think of anyone. I haven't been serious with anyone in ages."

I let out a breath in frustration before continuing. "We can't take any chances. I'm not letting you drive from Crossville to Prospect alone."

"Sam, I'll be fine."

"We're not having a debate here, Dixie. Just do this. Drive to Crossville PD. As soon as I can get a chopper in the air, I'll fly in, pick you up and drop off a man to drive your car back here. Ask someone at the nursing home for the location of the PD."

"Sam, this isn't necessary. And where are you going to get a helicopter?"

"I have friends. I'll call the Crossville chief and square everything."

"Okay, but—"

"No buts. Give me your cell number, and keep it turned on."

Dixie sighed. "Yes, sir."

I waved for John to come in.

"What's up, Boss? Dixie okay?"

I nodded. "Yeah. Call Crossville PD and ask the chief to babysit Dixie until I can get a chopper ride to pick her up. Ask him where we can land. Then find someone who wants overtime to ride with me and drive her car back."

"I could use some OT, Boss. My salary doesn't exactly put me in the *effluent* category."

I shook my head. "I believe you meant affluent."

"Yeah? You sure?"

"I'm sure. I need you here to work on the murder."

"I'm almost dead in the water. I need the crime scene pictures and reports and the autopsy results before I can do anything more."

"Okay, but no screwing around. Drive right back."

"Boss, that hurt. Have you ever known me to screw around?"

"Now you're full of effluence."

I went back to my phone, called WNXX TV in Knoxville and asked for cameraman John Leckmanski.

"How ya been, buddy?" he asked.

"Not bad. You know the deal—crime never sleeps."

"So I hear. Haven't seen much of you lately."

"Yeah, well."

He snickered. "I heard from Rachel last week."

"Uh-huh."

"She's doin' good up in Chicago. Says the station is really big-time."

"That's good. I'm happy for her."

He snorted. "I'll bet."

I didn't comment.

"So, what can I do for you?" he asked.

"No big thing. I need your traffic helicopter for a quick trip to Crossville."

He laughed. "Sure you do. Meeting someone for a round of golf?"

I explained my necessity.

"You gotta be kidding."

"Deadly serious. Tell your station manager I'll give you guys an exclusive on all the developments, and when this breaks, you get all the poop a day before the other stations."

"George isn't exactly rolling in dough. His operating budget gets thinner each year. Do you know how much fuel a trip to Crossville burns up?"

I really didn't need this kind of opposition. "Tell him he'll make Allen Peters, that prick you call the competition, look dreadfully inept."

"Hmmm. That may work."

"Remind him that my promise is good."

"Yeah. He knows. I'll call you back."

"Make it quick."

I called my wife to talk about Greg's murder and my plans.

"I'm glad you called, and I didn't hear about this on the five o'clock news." She sounded a little sarcastic.

"Yeah. I've been a little busy and called as soon as I could. Now I've got to fly to Crossville and retrieve Dixie Foster."

"Fly?"

I explained.

"You think she's in danger?"

"Who knows? I would never have thought someone in Prospect would kill Greg. I need to start getting straight stories from all the players in this."

"I see your point. Then won't it be dangerous for her to drive back to Long Island alone?"

"That's what I wanted to discuss next."

"Yes?"

"How about putting her in our guest room and me stationing a guard or two at the house to keep the pair of you safe?"

"I need a bodyguard?"

"Don't worry. It's just a precaution. Do you mind having Dixie around until I find the killer?"

"We hardly know each other."

"We can catch up over dinner."

She sighed audibly. "Sammy, the things I do for you."

* * * *

John Gallagher and I hopped into the WNXX Bell Jet Ranger as it sat on the athletic field next to Prospect Middle School. Moments later, the pilot gave us a thumbs-up, and the chopper lifted off and slowly moved northwest in a nose-down attitude until we cleared the trees. Then we climbed to 1,500 feet, and he gave it the gas. Cruising at over 100 miles per hour made the seventy air mile trip between Prospect and Crossville go quickly.

We met Dixie and her police escort at the helipad of the Cumberland

Medical Center just outside the city center. She looked stressed out and nervous.

I placed my hand gently on her shoulder. "Relax, kiddo. Everything's under control."

She didn't look overly confident. "That's easy for you to say."

Dixie handed me her electronic car key thingie, and I tossed it to John.

"Nice car, Dixie," John said. "Just get it?"

"Thank you, John. No, I bought it new a couple years ago."

"Oh," John said, like that was a miraculous revelation. "I can't afford new cars anymore. The Boss doesn't pay much."

I scowled. "Time for you to go, John."

He smiled like a little boy just given a new bicycle. "Okay, Boss. I'll call after I get back and lock Dixie's car in the city garage."

"Good." Then to Dixie I said, "Ready to travel?"

She shrugged. "I've never been in a helicopter before."

"There's no trick to it. We'll be back in Prospect in less than an hour."

"If you say so."

The chopper sat idling on the concrete pad. As we approached the aircraft, the pilot engaged the rotors that began a low RPM spin. As we stepped under the spinning blades, Dixie grabbed my arm and squeezed.

"You don't have to duck," I said. "The rotors are high above our heads."

"Do you ride in these things often?" She spoke louder than necessary.

"Not since I left the Army."

I opened the portside rear door, helped Dixie into the chopper and jumped in after her.

"Buckle your seatbelt," I said and handed her a headset. "Put these on in case the pilot wants to talk to us."

She nodded. The pilot brought the rotors up to flying speed, and the prop wash scattered particles of dust and ground debris. Dixie squinted and looked as nervous as a child sitting in a dentist's chair. After a few brief moments, we took off.

"Okay, folks," the pilot said, "relax and enjoy the trip. There won't be any stop lights to bother us."

Helicopter humor.

When he gave me an ETA in Prospect, I telephoned Stan Rose who met us at the middle school thirty minutes later.

After Stan drove away and we sat in my unmarked Ford, Dixie grabbed my hand. Hers was shaking.

"What's going on, Sam?"

I gave her a quick rundown on the DeCenzo murders, what little I knew about Greg's death, Dave Barry's impending visit, but didn't mention the letter I received from my pal Alphonse the Torch. I was wondering how I'd broach that subject with the women in my life.

I switched on the ignition and turned down the volume of the police radio.

"When did you see Greg last?" I asked.

"The evening after we left you. We had eaten a big lunch along the road that day, but Greg still wanted something for dinner. I wasn't hungry, but he said he'd walk over to the steak house next to the motel."

"Did you hear him go out or come back?"

"No. I was tired from the long drive. We left the Island at three a.m. to beat traffic to the GW Bridge and get on I-80. I took a shower, turned on the TV and fell asleep. I was on the road again before 7:30 this morning."

"You're okay now. Let's grab your stuff from the motel and get you settled into our guest room. I'll make a drink, and we can talk after dinner."

"Is your wife okay with me staying with you?"

"Not a problem." I hoped.

She squeezed my fingers. "Thank you, Sam."

"This has been one hell of a reunion so far."

"Has it ever."

Kate and Dixie had only met a couple of times—at Christmas parties when I worked as a detective in a general service squad. They were sitting in the living room getting reacquainted. Kate was sipping a Manhattan while Dixie was half way through her second scotch and soda, when John Gallagher called.

"I'm on 321 now, Boss. Be back at the garage in ten minutes."

"That was quick, John. I assume you had an uneventful trip."

"Yeah, Boss. No traffic and this is some car Dixie's got—like *fast*."

"Uh-huh. Tomorrow I've got to figure out how we can utilize the guys to protect Kate and Dixie. That letter from Alphonse opened up a can of worms. Who knows when some asshole might try to stick it to me?"

"I've been thinking about that, Boss. How are you gonna cover the sectors, give guys days off *and* get the mayor to approve overtime for a guard detail when you don't want to discuss the letter with too many people?"

"You've got a point."

"How about this? We call some of the old crew and see if they can help."

"People from the old office?"

"Sure. Frankie the Fool lives in Greeneville now. He'd come. Mike Rodriguez is only a day's drive away in South Carolina. Freddie liked working that Korean case with us, and he could pick up Maggie McDermott on the way up from Florida."

"That's asking a lot, John. These people have lives, and they are not getting any younger."

"No sweat, Boss. I'll make some phone calls tonight and see what I can turn up."

"Okay, thanks."

Chapter Thirteen

Before getting back with the girls, I called Bettye Lambert to ask a favor.

"How'd you like to do your favorite boss a solid, Blondie?"

"Sure, darlin'. Whatcha need?"

"For you to start work tomorrow instead of Monday."

"Okey dokey. What's up?"

I explained.

She didn't receive the information as well as I expected. "Sam Jenkins, what am I gonna do with you? How do you get yourself into these things?"

"Those are rhetorical questions, right?"

"I could just smack you."

"That's why I'm asking this over the phone."

"You are impossible."

"Be that as it may. Can you swing this? Will it be okay with Donnie?"

"It'll be fine. I didn't need four days to iron my uniforms."

"Good. Instead of going to the office tomorrow, come to my house in plain clothes. I'd like you to stay with Kate and Dixie until I can arrange for other bodyguards."

"I'll do the best I can."

"Great. Charge up your cell phone, bring two guns and lots of ammo."

"Oh, Lord have mercy."

* * * *

We sat in a corner booth at Sullivan's in Maryville. The diffused overhead track lighting cast shadows and gave the brick walls in the hundred-year-old converted furniture store a soft mellow look. The golden oak woodwork contrasted nicely with the dark red leather upholstery that almost matched Dixie's hair color.

Kate and Dixie sipped from glasses of chardonnay as I watched the head on my pint of Blue Moon settle.

"How's your aunt?" I asked.

Dixie shrugged. "About as well as can be expected. She's my mother's oldest sister—ninety last November. Physically, she's not bad, but she slips in and out of reality."

"Alzheimer's?" Kate asked.

"They say no. Hardening of the arteries causes dementia that doesn't get any better."

"She know you?" I asked.

Dixie nodded with a look of uncertainty on her face. "Most of the time. Once or twice, I thought we were in Never Never-Land. And she repeats herself constantly."

She closed her eyes and looked terribly sad.

"But overall, you had a good visit?"

"Yes. It was good to see her again. We went to the big outlet mall near the Interstate. She walks slowly, but gets around well enough with a cane. I bought her a couple of sweat suits. They seem to be what she likes to wear. And a nice wool cardigan. She's always cold."

"Is she eating well?" Kate asked.

Dixie smiled. "As much as me and she's still 110 pounds. We had lunch in a pretty little Chinese restaurant near the mall." .

"We know the place," I said.

Our waitress showed up with our dinners. Kate had picked something they call a Northshore Salad with grilled chicken, feta cheese, pecans, dried cranberries and balsamic vinaigrette. Dixie again said she wasn't very hungry and chose a Signature Salad—same as Kate's, but without chicken. I suspected the Chinese lunch hadn't dulled her appetite as much as the stress. Some people are affected like that. Stress makes me voracious. I ordered the Charleston Shrimp and Grits, a Signature Salad and baked creamed spinach. The waitress left with instructions to bring me another beer.

Kate managed to perpetuate the small talk throughout dinner. Dixie seemed understandably quiet, and as my wife sometimes describes me, I ate like a cannibal with table manners.

Half way through her salad, Dixie tossed in the towel. "I'm afraid that's it for me."

Never wanting to waste good food, I said, "Take it home with you."

Kate jumped in with, "If you don't eat it, he will."

Dixie laughed. I sneered.

"She's so cynical," I said, looking at Kate. "Bettye's coming back to work tomorrow. She'll be staying with you two until I work out something else."

Kate nodded and spoke to Dixie. "You'll like Bettye. She's Sam's desk sergeant and den mother to the POs."

"I feel like I'm being such a burden," Dixie said. "I should just fly home and have my car trucked back to the Island."

"Nonsense," I said. "You may want to see your aunt again. And this is the way I want to play it."

I ate a little more. There was a long moment of silence before Dixie asked, "Have you spoken to Greg's wife yet?"

"Steven Holmes took care of that. I don't know her very well."

"I feel so sorry for her," Kate said. "They've been married a long time, haven't they?"

Dixie nodded. "More than forty years."

Then she paused, but looked like she wanted to say more. We waited.

"On the drive down, Greg said he wanted to ask her for a divorce."

I wondered why she hadn't mentioned that earlier. I stopped eating and looked into her eyes.

"Did he follow that up with a suggestion that someone might take Joann's place?"

Dixie frowned. "What do you mean?"

I thought my question was simple enough. "Is he leaving his wife with hopes of someone else taking her place?"

She held my gaze. "I wouldn't know."

I'm sure Kate knew exactly what I was implying.

"Had he been to a lawyer yet," I asked.

"He didn't say that."

"Did his wife know of his intentions?"

Dixie dropped her eyes. "Maybe, but I don't think so."

"That's interesting. He bought a house in Florida and is ditching his wife." I popped half a shrimp into my mouth and followed it with a forkful of cheese grits topped with Louisiana hot sauce.

"Please excuse me," Dixie said. "Where is the ladies room?"

Kate told her, and Dixie slid out of the booth.

A few moments later when Dixie was across the room, Kate said, "You were interrogating her."

"I need to know things like that."

"Tonight?"

I took a deep breath. "She brought it up, and I asked."

"Sometimes you're like a fullback crashing into a defensive line."

"Aren't you the perfect football fan?"

Kate smiled. "Eat your grits, sweetie. Are they good?"

* * * *

A Saturday morning at the Prospect Municipal Building is about as busy as Martin Luther King Day at the Arian Nation clubhouse. I was it until ten after nine when John Gallagher showed up carrying a box of Entenmanns's doughnut holes. He dropped the box on my desk before fixing himself a cup of coffee.

"Ever wonder why you keep adding holes to your belt, John?"

He grinned like a little kid caught sneaking a look at his father's copy of *Playboy*. "I can afford to eat a couple of doughnuts, Boss. I only had cereal and a piece of toast this morning."

"And now you're ready for a second breakfast?"

"They're not really doughnuts, just the holes. Just a light snack."

"Every time you walk past a box of these, you pop one into your mouth. By lunchtime you've eaten enough calories to equal a Thanksgiving dinner."

He looked surprised. "No."

"Yes."

"You sure, Boss? Can't be."

"Don't make me hit you, John."

He tried his idea of method acting on me. This time it was how to look hurt.

"Boss, how can you say that? I spent all last night on the phone getting volunteers to protect Dixie and your wife and help find out who wants to kill you."

I pulled out the bottom drawer of my desk, set my foot on the edge and leaned back in my swivel chair. "Thank you, John. This is why you were always my favorite."

"Yeah? I'll tell Frankie. He'll be jealous."

"Who did you recruit? I assume Frank is one."

"Yep. Frankie will be here by lunchtime. I said you're buyin'."

"You're a real sport. Who else?"

"Mikey is on the way from Beaufort. He'll be here tonight. Then Freddie said he'd leave Port Saint Lucie this morning, pick up Maggie in Daytona and drive up. I'm not sure when they're gonna pull in. And listen to this. I called Wally Danko. He lives in West Virginia now. He's coming…probably tonight."

"Wally lives in West Virginia? Why?" I thought about my question. "Well, I guess if we live in Tennessee, somebody might want to live in West Virginia."

"Yeah. He likes all that hunting and fishing and outdoor shit. Says he's doin' good. Two of his kids work for a big auto dealer there. That's why he bought a place. Wants to see his grandchildren."

"Ah, the power of grandchildren. Something I don't understand."

John shrugged. He was a grandfather. "Anyways, Boss, we'll have a whole crew here soon."

"And I'll have to find motel rooms for them to stay in. Of course if someone looked at us, they might suggest temporary spots in an old folk's home."

"No sweat, Boss. I got that covered, too. My neighbor owns a vacation rental with four bedrooms. It's not booked for a couple weeks when he gets the Christmas rush, so he'll let us have it if we promise to clean it when the guys move out. I also said you'd buy him a bottle of that expensive scotch you drink. Okay?"

"Yeah, John, that's good work. Smart. Tell Frankie I said so. Make him jealous."

"So, who's looking after Dixie and your wife today?"

"Bettye came back to work a few days early. She got there before I left—brought a couple of guns—locked and loaded.

* * * *

At 9:30, Jackie Shuman called after being rerouted to the PD by my wife. Twenty minutes later, he showed up with folders full of pictures, diagrams and reports, and a shopping bag containing whatever he and David considered evidence.

"Man, I hate ta do crime scenes at mo-tels," he said. "Ya never know what's important ta the incident and what jest got left behind by some unrelated past guest."

"Yeah," I said, "I feel your pain."

"I took custody o' your Mister *Bug-a-relli's* property, but Dr. Mo got his clothes. David took the gun he's carryin' ta TBI for a work up, too."

"John said *Boo-gar-elli's* gun was in an ankle holster—something small. What was it?"

"Ruger nine millimeter. A model LC9. Nice li'l gun."

"Didn't find a Glock 19, did you?"

"Nosir, jest the Ruger. Why?"

"The Glock was our issue gun. Greg would have kept it when he retired and probably carried it when he went to work at the DA's office."

"Cain't he'p ya."

"I wonder if he had the Glock and the killer took it, and the Ruger was only a backup. I suppose you didn't see an empty holster that would hold the Glock?"

"No again."

"Who'd you give the Ruger to at TBI?"

"Bill Werner."

"Good. After I left the motel, did Mo say when he'd finish the autopsy?"

"Said he'd get a table over the weekend and give ya a call Monday."

"You gonna watch the post?"

"I hate them things, but yep, I'm the one."

"Okay, kid. I appreciate this."

He began to leave, and I asked another question. "You want some doughnut holes?"

"Shoot, I cain't eat them things. Gotta watch my boyish figure."

Chapter Fourteen

John picked up lunch at Howell's Pub. We sat at his desk in the lobby, eating barbeque pork sandwiches the size of half a soccer ball and listening to the county dispatcher handling calls for several PDs and the sheriff's deputies on a fairly busy Saturday.

I had a mouthful of food, so John answered the main phone line when it rang.

"Uh-huh. Howz it goin'?" he asked. "Yes, he's here. Right, will be all day. Sure. You got GPS? The address?" He recited it like a recording. "Okay. It'll take you about fifteen minutes from the airport. Right. Park in the back of the municipal building. The public entrance is open. We're on the right."

"Dave Barry?" I asked.

"How'd you know, Boss? You must be *psychotic*."

"You mean psychic."

"Yeah, that's what I said. You have your hearing checked lately? They do it for free at those *Beltrone* stores."

I grunted and took another bite of sandwich.

Dave Barry was in his early forties, had short brown hair and wore a navy blue blazer, plaid shirt and blue jeans. Anyone who knew his father would never doubt this was his son.

John played around with the reports and photos from Greg Buggarelli's motel room, while Barry and I adjourned to my office.

"I appreciate you seeing me on a Saturday," he said.

"John and I were trying to make sense of the work our crime scene guys brought us. We don't usually work weekends, but this is an exceptional case."

"I know. Steven wants me to say how much he appreciates your cooperation."

"You bet."

Steven. Not Steve or Stevie. I was working in a world different from what I knew.

We looked at each other for a long moment. I broke the silence.

"Steven mentioned that he sent Greg to see me. Greg never started a business conversation with me and never told Dixie Foster he was on a mission."

"I guess he wanted to get you alone, and he wouldn't have told Dixie. She wasn't in the loop on this one. She had no need to know."

"You sound like someone I know at the CIA."

He shrugged. "We've had problems over the last few years. Steven determined that we had to tighten security."

The Rackets Bureau has had information leaks since Perry Mason was a first-year law student.

"Dixie has been around a long time," I said. It sounded a bit protective. "She's trustworthy, and she is the DA's administrative assistant."

"Even the DA isn't totally aware of what we're doing here."

"Oh my."

"Much of this concerns you."

"I'm honored to be within the loop."

The look on his face told me he seemed to have taken offense at that.

"Look, you've got a history with Sonny Musucci," he said.

"I do."

"I believe we can be of mutual benefit to each other."

"Works for me."

"It's taken a while, but we've developed information that he's going to be taking over the family operations, and he's forming an alliance with people from out of town, specifically, another Italian crew in Providence and some of the Irish hoods in Boston."

"Why?"

"Yet to be determined, but it's happening. We think it's Sonny and the Irish mob that wants a piece of you."

I had an idea why, but I asked anyway. "What's their beef? Other than the obvious, that's very old business."

"You'd know better than me. Everyone back on the Island remembers you embarrassed the shit out of Sonny. Have you pissed off an Irishmen lately?"

I didn't have to think hard to remember a certain case where the IRA might not consider me their favorite American cop.

"Not lately," I said. "I've only been to Boston once, never marched in a St. Patrick's Day parade, but I've eaten my share of corned beef and cabbage pie."

"This isn't a joke, Chief. We believe Anthony Musucci and the Irish mob share mutual animus for you."

"Lucky me. Let's talk more about Musucci establishing this alliance with the Irish mooks."

Barry spread his hands to his sides indicating he didn't know much...or he wasn't prepared to say. "He's made trips up there, but doesn't spend extensive time with them."

"When he makes these business trips, how does he travel?"

"Far as we know, by car. His bodyguard, Victor Cinquemani, drives. They stay overnight or for a couple days at a few different high-ticket hotels and then drive back. Musucci may integrate pleasure with business."

Probably buys himself hot and cold running bimbos and the finest champagne.

"Who does he see?" I asked.

"Could be anyone of a few. They meet mostly in pubs. I'll make a list for you."

"Thanks. Tell me about this guy Victor. Cinquemani is a strange name. Means five hands. What's he all about?"

"They call him Bunny. He's pretty young for a job like this. Got his name from marrying a former Playboy model. They took his picture wearing her bunny ears at their engagement party."

"How'd he land the job?"

"Supposedly, his old man knew Gino Musucci. They weren't that close, but his brother Aldo, Victor's uncle, was. Aldo's son Vito is Gino's right-hand man."

"Hmmm. I met Vito recently. Big guy. What's Bunny like?"

"Pretty boy. A weight lifter. Greasy hair. Armani suits. Typical young wise guy."

"Have you had eyes on him over the last couple weeks?"

"I'd suppose. I'll check the logs and give you a call."

We spoke for another half hour about my dealings with Anthony 'Sonny'/'Moonface' Musucci back in the old days. I made coffee. We covered lots of the specific past history his employers sent him to cover. At one point, I took advantage of the lull in the conversation.

"How long have you worked with Greg Buggarelli?"

Dave Barry wrinkled his forehead as if he was thinking. "He finished thirty-five with the PD and in less than a year after he retired, he started with us. So, that would be about three years."

"Did he retire as a sergeant in Internal Affairs?"

"No. He was last in the 4th Squad."

"He have any personal problems with anyone in either the PD or DA's office?"

"Not that I know."

Barry was on his third cup of coffee. He shifted in the guest chair in front of my desk and looked like his back was bothering him.

"Damn seats on those regional jets are killers."

"The airline executives should be shot for what they do to their passengers," I said.

"At least."

"Did Greg tell you he was going to leave his wife?"

Barry frowned. "I think you've got that backwards. Greg told me his wife filed for divorce a couple weeks before he made this trip."

I raised my eyebrows. "That's interesting," I said. "A little different from what I heard. But I guess no one wants to admit he's been dumped."

"No, I guess not."

"I know you're still in the early stages on the New York end of this, but has anyone checked on his life insurance?"

He gave me another scowl. "You think his wife may have had someone do this?"

I shrugged. "It's not an unheard of occurrence. Do we know why she wanted him out of her picture?"

"He didn't say."

"If she already filed, the petition is public record. Maybe it's the time-honored catchall of *irreconcilable differences* or maybe she had her lawyer get more specific. People married for more than forty years usually have a good reason when they split up. If it's not in writing, you could ask her."

"I could."

I got the feeling Dave Barry didn't like being supervised. I wondered if *Steven* would concur.

"Thanks. Ever hear about Greg catting around?"

"Excuse me?"

"Catting around. Picking up women. Being unfaithful to his wife. Had Greg turned into a swordsman during his Viagra years?"

He shook his head. "I've never heard him brag about that."

"Greg supposedly purchased a place in Florida. I think it's a house rather than a condo. Did he go into the hole to buy that? Pay cash? Get a mortgage? Make a big down payment? Small one?"

"He's been talking about that. It is a house. In a place called The Villages. Big development with its own zip code. Another retired cop he knows told him about a good deal. Man died, wife was going to live with her daughter. She offered it at a good price for a quick sale."

"Lucky break. I wonder if the Widow Buggarelli will keep it?"

"I don't see how that could matter."

"If there was mortgage insurance on Greg's life, she might own it free and clear. She could sell it after the dust settles and make a nice profit. I'm wondering if Gregory was worth much more dead than alive."

"I'll see what I can find out. He did say he took the longest mortgage the bank would offer. He wanted to buy it with someone else's money."

"Not a bad idea if you're going to use it as a rental and don't mind paying interest."

"Everybody's got their own ideas about that."

It wasn't time to discuss real estate philosophy.

"So," I said, "I guess financially Greg was doing okay. Thirty-five years would give him about a seventy-five percent pension from the job and whatever you pay him per diem. I'll run a credit check to confirm that and see what his charge cards look like."

"Good idea."

"Happen to know what kind of wheels they own in the Bugarelli household?"

"He drove a company car to work. I never saw his privately owned vehicle."

I nodded. "When I worked with him, Greg could be abrasive at times. I'm sure that trait didn't diminish during his long time in Internal Affairs. Did he ever talk about a cop or cops who he prosecuted—people with a serious grudge—who might look good for this?"

"You think—?" He stopped himself. "I'll call your IAB and see if someone can dig up any information."

"I can do that myself. I still know a few people at the main office."

"Okay."

He was beginning to look weary of my questions, but I had a few more areas I wanted covered.

"How about Greg's work habits," I asked. "Was he a hard charger? Go that extra mile to pursue the goombahs? Ever get into other organized crime ethnicities? Russians, Albanians, Haitians, Columbians, Klingons?"

Barry took a moment to formulate his thoughts. "We had him dealing strictly with the Musucci family and those who supported their enterprises." He shrugged and appeared as if he didn't want to elaborate too much on Greg's character or performance. "Greg was diligent. Competent. Did what he was told. Got along well in the team."

That sounded like something a supervisor might say when not wanting to sound harsh about a mediocre worker.

"But he was no ball of fire like your father or Jackie Lynch—guys who drummed up their own cases all the time and broke lots of balls and cost the mopes lots of money."

Barry sighed. "No, Greg was not like that."

"So, it's doubtful this was an ordered hit because Greg was a huge thorn in anyone's side?"

He shrugged again.

"Except maybe his soon-to-be ex-wife."

"I wouldn't draw that conclusion too quickly."

"No one's ever accused me of tunnel vision."

He nodded.

"Another thing is puzzling me. Greg was killed, and all his belongings seemed to be left untouched. If a pro did this, why not try to throw us off by making it look like a robbery?" I didn't give Dave Barry time to answer my rhetorical question. "Greg was carrying a little Ruger automatic. Something I'd consider an off-duty piece. He was on official business, but we didn't find the Glock 19 the PD would have issued him and he took with him after he retired. Can you do me a favor and see if he left it home, or should I assume it's in the wind somewhere around here?"

"I'll have someone check with his wife. If she's got any weapons around the house, we need to take them into custody. I doubt she was licensed to own a handgun."

I smiled. "Great. That would be a big help. I don't have much of a budget or time for out-of-state travel."

"Anything else I can do for you?"

I just got the feeling that Dave Barry considered our recent chat one-sided.

I looked up to see John Gallagher standing in my doorway.

"'Cuse me, Boss, but I might have something important here. At least it's interesting."

"Come in, John. What have you got?"

"Jackie Shuman dumped Greg's cell phone."

He stepped around to my side of the desk and laid several sheets of paper on my blotter.

"Look at the last number he called. Last night within the possible time of death. I looked it up."

Next to a 631 area code number, John had penciled in Shore Manor.

"That is interesting." I recognized the restaurant as one owned by a very connected guy.

"That number appears a few more times," John said. "Now get this." He pointed to different blocked numbers down the page. "Incoming calls from untraceable phones show up numerous times. How about that?"

I looked up at John and smiled. "Well, won't we be dipped in shit?"

"Interesting, huh, Boss?"

"What?" Dave Barry asked, obviously feeling left out of the loop.

"Does Monk LoScalzo still own the Shore Manor? That's one of the interesting numbers Greg has been calling."

Barry frowned, but nodded. "On paper, he does. He shows up at the restaurant often enough, but really to just hang out with his circle of old Mustache Petes. His son Pasquale Jr. runs the place with his wife."

"Patsy Jr.—that was one scumbag. A professional knuckle man."

"Still is. And you should meet his wife Amber. A real Dragon Lady."

"Amber? Is she Italian? There can't be a Saint Amber."

"She is. Amber Marie Provanzano. Her brother is Franco. Know him?"

"Sure. Sonny Musucci's dealer. Frankie Pro was quite the card player."

"That's the one."

"There was always a big ticket after-hours game going on at the Shore Manor," I said. "Monk ran the cards and chopped the pot, but Sonny sent Franco to sit in as the dealer and loan shark. Do you guys keep that place under surveillance?"

"No need. The uniform cops work it. You know, stop cars that leave the parking lot, write chicken-shit tickets, maybe pop a DWI when they can, generally break balls and send in field interrogation cards so we know who was playing."

"Was Greg working any cases concerning that restaurant or the Canaan Lake Club?"

He shook his head. The embarrassment on his face was indescribable. "Not with the Shore Manor—maybe he had a snitch there. I'll check the CI files. We all worked on the Canaan Lake Club case."

* * * *

Dave Barry remained with us until just before five p.m. He said he wasn't in the mood for dinner, so John and I showed him out through our private rear entrance to the police parking area. He drove his rental car toward the Fairfield Inn across from the airport in Alcoa where he'd spend the night before flying out the next morning and landing at LaGuardia before noon on Sunday.

I had given him a lot of information, but to a point, received only a few tidbits in return. I felt like a young Bob Dylan in reverse—I should never trust anyone under a certain age. And I knew I could never work alongside someone like Barry unless I called the shots.

75

When we returned to the lobby, we found Frank O'Brian sitting in John's chair with his feet on the edge of the desk.

"Whaddaya say, Frankie?" I said.

He swung his feet down and stood. "Hi, boss. And hello, stupid," he said to John. "You gave me the wrong address for this place. Good thing I've still got my superior police abilities and found it."

"No, Frank," John said, "you must have written it down wrong. I know where we work. And you know what, you fool, you were never really the Boss's favorite. He told me. It was always me. He hates you." He sounded like a sarcastic adolescent.

I gave my children the international time-out signal. "Enough, boys. It's late. I'm not in the mood to watch a gunfight before dinner."

"Sorry, boss," Frank said, "but you know how much I hate Gallagher."

"Speaking of dinner, what are you guys doing?" I asked.

Frank answered, "Stupid said his wife was handling that."

John said, "The fool here wanted to come directly to the PD because he was close, but I told everyone else to come to my house, get something to eat, and then I'd take them to the rental cabin."

"Okay, good." I said. "I guess Mazzio and Maggie will pull in sometime tomorrow. Once everyone's here, give me a call, and we'll talk strategy."

The Dead End Kids nodded.

"Hey, Frankie," John said, "know who we just spent the afternoon with?"

Frank shook his head and rolled his eyes, his expression indicating he thought John's question was inane. "How could I possibly know, you nitwit, I got here after he left."

John seemed immune to Frank's venom. "Dave Barry's kid. He's a senior investigator at the DA's office."

"I remember Dave Barry, but never met his kid. What did he want?"

"To swap information," I said. "Only I'm not sure he was exactly forthcoming."

"You gave that kid a lot of info, Boss," John said.

"Yeah, but I feel like I swapped a sawbuck worth of information for two bits of incite."

John said, "I heard a lot of what you said, Boss. You gave him lots of stuff no one would have remembered. I wanted to tell him he should be grateful you have a *photostatic* memory."

Frank smiled. I looked at John for a long moment.

"I'm glad you didn't, John. We wouldn't want that to be general knowledge."

"Yeah, right. How'd you like it when I brought in the records of Greg making phone calls to that wise guy restaurant? He almost shit himself."

"That pissed me off," I said. "Informant, my ass. Compared to Barry, Greg is old school and remembers when a confidential informant was really confidential. Only you and your partner knew the identity. That's not the case today. Guys get jammed up for not registering a snitch. If Greg had an informant at the Shore Manor, his boss would know."

"I don't know what happens at the DA's office," John said, "but nowadays in the PD if you use a stool that's unregistered and something backfires, you get at least a two day rip."

"What do you think? He called to make reservations and said, 'By the way, before you go, let me talk with my stool pigeon?'" Frank said. "In a place like that, every employee is connected somehow. You don't call a main number to squeeze your snitch. Greg was checking in with someone."

Frank was never a Greg Buggarelli fan.

"Barry got caught with his pants down," I said. "Greg wasn't the kind of guy who stretched the rules. He wasn't clever that way. Something is wrong here. He might have been undercover, and Barry doesn't consider us worthy of knowing, or Greg's involved in something that could embarrass the DA's office."

"Now that Greg's dead," John said, "Maybe they want any problems to just die with him. I mean, he was one of their own."

"I never trusted Buggarelli," Frank said. "Everyone thought he was too enthusiastic about bagging cops when he was in IAB."

Chapter Fifteen

The wheels of the Crown Vic crunched over the gravel driveway, and I backed into the turnaround between the barn and our three-car garage. Immediately, I saw that someone had forgotten me. The garage door, usually up and waiting to admit me into the back of the house, was locked down tighter than a prison cellblock. So, I walked past Bettye's VW, along the path to the seven steps to the porch and approached the front door. I listened for a moment, heard a Phil Collins CD I'm not particularly fond of, stuck a key into the doorknob and entered the foyer. Three females laughed. I peeked into the living room and found Kate and Dixie sitting on one of the loveseats and Bettye on the other. Kate and Dixie held wine glasses half-full of something red. Bettye juggled a coffee mug.

"Hi, ladies"

"Hello, sweetie," Kate said and wiggled her fingers at me.

"Hi," Dixie added,

"Hey, darlin'," Bettye said.

I felt horribly outnumbered.

Bettye left with a promise to see me on Monday. It took me less than two minutes to determine that Kate and Dixie were half lit from no food and a bottle of merlot, so I prepared baked ravioli for dinner—good sense told me that the girls should stick with red wine.

I did my best to entertain the ladies during dinner. I heard an appropriate ratio of giggles to my foolish stories and thought about how civilized our relationship was.

After the meal, I washed, Dixie dried, and Kate racked up the dishes.

Dixie hung the towel on a bar to dry and asked, "Did you get anywhere with the investigation today?"

"While I'd like to tell you I've got everything wrapped up and ready to make an arrest, I can't. But I can give you two a run down on what happened."

Kate said, "We'd love to hear that, Sammy, but before you start, can I get you two anything?"

Dixie shook her head. "Maybe later, thanks. I usually don't drink this much wine."

"How about a Glenfiddich, Kats?" I never worried about my temperance.

"Coming up."

Dixie and I sat in the living room while Kate fixed two drinks.

"Did you know that Steven Holmes sent Greg here to see me?"

"Steven did what?"

Her question was an answer.

"Supposedly to pick my brain of what I know about Anthony Musucci and tell me that with him taking over the family crime business, old Moonface might want to do me harm."

Sheepishly, Dixie said, "Greg didn't tell me a thing. And no one back on the Island ever mentioned it before I took vacation."

"I don't doubt that. I also spent five hours with Dave Barry Jr. today discussing Musucci the younger. Between Holmes and Barry, I felt like I was talking with a pair of yuppie Feds—two guys who definitely don't lay all their cards on the table."

"Sam, there are not many left like you," Dixie said. "This is a whole new generation of police officers."

Before I could tell Dixie that even her boss wasn't privy to Holmes' plans for this particular operation, Kate walked in and placed a short glass of single-malt on the lamp table next to me. In her left hand, she held something that looked like Canadian whisky and ginger ale.

"Here ya go, Sammy. What was that about Sonny Musucci wanting to harm you?" She batted her eyelashes. "Something I should know about?"

"Pfui," I said. "Sonny Musucci is a—excuse me, ladies—a piss ant. While I will take precautions to protect the likes of you two, I place little credence on what Moonface the Moron can accomplish."

"Greg Buggarelli did get killed, Sam," Kate said.

"Well, there is that. But I'm not off guard. And I'm not convinced Musucci had it in for Greg. But I will find out." I took a sip of scotch and waved my hand dismissively. "Besides, the beef Musucci has with me goes back so far that even he couldn't hold a grudge this long."

"What is this grudge all about?" Dixie asked.

"You haven't told her?" Kate asked.

"Ancient history," I said. "I'll see Gino next week and see what he knows about his idiot son's short term plans."

"Sam," Kate said, "Dixie has a right to know."

"Why do I let you women bully me?"

"You know we love you, Sammy," Kate said, "and all this does make for a relative and interesting story."

"Oh, for god's sakes. I locked him up a long time ago. It was no big deal."

"It was a little more elaborate than that, sweetie. I could tell the story if you'd like."

I let my shoulders drop three inches and expelled a large volume of air. "Sometimes I wonder why I'm not a misogynist."

"That's not possible, love. Tell your story."

I was too tired to argue.

"Right. Sonny Musucci sanctioned or ran a few high dollar card games in the 5th Precinct back in the day—at a couple of restaurants, the beauty shop he owned in his wife's name and that sleazy billiard club near the tracks in Patchogue. Everyone knew about them. The precinct cops kept an eye on most of the players and forwarded information to the squad. Only most of the dicks were too busy dealing with their usual squeals to care. But not stupid me. I took an interest, and after working on it for a while, Musucci must have considered me a royal pain in the ass."

"I can't imagine why." Kate needed to interject that before taking a sip of her highball.

I scowled. "Yeah, but maybe he could. Anyway, my father lived not too far from the precinct house and without thinking something might happen because of me, he put his name prominently on his mailbox. One of Musucci's goons, I assumed it was his number one henchman, Franco Provanzano, decided to drop a couple of M80s in the mailbox and light them up. In case you didn't know, 2 M80s are roughly the equivalent to a half stick of dynamite. Frankie Pro blew up my old man's mailbox, sent shrapnel flying and broke some glass. All that scared the shit out of Daddy, his second wife and the four new kids."

"I remember when that happened," Dixie said.

I nodded and paused for a sip of scotch.

"Even though it was damage done by using common fireworks and usually would have been handled as a criminal mischief, technically it was an arson first degree done to a cop's family member. Everyone in the precinct and the squad was looking for revenge, and I really wanted to arrest someone, but never could get enough evidence to put Provanzano at the scene. And that really pissed me off."

"And?" Kate prompted.

I violated a basic rule of single-malt drinkers and took a gulp of whisky.

I growled almost audibly before continuing. "And that *pissed* me off. Someone violated the unwritten rules of cop/wise guy relations. I couldn't let that go."

"What did you do, darling?" Kate likes to make me squirm.

A little more distilled water from the River Fiddich allowed me to elaborate. "I knew Sonny didn't do it personally, but he either ordered it done or Frankie Pro took it upon himself to do it on his behalf. Neither one mattered. Musucci could put a stop to any future bullshit."

I had drained my glass and needed more scotch. Or maybe I just wanted it. Before continuing, I rattled the ice cubes.

"I knew Sonny's daughter went to the Canaan Lake Elementary School. So I checked out a camera with a telephoto lens and took the kid's picture when she walked toward a school bus." I shrugged. "That was it."

"And what did you do with the little girl's photo, Sammy?"

Kate was enjoying herself too much. I almost asked Dixie to run away with me.

I screwed up my nose and gave Kate a dirty look. "And I used a grease pencil to draw a circle around the girl's face and centered cross hairs on her forehead. It looked like a rifle scope. Across the bottom of the picture, I wrote: ENOUGH. I had no problems after that."

"You never told me you did that," Dixie said.

"Not something you spread around."

81

Wayne Zurl

"Was that the end of your business with Sonny Musucci?" Kate knew the answer before she asked.

"Noooo. When I had obtained enough to arrest him for promoting gambling and criminal usury, I obtained a warrant and arrested him in his home in front of his wife and children. I cuffed him and hauled him out."

Dixie tilted her head. "That must have been embarrassing. Perhaps he still harbors a grudge?"

"Are you two in this together?" I sounded exasperated to myself.

Dixie looked at Kate. "Maybe I will have a scotch and soda now."

"Yeah, Katherine, you could refresh my drink as well." I didn't sound as polite as Dixie.

Having finished my ripping yarn, Kate made drinks for her and Dixie and set the bottle of Glenfiddich next to me. I would have liked new ice and frowned. Kate smiled; she knew it would annoy me.

"You said Frank O'Brian came to help," Kate said. "Who else will be working with you on this?"

I didn't answer quickly enough before Dixie commented. "Frank has been retired longer than you. Where is he living now?"

"Greeneville, Tennessee," I said. "About two hours away."

"And who else?" Kate repeated.

"Mike Rodriguez and Walter Danko should be here tonight. Fred Mazzio and Margaret McDermott are coming from Florida—sometime tomorrow."

Kate asked Dixie, "Do you know these people?"

"Other than Frank, I know Mazzio and Maggie," she said. "I must have transferred to the DA's office when the others worked in Sam's section."

Kate smiled. "Sam's Over the Hill Gang. Fred was here last year. He ended up working a case with Sam and John. But he's not the only one who's dropped by to visit with the old boss."

"Where are all these people going to stay?" Dixie asked.

"John's neighbor owns a rental cabin," I said. "It's big enough to house the whole bunch. I need security for you two and with only twelve cops, I can't run Prospect PD and take on the extra work. They volunteered to help."

82

"Oh, my God," Dixie said.

Kate sipped her drink.

Chapter Sixteen

Hanging out with Kate and Dixie was no hardship. The only difference in that Sunday and others was that I kept a handgun within easy reach at all times, and I loaded up my CAR-15, a short version of the standard Vietnam-era assault rifle and three additional thirty round magazines and stashed it in the dining room closet.

As usual, I got up around 6:30, while the girls slept later. When they finally made their appearances, I had coffee ready and fixed cheese and mushroom omelets.

After breakfast, Dixie went upstairs to shower, and Kate helped me clean up.

While drying the coffee pot, Kate said, "I feel so sorry for her."

I interpreted that to mean one thing and responded accordingly. "She seems terribly nervous, but I don't think anyone is after her. However, I always plan for the worst."

"I didn't mean that. Don't you wonder why a sweet and beautiful woman like Dixie never married?"

I stashed the drain board below the sink. "I'll bet 1,500 cops were trying to get into her pants back in the day, but she never found the right guy."

Kate slid the pot into its place in the coffee maker. "How many times do I have to call you an idiot?"

"I beg your pardon?" I tried to sound offended.

"And because you are not a fool, you know exactly what I'm saying."

I canned the offended act and switched to sarcastic. "Why don't you tell me?"

"She found the right guy, but he wasn't available. Capiche, Sammy?"

I looked her square in the eye. "I never took advantage of that girl."

"I'm sure you didn't. That's not you. You're the hero type, and none of your role models would have done that. It's not a cowboy thing."

"Do you have a second point?"

"Other than it's obvious that she loves you, have you called or contacted her since you retired?"

"No."

"Then you haven't been stringing her along. You're a good boy."

"That's it?"

"That's it."

"Thank you."

"You're welcome. Just don't tell me you look at her like your little sister."

"Did I say that?"

"No," she said.

"Are you okay with having Dixie here?"

"Yes. I like her. She's intelligent and good company."

"Good."

She hung the dishtowel up to dry. "Are we going to be virtual prisoners in the house until you catch the person who killed Greg?"

"No. If you want to go out, we can. Just not to a dark movie house. Before we leave, I'll issue you girls handguns just to make things more secure. You don't have to strap them on like Annie Oakley, but keep them handy while you're in the house. After that, we can do whatever you like." I leaned against the counter and stuffed my hands into my pockets while pointing out, "I'm dreadfully good at spotting a tail and better at losing them. We'll use my police car. With only one radio call, I can have hundreds of comrades coming to our rescue."

"Stop joking for a minute and tell me, do you think this supposed threat has any validity?"

"Against me? Maybe, but I can't imagine resurrecting something after all this time. Why would Musucci all of a sudden get a bug in his shorts? And why would some Boston hoods care if the IRA has issues with me?"

"You didn't mention the IRA before."

"Must have forgotten. I'm going to call Ralph Oliveri and ask him to check out a few things. I don't like how Holmes and Barry are doing business."

"You're looking out for Dixie and me, but please think about yourself. Have a partner travel with you. You need someone to watch your back."

"Okay. I'll take John or maybe Frank. He's not specifically doing any guard duty here."

"Thank you."

I nodded. "I'll ask Mike and Maggie to stick with you all day, but I still want you to have a gun nearby."

"You think that's necessary?"

"Better to be prepared and not need it. Be sure you keep it handy if, for some reason, my ex-cops are taken out of the picture."

"Don't even say such a thing."

I needed to lighten up the conversation. "You know me. I sometimes confuse a simple job with one of my Army special operations."

Kate nodded and then let the lashes over her big browns flutter. "Are you sure you want me armed while your ex-girlfriend is in the house?"

"Pfui. Who said she's my ex?"

I'd carry my Glock to provide me with lots of firepower and give my regular duty weapon, an old Smith & Wesson service revolver to Kate who needed no refresher on safe gun handling. Dixie got my snub-nosed off-duty Chief's Special. I briefly covered the fundamentals of good shooting with her and basically said, "If you have to, yank the trigger a couple of times and run like hell to the nearest phone."

I neglected to tell Kate that I had once taken Dixie to the police range and taught her to shoot. It didn't seem important at the time.

At eleven o'clock, I got a call from John. Fred Mazzio and Maggie McDermott had arrived. Now the entire crew was housed at the rental cabin.

"Go pick up Chinese for everyone," I said. "I'll spring. When I get there, we can iron out the assignments."

"Okay, Boss. What do you want?"

"Whatever Frank is having."

I knew he never ordered anything but pepper steak, and I could live with that.

I called PO Bobby Crockett to babysit Kate and Dixie. He'd be good company for them. He'd flirt with Dixie to cheer her up, and he was highly

86

competent.

* * * *

The rental cabin looked something like Ben Cartwright's Ponderosa ranch house with a three-car garage. It had four bedrooms and a pair of foldout couches in the living room. Everyone could sleep alone.

John had brought in the Chinese food just before I arrived, and everyone was waiting for me.

Frank O'Brian, Wally Danko and Fred Mazzio were drinking from bottles of Tsingtao beer. John and Mike Rodriguez held sodas, and Maggie was making tea. Frank handed me a Tsingtao.

"Here ya go, boss."

"Thank you, Francis."

Then I started the greetings and handshaking.

"Whaddaya say, Wally? It's been a long time."

"Hey, Sam, you're looking good."

Wally Danko was the oldest of the group and the biggest. A neat mustache topped off his big smile.

"Mikey, thanks for coming. Man, you never look any older."

"Good to see you, Sam. But I never had this white hair before."

I shrugged, happy to still have hair of any color.

"Freddie, you keep working here and I'll have to get you a badge like Gallagher."

As usual, Mazzio was dressed in a Hawaiian shirt and jeans. The Italian Don Ho.

"Howzit goin', Madman? Hey, I gotta tell you, you owe me for this. McDermott didn't shut her mouth from the time I picked her up in Daytona. Yack, yack, yack. Drove me crazy."

Maggie McDermott turned off the tea kettle and walked over. "Oh, shut up, Freddie. Driving with you was misery."

"Yeah," Freddie said," I had the '60s station on the satellite radio, and she wanted the '70s. Pain. In. The. Ass."

She ignored him. "Hi ya, boss-man. Gonna give me a hug?"

"I'd love to, Margaret. How've you been? You still look like you're thirty-nine."

In fact, Maggie was the youngest but creeping up on sixty. Her platinum blonde hair looked exactly the same as the last time I saw her.

"You are such a liar." She put her arms around me and squeezed. "Now, tell me why someone wants to kill you."

"Yeah, boss," Wally said, "how do you always get yourself into these situations?"

I looked at John Gallagher and pointed at Danko. "Who invited him?"

John frowned. "Don't look at me, Boss. Maggie gave me his phone number."

I looked at her. "You know this old coot loves to break my chops. If you wanted a father figure around, what's wrong with me?"

She pinched my cheek. "Sammy, I always looked at you as a sex object."

That drew a round of catcalls from the roomful of miscreants.

I raised my eyebrows twice. "Now you tell me."

With lunch out of the way, we sat around the oversized dining room table for a war counsel.

"The ladies will want to go places occasionally to keep from going crazy," I said. "Maggs, it would look more normal if you took the day shifts and make it three girls travelling together."

She nodded. "Sure, boss."

"And since Mikey is the most mannerly and civilized-looking out of this motley crew, you tag along."

Mike nodded. "Okay. I like hangin' out with girls."

Frank O'Brien frowned. "What do we look like?"

"A bunch of old thugs," I said.

That caused a few remarks and flagrant mumbles.

"Oh. Just checkin'."

"I'll be home at five o'clock each night unless something pops up. So, that leaves from midnight until eight. Suggestions?"

"One inside and one outside," Fred said. The weather's good. Sitting in a car for a few hours is no hardship. Dank and I can use your PD car. There's a radio if we need it."

"Okay," I said. "I can activate the perimeter alarm in the house. That way, we can move around inside, but if anyone sneaks past the outside man and tries to break in, the siren goes off, and the county cops get dispatched.

"Sounds easy," Wally said. "Everybody bring guns?"

Everyone nodded.

Maggie said, "I brought two."

"Thank you, Mrs. McDermott," I said.

She smiled.

I've got two shotguns in the car," Wally said.

"Why am I not surprised?" I said. "I've got an 870 .12 gauge and a CAR-15 in the house."

"You mean I can rock and roll if the balloon goes up?" Mazzio asked, referring to the possibility that my CAR was fully automatic.

"It's not like the 1st Cav, Frederick," I said. "Semi-automatic."

"Good enough. I want that CAR."

Danko jumped in. "Don't give him all that firepower, boss. The man's unstable."

"Up yours, Commander Kielbasi," Fred said.

"Margaret, can you do something with these people while I'm gone?"

"I'll try, boss, but no guarantees."

"Okay. I'll see you and Mike tomorrow morning. Make it about 8:30. And two others at midnight."

Everyone nodded, without questions.

"Anyone who wants to join the hunt for Buggarelli's killer, show up at the PD. John and I get in at nine. Frankie, you and I will partner up to do whatever. Now, I'm going to take a couple of beautiful women for a ride through the national park. I hope the scenery takes their minds off the problem and no one follows us."

Chapter Seventeen

I remember many bad days in my life, but Monday was one of the worst.

It all started with a visit from Mayor Ronnie Shields. He rarely walks into the PD, and I just didn't buy his story about wanting to welcome Bettye back.

"I'm glad she's here," I said. "That woman can run a department as well as anyone I've ever seen."

"Yes, sir. Yes, sir. She's a good woman," he said while fiddling with a rolled-up piece of paper.

"So, how was your time off?" Ronnie had been away for a long weekend. "Go someplace special?"

"We did. LaDonna wanted to spend a few days at the Grove Park Inn over ta Asheville. You ever been?"

I nodded. "Went for their Sunday brunch once."

"Oh, that was goo-ood, wasn't it?"

He sounded like Andy Griffith doing a Ritz Cracker commercial.

"It was. But expensive."

I'll admit that I sometimes enjoy making our mayor uncomfortable— especially when it concerns some dodgy political shenanigans he or one of his cronies are into, but he walked into my office showing enough stress for five young husbands with nine-month pregnant wives.

"How ya doin' with the new homo-cide from last week."

He makes *homicide* sound like the destruction of a sexual persuasion.

"It's a bit complicated and puzzling at the moment." I took a stab in the dark and pointed at the paper he was strangling. "Is that the memo about it I gave to Trudy on Friday?"

"Oh, this? Well, yes."

"The forensic report is in, but not the autopsy. We should learn those results today. As you know, the victim was a cop, so we're asking his agency for help."

"Did ya talk ta Darnell about this?"

I shook my head. "No. After I spoke to you on Thursday, I relayed some new information to Trudy and gave her an account in writing—for you. If she thought Darnell should know about it, I assumed she would tell him."

"He is the deputy mayor, Sam. Woulda been nice if he heard it from you."

I tossed the pen I'd been holding onto my desktop and sat forward in my chair—probably a little too aggressively.

"I don't like Darnell. I don't want to talk to him—ever. And there is nothing he could have done to help me."

Ronnie shifted in my guest chair. He fidgeted, re-crossed his legs and looked generally uncomfortable for several moments.

"We cain't have that, Sam. No, sir. Cain't have that at all. Darnell is the deputy mayor, and in my absence, he's in charge."

I wanted to reach across my desk and mess up his lacquered hairdo. I didn't even attempt to mask my attitude. "I guess he complained to you. The average man would have called me himself if he felt slighted. Your deputy is not only ignorant, he's a candyass."

Ronnie only addressed one of the issues I mentioned. "Uh, he did mention it."

"Humpf. So, in your absence, you want me to report to him on a regular basis?"

"Uh, well, not if nuthin' important is happenin', no. But with somethin' like this, ya should discuss it with him."

"Why? He knows nothing that could possibly assist in my work."

"I think you should."

"Opening a dialogue would only give that young fool a chance to offer incompetent advice that would just piss me off, or he'd attempt to do something and make a mistake."

"Sam, the man's a lawyer. He's not a fool."

"He *was* a law clerk. He is not a lawyer. He isn't capable of passing a bar exam."

91

We sat through a long moment of Ronnie mustering up the fortitude to issue me an order.

"Sam, this is the way we want it."

I wondered who *we* was.

I shrugged. "Orders are orders."

Ronnie looked very uncomfortable.

"No hard feelin's, Sam, but that's the way we want it."

Was he using the royal *we*?

"You already said that, Mr. Mayor."

"So, you'll comply?"

"And I agreed to that."

"But you disagree with the premise?"

"Of course I disagree. It's a mistake to trust Darnell to run this city— even for a brief time. Watch your back. He's a political hack and an idiot."

Ronnie turned a little pink.

"I'm sorry you feel that way," he said as he left.

* * * *

I grabbed my sport jacket and walked out to the lobby. Bettye was at her desk, and Frank O'Brian sat next to John Gallagher, looking at a few documents.

"Betts, I've got to take my Glock to the TBI lab and satisfy that shitbird from county IAB that I didn't shoot Bo Stallins' victim."

"I can't believe he's doing this to you, Sam. What is he thinkin'?"

"You're giving him too much credit. He's incapable of thinking. He's doing this for some politician who wants to bust my chops. Bo understands that we'll clear his murder case because of my connection to the vic, but little Rodney, the annoying, ineffectual, petulant, juvenile, snot-nose, shit-for-brains captain wants to waste his time and mine."

John Gallagher said, "Watch your blood pressure, Boss. Don't let that turkey get to ya."

"What are you two doing?" I asked.

"Reading over the crime scene reports, looking at the diagrams and pictures, statements and timelines," Frank said.

"John can do that. Let's take a ride. When we get back, all four of us can take a look at what Jackie Shuman calls evidence. Maybe one of us will spot a clue."

Frank stood up. "Gotcha back, Sambo. John, stay out of trouble. Sarge, see ya later."

"Be careful, boys," Bettye said.

In the car, Frank asked, "What's the story with Buggarelli's gun?"

I shrugged. "From what the evidence technician described, it could be an off-duty gun, but kind of small to use every day."

"Our Glocks weren't that big," Frank said. "Why swap seventeen shots for some little thing. What's it hold?"

"I looked it up on the Internet. 8 shots."

"Well, Buggarelli wasn't the brightest light bulb."

"Frankie, I know you didn't like him, but do you say that for a specific reason?"

"Specific? No. The guy always gave me bad vibes."

* * * *

"You're a suspect in a homicide?" Bill Werner, one of the TBI's firearms examiners asked.

"So Captain Rodney Burchfield thinks," I said.

"Based on what?"

"My phone number in the stiff's pocket, his being shot with a nine millimeter, and me owning a Glock 19."

"That's it?"

"And Rodney is an asshole."

"Never heard of him." Werner said.

"Bo Stallins told me Rodney worked patrol for about a year, then went to Jail Admin, got promoted twice, then came over to Plans and Operations. He got promoted again to take over Internal Affairs Bureau when Clifford Barkens got canned."

"He's investigating cops, and he was never a detective?" Bill Werner spoke with a typical Michigan/Great Lakes accent.

"Sounds like he was hardly ever a cop," Frank said.

"Makes you wonder," Bill said.

"Don't be surprised if you see him as chief deputy someday—or even sheriff—when Joe Dee Hartung goes to Nashville or Washington or wherever he wants to go when he gets elected as something else."

"Makes me like the New York civil service system more every day," Frank said.

"Listen, guys," I said, "while we'd love to fix the world polluted by politics, I doubt we will. So how about it, Willie? Want to fire my Glock?"

"Whenever you're ready."

I turned away from my two colleagues, drew the handgun and dropped the magazine. After sticking the magazine under my waistband, I racked the slide to the rear and caught the ejected cartridge in my left hand.

I handed all three to Bill Werner. "Here ya go, doctor. When that bullet doesn't match those dug out of Carlo DeCenzo, send Bo Stallins the report. It might make Rodney feel slighted."

"Sure, let's do this now."

Werner fitted a pair of shooter's earmuffs over his head, and we all stepped next to a water-filled tank. Werner pushed the ejected cartridge into the magazine, slammed it home and released the slide.

"Hold your ears," he said.

With a round in the chamber, he aimed the muzzle end at a protective tube just above the water level and fired. The expended cartridge bounced on the tile floor, and the slide locked open to the rear.

Bill made the gun safe, recorded the serial number on a TBI test fire form and handed it back to me. "There ya go," he said.

"Thanks. Do me another favor?"

"What do you need?"

"Will you check the Ruger that David Sparks delivered the other day? The guy killed at the Foothills View Motel was carrying it, and I'd like to get moving on the case."

"I can move that one up on the list of things to do. Want a full package?"

"And you might want to compare at least the type of round from that gun to the same ones that killed DeCenzo."

"You're kidding?" Frank said.

"No," I said. "This whole affair stinks. Too many coincidences. Too many bodies."

"Like Abbott and Costello," Bill said. "Who's on first?"

"Yeah," I said. "And if you don't mind, as soon as NCIC tells you what they know about the gun, give me a call."

"Like I said before, I'm sure DeCenzo was killed with a Glock. They have unique rifling, but you got it. Who knows what we'll find? And, my friend, I'll get that one done as soon as possible."

"Willie, you're a fine American."

* * * *

Back in the car, I slapped the steering wheel three times. "Shit, shit, shit!"

"Don't lose it, boss." Frank looked at me as if he might have to take me in for an involuntary committal.

"No, Frankie, I've got it wrapped pretty tight. But now I'm going to do something I'll bet you never thought you'd see."

"You're not getting a sex change, are ya?"

"Worse. I'm asking a Fed for some serious official help."

We sat in what they call a squad room at the FBI's Knoxville field office on Locust Street in the old city. Actually, it looks more posh than an office at a multimillion-dollar Wall Street brokerage.

I looked at Frank. "This is the guy I told you about. Ralph Oliveri, Frank O'Brian. Frank retired from my old job. Frank, Ralph isn't quite as bad as all the other G-men we knew. He's from Ozone Park."

"How many times do I have to tell you? South Ozone Park. There's a big difference. Nice to meet you, Frank. Are you suffering from dementia, or is there a legitimate reason for you to be hanging out with this guy?" Ralph pointed at me. He was sitting at his desk wearing a white dress shirt, conservative striped tie and gray slacks.

"He's very caustic for someone so young." I said.

Ralph is in his mid-forties.

"Every time people see me with Jenkins," Frank said, "someone asks if my mother dropped me on my head when I was a baby."

"Ah, another dump on Sam day," I said. "Okay, I came here for some interagency cooperation, but I see I'll have to file a formal request to the SAC. Is Carl in today, Ralph?"

"You see, Frank, he thinks I'll get shaken up by that. Ha. He owes so many favors, he'll have to live to be a hundred to pay me back."

"Ralph, you don't know me and don't owe me spit," Frank said, "but I'm beggin' ya. Help him out here, or I'll have to listen to his bitchin' and moanin' all the way back to Prospect."

Oliveri made a production out of thinking that over. He's so Italian looking, he probably has tomato sauce in his veins. "Yeah, why not? What's one more favor?"

"You're a peach, Ralphie." I said. "Do you know anyone at the Melville field office?"

I briefed Ralph on the entire affair as I knew it and then asked the favor.

"Do you know for a fact that our Long Island office has a wiretap on this Shore Manor?" Ralph asked.

"No. That's why I'm asking. If I can believe that DA's investigator," I said, "I know the county does not. The 5th Precinct cops are hammering the after-hours gamblers—probably looking for an informant. But if any Federal agency has a wire on the LoScalzos, maybe they can shed some light on the conversations Greg Buggarelli had with whoever answers the phone there. While you're at it, see what they know about the Canaan Lake Club, a place owned by Anthony Musucci, son of the infamous Gino Musucci. The county wire picked up a vague conversation that they interpreted as being a discussion about the contract on me. But the connection was bad, and they cannot ID either party."

Ralph snorted. "Gino, your new buddy and soon to be resident of Prospect."

"What can I tell you? A man's gotta do what a man's gotta do."

Ralph shook his head and looked exasperated with the situation. "You think this Buggarelli could be dirty?"

"Who knows? His recent home life seems to be somewhat sullied. Maybe he's got an illegitimate connection to those humps. Maybe he plays cards and doesn't win. I really don't know."

"And right now, you don't like anyone for his murder?"

"Haven't got a clue. He's never been to Tennessee before. As far as I know, no one down here knows him. My next stop is Gino Musucci. Maybe Buggarelli's name rings his bell."

"Okay, paly," Ralph said. "I'll make a call."

* * * *

When Frank and I returned to Prospect PD, I called the Jupiter Hills Security Police station and asked for Chief Baxter. A moment later…

"Sambo, you're back. What's goin' on?"

I told Jim Baxter all about the new happenings and asked another favor.

"Some shit, huh?" he said. "Buggarelli was never my favorite guy, but nobody deserves to get beaten to death. Yeah, I'll talk to Marie again. Tell you what. How about you fax or email me a list of questions so I don't forget anything?"

"Great idea," I said. "I'm glad you know all these technological things."

"Yeah, I'm a real techno-wizard. My grandson taught me how to use a cell phone."

"You're a wild and crazy guy, James. Before you go, guess who's here working with me."

"Besides Black Cloud Gallagher?"

"Yeah. How about Frank O'Brien?"

"Frankie the Fool?"

"Hello, Jimmy." Frank yelled in the background, using an almost falsetto voice.

"Sounds like the Fool. Lemme talk to him."

I handed the phone to Frank and stepped over to the evidence closet to grab the bag of items Jackie Shuman had dropped off.

While Baxter and O'Brien behaved like children, I began rummaging through the small baggies of evidence. One item stopped me cold. I slipped that plastic bag into my jacket pocket and carried the carton into my office.

"Okay, Jimmy," Frank said, "good talkin' with ya. Next time I'm down there, I'll stop in. Yeah, you can introduce me to Burt. All right, I'll see ya."

Frank hung up and asked, "He really works for Burt Reynolds?"

"Huh?" I heard the question, but was still focused on what I had found. "Uh, yeah. Burt owns the corporation that built the community."

"I'll be damned."
"Yeah."

Chapter Eighteen

I placed a small cardboard evidence box on John Gallagher's desk as Frank sat in the chair next to him.

"This stuff has been here since Friday, John. Let's trash Shuman's bag and use our case box."

"Sure, Boss. Out of one and in the other."

"Don't sound so happy. We should be ashamed of ourselves for not checking everything before now."

John tried to look ashamed, but couldn't pull it off. "You know, Boss, in the old days, I'd blame Frankie. But he just got here. I guess I'll have to blame you."

"That's right, John, you Irish weasel, never take responsibility for anything."

"Why don't you fire him?" Frank said.

"I only keep him around because Bettye likes him."

"You take in stray cats and mangy dogs, too, Sarge?" Frank asked.

"Gentlemen, I refuse to take part in this conversation. Sort through your evidence like good little detectives."

"Don't get excited, Boss," John said. "Jackie said he didn't see much here that's worth anything."

"I know. He thinks the stuff not specifically tied to Greg is all from prior guests. There doesn't look like much here."

John reached into the box and pulled out a standard motel scratch pad, one with a Best Western logo on top.

"Looks unused." He thumbed through the pad. "No indentations on any of the pages." Then he took a pencil and colored in the top page. "See? No invisible writing."

Frank grabbed the pencil and threw it at John. "You think you're

James Bond, stupid? You didn't need a pencil to see nothing was there."

"You're just jealous, fool. The Boss relies on my detective skills all the time."

"Skills? You can barely wipe your—" Frank looked at Bettye and turned a little pink. "Go look in the mirror, moron. There's invisible ink on your forehead that says, 'Punch me. I'm an idiot.'"

I whistled through my teeth. "Knock it off…please. Fight after 5 p.m."

John said, "Okay, Boss. But it's Frankie's fault."

Frank sent ocular darts toward John and then looked at me. "You can't boss me around anymore. I'm not on the payroll."

I shook my head. "Francis, must you?"

He shrugged.

I picked up a box of stick matches from Johnny Milton's Paradise Found Steak House, the restaurant next to the motel. There were only matches inside. It too appeared unused.

"Dixie said Greg intended to get something to eat here," I said. "Put them on the list. Take one piece of his photo ID and ask if anyone there remembers him, and if so, did he meet someone."

Frank wrote that down as I began taking more items from the bag. A pen with motel markings looked new. A used tissue was the only piece of trash collected.

"The ETs did a good job of looking," John said. "Before I left, they moved the furniture, checked the drawers top and bottom. David was crawling under the bed when I walked out."

"If this is all they found, that's one clean motel," Frank said.

I nodded. "Yeah. Go ahead, John. What's next? Let's put a location on this stuff."

He extracted a couple more items. "Paper clip. Tag says back of dresser. No help there."

He placed the small plastic bag in the box with the other previously seen items.

"Q-Tip. Under bathroom vanity. Greg didn't look like a Q-tip kinda guy."

"How do you know, stupid?" Frank said. "Did you check his ears for wax?"

"Shut up, fool." John said. "Oh, here's something that might be good. Earring back. Maybe a woman killed him. No, probably not. Came from the closet floor. Just something the maid missed."

I looked into the bag. "The rest looks like his personal effects." I pulled out a black leather shield case and opened the snap. I laid the gold-colored detective investigator's badge on John's desk. Next came a dark brown ankle holster. Gallagher picked out the last item, a brown leather wallet.

"I looked through this in the room, Boss. Nothing interesting. Driver's license, ID cards. Credit cards. Couple of pictures. Some cash. But no secret messages or unexplained items. Really pretty clean and orderly. I guess Greg had a type A personality."

Frank couldn't let that go. "Your wallet must look like a dumpster, stupid. You've got a type Z personality."

John was about to speak when I exercised my supervisory prerogative. "Don't start! When I work with you two, I get a headache in ten minutes. John, did you check his suitcase in the motel room?"

"Yeah, Boss. He hadn't unpacked…just opened the case."

"Do it again. Spread out in the squad room. Check all the cloth. Check the lining of the case and anything else you can think of. It's on the floor in the front of the evidence closet."

"Okay. I'll get the fool to help me. What are you gonna do?"

"Pay Gino Musucci a surprise visit. He must be a card player. Let's see what he says about a pair of dead DeCenzos and one Buggarelli."

* * * *

To reach Gino's rented home, I drove to an area called Kinzel Springs and turned off US 321 onto Brian Branch Road. At the end, I crossed the narrow stream on a private bridge and ascended a steep driveway with a mix of deciduous trees and tall Virginia pines on both sides. On top of the hill, a cleared and landscaped lot afforded the homeowner killer views of Fence Rail Gap to the west and the private community of Laurel Valley to the east. The modern-styled place looked beyond expensive, but disappointing, the design more suited to an Atlantic beachfront in the Hamptons.

I parked and strolled over the tan pea gravel to the leaded glass front door.

Westminster chimes sounded off when I pressed the illuminated bell button. Sixty seconds later, Vito answered the door. He looked me over as if he was passing judgment on a side of US prime beef.

"Howzit goin'," he asked.

"Not bad. You doin' all right?"

"Eh, can't complain. You lookin' for Gino?"

Vito's turtleneck of the day was pearl gray over black slacks. His shoulder holster was a stunning creation by Bianchi in a tasteful saddle tan.

In answer to his question, I said, "Who else?"

"He's in the crapper. Come on in."

Vito led me from the foyer through the living room. If I disliked the modern exterior, I really hated the stark interior. Everything was white—walls, ceiling, carpets, furniture, lamps. A polar bear could hide indefinitely if he closed his eyes and covered his nose. The room had all the ambiance of a new fiberglass porta-potty.

From the living room, two steps down put us in a family room with one wall totally glass, offering a spectacular view of the mountains. The interior decorator must have felt exceptionally bold one day. The carpets were beige. The upholstered sofa and chairs were two shades of beige. The wooden furniture and built-in wet bar were all natural light oak. To scramble the otherwise soothed senses, a long rectangular painting, resembling abstract art and done in mostly primary colors, hung over the couch. It reminded me of the inside of a baboon's brain after he'd been on a three-day bender.

"Nice painting," I told Vito.

"Yeah? You like that shit?"

"I hang finished jigsaw puzzles on my walls."

"Oh, yeah?" He shrugged, but didn't say, 'It takes all kinds.' "You want somethin' ta drink?"

"I'll wait for Gino."

That satisfied him.

"All right." He pointed to a chair. "Take a load off."

Vito left the room, moving with surprising lightness for a guy whose last day under two-seventy-five was a distant memory.

I stared out the big window. A powder blue haze hung over the darker blue peaks. One look let you know why the Cherokee called them the Great Smokies.

After ten minutes, I began feeling neglected.

I turned when Gino spoke. "Been here long?"

"Robinson Crusoe wouldn't call it much of a wait."

"Ha. Like I said, you're hot shit. Okay, I'll use your words. To what do I owe the honor?"

He wore a banana yellow polo shirt under a green Argyle cardigan over pale green slacks.

"You look like you're on the way to play golf," I said.

We shook hands—old friends now. Best buddies.

"Nah. I don't play golf. Stupid game. I'd rather go to the track." He wasn't talking about running a 440 for exercise. "That's one thing I'll miss livin' down here."

"Maybe you'll develop an interest in college basketball," I suggested.

"Yeah, right. The goon sport. What do you go, about six foot?"

I nodded.

"Tall for an average guy, no? In that sport, you'd be a midget."

I laughed.

"Want a drink?"

"What are you doing?"

"I'm having scotch."

"Okay," I said, "over a pair of cubes."

He walked to the wet bar, took two short glasses off a shelf and poured two inches of something from a crystal decanter into each. He reached into the mini-fridge below the counter, plucked out a couple cubes for each glass and added soda to his.

Gino handed me a glass and raised his. "Salute."

"Salute," I said. The whisky tasted like Dewar's.

"So," he said, "wha' can I do for ya?"

"I was wondering if you knew that a mutual acquaintance died the other day—and not of natural causes. Alphonse DeCenzo."

He nodded. "I heard."

"Mind if I ask how?"

"How I heard or how he died?"

103

"I know the last."

"My brother-in-law called. He knows some people."

"Does he know who did it?"

"No. Just ideas. He didn't say."

I pulled the letter Alvie Greenblatt delivered from my jacket pocket and handed it to Gino. "Alphonse wrote me a note before he got killed. His lawyer made sure I got it."

Gino read it slowly, maybe twice.

"Jesus Christ."

"Too many coincidences happening," I said. "Carly DeCenzo gets popped with my name and number in his pocket. Alphonse buys the olive farm in Florida. I get this note, and a cop I used to work with gets murdered in a Prospect motel. Makes me wonder what's next."

"Who's the cop?"

"Ever run across a guy named Greg Buggarelli?"

"He work for you?"

"He was in the same team when I worked in the 5th Squad. But after that, we went our separate ways. Recently he was a contract investigator for the DA."

I showed Gino Greg's photo ID with the most recent likeness. He looked carefully, but shook his head.

"I don't know this guy. Never saw him in Jersey. He ever deal with Anthony?"

"I assume so, but I've got no details yet. Should I put your son on my list of people who might want to see my wife collect a death benefit?"

"Anthony?" He sounded surprised. "When's the last time you saw him?"

"We were never cordial."

"Yeah? So what? You locked him up when? Almost thirty years ago? You two are past history."

"He told me he'd never forget."

"Anthony's got a big mouth. He says stupid stuff. Call him and ask."

"Sure, I'll invite him down here. We can have coffee and chat."

"All right, all right. I'll check into it. What you're sayin' goes against the grain, but if that fuckin' kid does anything ta jeopardize me and Theresa livin' here in peace, I'll—"

I interrupted. "I really don't want you to finish that sentence."

Gino rolled his eyes. "Yeah, right. Okay. Like I said, I'll look inta this."

"Thanks."

"I'll call ya." He took a healthy pull on his drink.

After a long moment of us sipping in silence, I broached a new topic. "I don't want to seem like a nitpicker, but I really should ask about one of the few laws Tennessee has regarding shootin' irons. Does Vito have a carry permit for the cannon he wears under his armpit?"

He laughed. "I knew you'd check, so, yeah. Soon as we got here, he applied for a carry permit. He's got a clean record. No problems. Had ta go ta safety classes, too." He laughed again. "Then he bought a new gun over the counter at someplace in Maryville."

"I knew Vito looked like a good boy."

"You didn't check up on him?"

"I don't know Vito's family name," I lied.

"Easy one ta remember, Cinquemani." He gave it an old country pronunciation: Chink-qua-moni.

"Five hands. You're right. Easy to remember."

* * * *

I walked back into the PD and found Bettye alone.

"Hey," I said.

"Hey, yer own self."

I pointed at John's desk. "Those two on the road?"

"Uh-huh."

"That's a potentially dangerous situation. They might kill each other. But the public is probably safe."

She smiled.

A radio call came in from Vern Hobbs in unit 506. He said he'd be checking a possible stolen car dumped in a wooded area. Bettye acknowledged the call and jotted down his location before looking back at me.

"You going out for lunch?" I asked.

"I am."

"Would you stop at Quizno's and get me a turkey, bacon and Swiss

105

with mayo?"

"You figger your arteries need a little cloggin', darlin?"

"Be nice to me. I spent the morning with two gangsters."

She fluttered her eyelashes and handed me a pink telephone message slip. "Give Dr. Mo a call. He's got the results."

"Morris, Morris, Morris," I said. "I love you. Everyone should be as punctual. Who's my killer?"

"You overestimate me, boychek. I know how the man was killed...not who killed him."

"Isn't that splitting your infinitives? Shouldn't it be, by whom he was killed?"

"Who, whom, who-ha. You want to know what I know or what?"

"Tell me."

"Very simple. Two shots to the temple with an oblong blunt object."

"Ouch. If I wanted to kill someone quietly, I might go for his temple."

"It's a sensitive spot. The first blow probably put him down. The second—a more focused and forceful one—killed him. Quickly."

"Rather straight forward."

"Don't go away, young man. There's more. The object left a unique mark. Waffling. I'm thinking blackjack."

"Like an old-fashioned lead jack covered by woven leather strips?"

"Exactly. And a big one. Probably pushing a pound."

"Hmmm. I used to carry one of those. Fourteen ounces, to be exact."

Chapter Nineteen

While Bettye was out, I sat at the desk and listened for the phone and the radio. It was unusually quiet, so I called Bo Stallins.

"I've got something for you to check that may help you or me or us," I said.

"What's that s'pposed ta mean?"

"I need to know what kind of gun is listed on the concealed carry permit for one Vito Cinquemani. The paper should be newly issued. Supposedly, the gun came from a store in Maryville."

"What the hell kinda name is *Sink-queer-manny*?"

"It's Vito's name, sir."

"Very funny. Spell it."

I did.

"And how might this he'p me?"

"If it's a nine millimeter Glock, use your imagination."

"Hmmm. By the way, I wanna give ya a heads-up. Burchfield is sendin' a subpoena ta yer lawyer demandin' that you appear with him and answer questions about the death of that man at the Foothills View Motel. I guess now he figgers you killed him, too."

"That stupid son of a bitch. Like I've got nothing else to do than talk to him about something that's none of his business."

"Jest lettin' ya know, bud."

"Yeah, thanks. Let me know what Vito purchased, okay?"

"I'll call ya."

After a few 9-1-1 calls and twice as many radio transmissions came in, Bill Werner called with news.

"First, I'll have you know, you did not kill Carlo DeCenzo. At least

107

you didn't with that Glock 19 of yours."

"Wow, that's a relief. For a minute there I thought I might have."

"Yeah, I could hear the apprehension in your voice. Sounded like you were sweating that one. Now, that other item, the Ruger LC9. I'm afraid that one's a jackpot."

"Ooo, tell me."

"Well, it didn't kill DeCenzo, but I knew that because the rifling is nothing like a Glock. NCIC says it's hot. And guess who's got the open case?"

"Hmmm. Wait while I gaze into my crystal ball. Hmmm, the name of the actual cop is a little fuzzy, but I bet he works on Long Island."

"Give that man a stuffed panda. 1st Squad Detectives from your old job. It's proceeds from a very large commercial burglary at a place called Gun Central."

"On Route 110 in Farmingdale, owned by an ex-cop named Angelo Garafola who retired on disability and became an arms dealer."

"I don't know who owns the store, but Gun Central is the place."

"Is the detective's name and date of occurrence on the file?"

"Happened November 18th last year. Handled by Detective Thomas Woods, shield number 797, team 2, 1st Squad.

"Thank you, William. Have I ever told you you're my favorite firearms examiner?"

"You've got some line of shit, buddy."

* * * *

Every time I heard the name Rodney Burchfield Jr. I'd grit my teeth. Thinking about him created the same feeling I'd get if I learned that vandals had driven ice picks into all four of the horribly expensive Michelin radials on Kate's new Infiniti. But I assumed that he'd have to be dealt with. I called Joe Costello's office, gave his secretary Stephanie Garner a head's up and made an appointment to discuss the young nincompoop with my attorney.

That out of the way, I called Pat Herlihy on Long Island and explained about the Greg Buggarelli murder and the little gun in his ankle holster.

"Jesus, what kind of place do you work in?" he asked. "You got more murders in a week than Detroit."

"We're having a bad season."

"Yeah, right. What's next? You better keep an eye on Gino Musucci. He might be giving you the biggest snow job since the blizzard of 1947."

"You're a dismal bastard."

"Yeah, I'm just sayin'."

I wanted to change the subject before he had me contemplating suicide.

"You know any of the precinct cops harassing the gamblers at the Shore Manor?" I asked.

I could almost see him thinking and nodding. "Sure. There are a few enthusiastic guys doing a lot of ball breaking over there."

"Do me a favor, and ask if anyone has ever stopped Greg Buggarelli after the game broke up."

"You're kidding."

"Afraid not. Greg's boss at Rackets Bureau says he had no active cases on either the Shore Manor or the LoScalzos. Yet, John Gallagher found the restaurant's number on Greg's phone."

"Was he a gambler?"

"Who knows? He was talking to someone at the Shore Manor, and anyone can find quite a few nice restaurants between Montauk Highway in Shirley and where Greg lived in Smithtown. Even I wouldn't drive that far for good Italian food."

"So, you figure if Greg got stopped, he'd tin the cops and give them a story about working undercover?"

"Wouldn't you?"

"I hope you're wrong."

"I hope I'm right. He's dead now, and something was wrong with him. A good cop doesn't carry a gun stolen during a commercial burglary. How'd he get that? Connecting him to Patsy LoScalzo and Sonny Musucci would fill in some empty gaps."

"We should be glad you never worked in Internal Affairs."

"The good guys would have had nothing to worry about. And this does seem like Greg may have been complicit with the plot to whack yours truly."

Pat sighed. "Holy shit. What a can o' worms. Okay, I'll track down a few cops and ask."

"I've got a local agent asking if the FBI in Melville have wire taps on the phones at the Shore Manor and the LoScalzos or the Canaan Lake Club and Moonface Musucci. Maybe we can piece together a few of these dangling facts."

* * * *

I was munching on the sandwich Bettye brought back for me when Jimmy Baxter called from Hobe Sound.

He snickered. "Marie DeCenzo made coffee, gave me a few cannolis and we had a long chat."

"You want a drum roll before you tell me what she knows?"

"Jeez, Sambo, you're always so impatient."

"I've got a young asshole from Sheriff's IAB now accusing me of beating Greg Buggarelli to death. Excuse me for getting antsy."

"What kind of place do you work in? Is this guy serious?"

"He's stupid. That's worse than serious. If he continues to annoy me and run up my legal expenses, I may be forced to toss this little captain out a second floor window."

Jimmy laughed. "If he's that bad, don't open the window."

I sighed. "What do you know, James?"

"Well, Marie still doesn't definitively know who killed Alphonse or Carlo. But you know the deal. One of those wives would have her tongue cut out before blowing the whistle on another wise guy. Then she gave me that crap about not being able to prove anything. When I pushed her to cut the bullshit, she figures it had to be Sonny Musucci. Said he's always had a hard-on for the men in her life."

"Maybe Sonny knew Alphonse had been feeding me info for years, but why Carly?"

"Just a guess, but Carly inherited the vending machine business and owns the machines in the Canaan Lake Club and the Shore Manor. Maybe he saw or heard something that was none of his business."

"Hmmm. Or now that Sonny is taking over Gino's operation, maybe he wanted to give that lucrative vending territory to one of his people. But the DeCenzos had been granted the area by Gino himself. Only way to undo Gino's edict is to kill off the heir apparent."

"Could be."

"But if Carly heard something mentioned about me at one of those places while tending the machines, maybe he told his papa."

"That's what I'm thinking," Jimmy said.

"So maybe Patsy LoScalzo got suspicious and dropped a dime on Moonface."

"Or somebody in Musucci's place knows something."

"Those are easy answers," I said.

"Nothing new under the sun."

"Marie say anything about the Musuccis going to bed with the Guinzos in Rhode Island or the Micks in Boston?"

"Jesus Christ. You're gonna need the United Nations to sort this out."

"I'll take that as a no."

* * * *

Ten minutes and several bites of sandwich after I hung up on Jim Baxter, Bo Stallins called.

"Got me that info on yer boy *Sink-queer-manny's* carry permit," he said.

"Why do you people have such trouble with Italian names?"

"Do what?"

"It's a good thing the Russian mob doesn't come down here."

"Russians?"

"Forget it. What kind of gun is Vito packing?"

"Smith & Wesson SD40. Brand new in the box."

"I take it that SD40 means a .40 caliber automatic?"

"Yep. Full size. Ten in the mag and one in the chamber."

"That complies with all the rules in any state."

"It does."

"But doesn't hardly shoot nine millimeters."

"It don't."

"Doesn't mean he might not have something off paper."

"Got that right."

"Thanks, buddy, but you're no help at all."

"Up yours."

* * * *

At twenty to five, I left the PD heading for Joe Costello's office in Maryville. The sun began dipping into the horizon and gave off the color of a blood orange. I squinted, looking into its brightness, as I drove due west on US 321. The sky was clear, the air cool, and if I didn't have so much on my mind, I would have thought life was as good as back in the days when every suit came with two pair of pants.

I parked the Ford, walked over a red brick path flanked by grass nice enough to be mistaken for a putting green and opened the door to Joe Costello's waiting room. The beautiful Stephanie greeted me like a long lost uncle.

"Nice outfit," I said. "Royal blue is a good color for you."

"Well, thank yew. Aren't you jest so sweet?"

"I am and modest, too."

She smiled and started to pick up her phone.

But Costello had heard us talking, stepped into his doorway and waved me toward his office.

His dark gray suit jacket lay across the corner of his Hepplewhite-styled solid cherry desk. His sleeves were rolled up on his forearms, striped tie undone and collar open, and he looked tired.

Joe slumped into a brown leather swivel chair big enough to hold Henry VIII, and I dropped into a yellow, tucked and buttoned leather guest chair that must have cost more than my annual property taxes.

"You look tired," I said.

He shook his head, but wasn't disagreeing. "I'm gettin' too old for this aggravation."

"You're a lot younger than me."

"Which makes me ask why don't you really retire."

I shrugged. "Adrenalin junkie?"

"I'd find a twelve step program and kick the habit." He didn't wait for me to offer a clever comment before he continued. "What have you done to this Captain Burchfield to warrant this treatment?"

"If you don't count calling him an asshole, nothing." I waved a hand dismissively. "Little Rodney takes his orders from someone who doesn't like me."

"The sheriff?"

"Joe Dee and I get along alright."

112

"Then who?"

"Probably a cast of thousands. I'm wondering if I should just dispel the myth of me killing those two people or start my own background investigation and dig up a conspiracy."

"To what end? Do you have time to prosecute this?"

"No, but I'd like to stick it up someone's ass."

"Don't you think stickin' it to someone got you into this predicament?"

"Hey, I pay you. Why are you raining on my parade?"

"I'm a lawyer. We do stuff like that."

I took out my Alphonse DeCenzo letter as delivered by Alvie Greenblatt, emissary of Sheinbaum. McCluskey and Clancy, PC and handed it to Costello. "Perhaps Burchfield will see the futility of his investigation if he gets the bigger picture. Or maybe he'll just cross his fingers and hope I'm the next victim."

Costello frowned as he read. When he finished, he looked up. A wrinkled brow and hard dark eyes made me think he took the message seriously. "May I copy this?"

"Sure."

"I assume you're taking precautions?"

"You think I should wear a condom?"

He made a face and shook his head. "Not what I meant."

"Yeah, the most cautious kind."

"You don't seem overly concerned."

"I'm watching my back and so are other people."

"Your cops?"

"To some extent, but I've arranged for some non-local talent."

"Do I want to know about this?"

"Probably not."

He raised his eyebrows.

"I arranged for a few *security specialists* to lend a hand. And I've got a county PD, DA's office and Feds in New York working a few angles for me. Also, the father of my best suspect would like to get on my good side. Google a guy named Gino Musucci. He and I are becoming fast friends."

Joe shook his head. "I don't need to Google Gino Musucci. You play with some strange people."

"They came with the territory."

Costello sighed, and his shoulders dropped. He looked even more tired. "Okay. I won't try and tell you how to run your business. We've got a 9:30 date with Burchfield tomorrow."

Chapter Twenty

Joe Costello was already in the parking lot of the Justice Center when I pulled in at 9:20. He locked the doors on his black Lexus and met me on the asphalt.

Joe kicked off our meeting with Burchfield by admonishing him for his witch-hunt. He cited legal reasons why Rodney's investigation was foolish and any suspicions would turn out unfounded.

"For God's sake, Captain, you can't even articulate a reasonable suspicion why Chief Jenkins is involved in these murders."

Burchfield allowed his petulance to show again. "That's not the way I see it."

"Thankfully, the courts have established criterion on the levels of proof necessary to prosecute a criminal matter. Perhaps you should brush up on the Tennessee Code before you continue to waste taxpayer's money."

Rodney did that mouth thing I'd grown to hate and said nothing.

"Read this," Costello handed the little runt a copy of DeCenzo's letter. "That was delivered by an investigator employed by a law firm from Stewart, Florida. That's in the proximity where Mr. DeCenzo senior, father of Carlo DeCenzo, our decedent, was recently murdered. That in itself casts more than a reasonable doubt on the chief's involvement. The letter tells us Chief Jenkins may be targeted as an intended victim. He's not a killer."

Burchfield dropped the letter onto his desktop and renewed his facial gymnastics. "I'll look inta this."

Costello shook his head in frustration.

I had been sitting quietly, allowing the attorney to earn my portion of his astronomical salary, but now Rodney had gotten on my nerves.

"Let me give you a little advice, Captain," I said. "Don't look too deeply into this, or you'll place yourself in a world of trouble."

Burchfield sat forward abruptly like he had been mortally offended. "What's that s'possed ta mean?"

"It means, shit-for-brains, that your investigation is heading nowhere but into the toilet, and if you interfere with my *official* investigation of multiple homicides, you might find yourself charged with obstructing."

"You cain't—"

"Shut up! I can, and I will. This case has become so far-reaching that you wouldn't be able to tread water for two minutes as you floundered around in the complications. I've called in two law enforcement agencies from New York to assist me." He opened his mouth, but I didn't even take a breath. "And because of the probability of an interstate conspiracy, I've enlisted the local FBI field office to secure help from the FBI in New York to cover additional territory. Soon enough, we may be involving local and Federal investigators from Rhode Island and Boston. So, sport, if you stick your nose into my business too far, I'll ask my FBI friends to toss your ass into a Federal slammer until you cease and desist on this fool's errand. Capiche?"

"You threatin' me ag'in?"

I shook my head in disbelief. "Yes, you moron, I am. Go tell your handler that this political master plan to break my balls will not fly. I'll make it my life's work to prove you and them guilty of a conspiracy. And after I finish with you in criminal court, I'll have Mr. Costello sue you all in civil court, and I'll own everything that's yours."

Rodney listened to me while squinting and moving his nose around like an angry squirrel.

"If you think I'm bluffing, Rodney old boy, discuss this with a lawyer connected to the politician who sent you after me." I stood abruptly and sent the chair I'd been using sliding across the small room. "We're done here."

Rodney's mouth hung open like a slack-jawed drunk. Costello looked up at me. I gestured for him to follow.

Joe smiled and spoke to Burchfield. "I'll be finishing this conversation with the sheriff." Then he followed me into the hallway.

In the elevator, Joe asked, "All that noise true?"

"I speak with straight tongue, paleface Irish lawyer."

"Is a straight answer from you possible?"

"Close enough to the truth for that nitwit."

"Good. I'll make an appointment with Joe Dee. After that and what you said, maybe Burchfield will stay off your case."

"It would be in his best interest."

* * * *

I found Kate, Maggie and Mike playing cards in the dining room. A footed glass of white wine sat next to Kate while Maggie drank from a Diet Coke can, and a can of grape soda adorned a coaster at Mike's right hand.

I looked over Mike's shoulder at the cards he held. "Hmmm."

"What?" he said.

"Anyone who drinks grape soda has no right to ask questions."

"Gimme a break."

Maggie dropped an eight of clubs on the discard pile. "Hearts."

Mike groaned and picked up a new card. Kate kept a straight face and discarded a queen of hearts. I had no interest in making the game a foursome, so I walked into the living room and found Dixie reading. What I assumed was a scotch and soda sat on the lamp table to her right. Her eyes were a little cloudy, and her brow wrinkled. She looked hard at work.

"Hey, kiddo," I said, "you really concentrating on that book or feeling unhappy?"

"Hi." She marked her place and set the book aside. "Just weary, I guess. We didn't do much today."

From the dining room, we heard Mike. "Damn." Several cards hit the table with a little force. "I haven't won a game yet."

"Cheer up, Mikey," Maggie said. "You get to play with two beautiful women."

"Big deal," he said. "I'm getting hungry."

That drew my attention. "What are you guys doing for dinner?" I asked.

Mike answered. "Stupid said he's bringing steaks to the cabin. Dank volunteered to man the grill."

"Which *stupid* are you talking about?" I asked.

"Frank," Maggie said. "John's wife wants him home tonight."

"What have you got in mind, Kats?" I asked. "I don't smell anything cooking."

"I thought you'd like to take two of the women in your life out to eat."

"It's a good thing I've got two pensions and a decent job. I'm romantically involved with a pair of gold diggers."

I walked into the dining room. Dixie followed.

"How about the Villa Napoli?" Kate asked. "I thought Dixie might like a touch of back home."

"Works for me. Everyone likes Italian food. Right, Dix?"

"Sure. I'm up for a drive."

As usual, Nick Cutrone seated us at his table, table 35, on the raised portion of the dining room, four steps above the main floor.

Nick's son, Tommy, had prepared a special batch of butternut squash ravioli with onions, garlic, and prosciutto, topped with a creamy wine sauce. We all ordered the special and thought that an imported pinot grigio would be a good accompaniment.

Around the time Nick's grandson, Vinnie the bartender, delivered the wine in a silver-plated ice bucket, Kate excused herself and headed toward the lady's room.

Dixie began a conversation. "I'm due back at work on Monday. How long do you think I have to be here with my bodyguards?"

I had expected the question sooner rather than later. "Aren't you enjoying my company?"

She offered a halfhearted smile. "I should have remembered it's impossible to get a straight answer from you."

"I'm shattered."

"You also seem to be the target of someone from your former life."

"Well, there is that, too."

"You could have an ax embedded in your head and make a joke out of it."

"Maybe not. But don't you want me to keep you safe?"

"Why would the person who killed Greg want to kill me?"

"Honestly, he...or she...probably wouldn't. You didn't witness anything. I'm just being cautious."

"I wanted to see my aunt again."

"That's not such a great idea. Call her again. Tell her you had car trouble and the repairs are taking longer than you anticipated. She'll understand."

"I suppose."

"You want to go home?"

"I have to, don't I?"

I gave her one of my most endearing smiles. "I was thinking of becoming a Mormon and could use an extra wife or two. Interested?"

"You're such an idiot."

"Who me?"

She smiled again, this time, a genuine big one. "Yes, you."

"But I'm good at it. So, how do you want to go back? I see two choices."

"And they are?"

"You can drive back. Wally Danko could escort you to, let's say, Pennsylvania. That would be close to his place in West Virginia. Then, I'll get Steven Holmes to send an investigator or two to meet you and finish the trip to Long Island. Option two is a flight back. I'd arrange for an air marshal to keep an eye on you in the plane. Steven could have someone meet you at the airport. Your hot little IS350 could be trucked back."

"I'd rather drive."

"I thought so."

Kate approached the table. I stood and pulled a chair out for her.

"He's such a gentleman in front of you, Dixie," she said. "He's never this chivalrous when we're alone."

I scowled. "The woman is a liar."

Dixie grinned a little.

"What were you two discussing?" Kate asked.

"Dixie's exodus," I said.

"Oh, when?"

"I guess Friday," she said. "That will give me a day at home before work on Monday."

"Okay, then," I said. "I'll get to work on the logistics."

"And you think this is a safe and good idea?" Kate asked.

"I think so," I said.

"It's been good to see you two," Dixie said, "after such a long time."

I took a long sip of wine and changed the subject. "Did you see Greg immediately before driving down here?"

"Immediately?"

"Like within two or three days of leaving?"

"Uh, no. I think he was off. The day we left, he parked his car outside the office. I picked him up in the parking lot, and we got right onto the Expressway heading here."

"Hmmm. That gives me a problem."

I explained about Greg having been in telephone contact with Patsy LoScalzo or someone else at the Shore Manor and the stolen gun he'd been carrying.

"So what are you saying, Sam?" Dixie said, looking more at her wine glass than me.

"I'm asking where Greg was because I think he had time to get down here, kill Carlo DeCenzo and get back to New York and meet you."

Dixie raised her eyes cautiously, somewhat like a small child approaching an open coffin. "Is that possible?"

"Sure it's *possible*. No one seems to be able to explain little things about Greg's behavior. I've asked Holmes to question his wife and latch on to Greg's Glock for a comparison to the bullets that killed Carly. But he hasn't called back yet."

Both Dixie and Kate were about to speak when I continued. "The big question is, why was he packing a Ruger stolen from a Long Island gun shop. And why was he communicating with LoScalzo or one of his goons?"

Kate looked shocked. "You think he was sent here to kill you with the stolen gun?"

"That's not possible." Dixie said.

I shook my head. "Oh, it's possible. I would hope not, but—"

"So who killed Greg if he was sent to kill you?" Kate asked.

"Don't know, but I'd like to buy that person a beer."

Chapter Twenty-One

A white, late model Corvette pulled out of the Villa Napoli parking lot moments after we did. I turned right on Washington—so did the 'Vette. At the next traffic light, I took the gentle curve left onto US 321 heading east. The Corvette followed three or four car lengths behind. I saw no front license plate, so assumed it might be a local car. We passed the Justice Center and the hospital. I maintained the forty-five mile per hour speed limit. So did the Corvette, while other cars breezed past us.

When the limit changed to fifty, I increased my speed and shifted to the right lane. The 'Vette switched lanes and held fifty miles per hour. More cars passed us doing fifty-five or sixty.

My quandary: Coincidence, or was someone purposely following us? With backlighting from a couple of well-illuminated gas stations close to the road, I could make out a pair of heads in the two-seater. Being outnumbered is never a good thing, but it wasn't like I might be getting ambushed by a platoon of infantrymen. Any good shooter can take out a pair of hoodlums if he acts first, and I'm better than good. If necessary, this duo would be dead before they could react.

I really didn't want to alarm Kate and Dixie, but to pull off what I had in mind, I'd have to tell them my plan.

"Don't get excited, ladies, but I think someone's following us."

Kate turned to face me, and her shoulders dropped. "Oh, great. Who?"

"Good question. It's a Corvette, so I can't outrun them. I'm going to make a few turns and then take evasive action."

"*Oh, great* is right," Dixie said.

"I'll just make a few right turns that make no sense. If they follow, I'll know for sure they're up to no good and then make a move."

"Describe this *move*," Kate said.

121

"Not exactly sure yet, but you'll know when it happens. When I stop the car, keep your heads down."

"Why us?" Kate asked.

Without using a turn signal, I made a quick right onto Grandview Drive. Seconds later, as we passed a cemetery on the left, the Corvette headlights appeared behind us. I floored the Crown Vic. The 'Vette picked up speed. At Tuckaleechee Pike, I turned right again and stepped on it. At the next corner, I took another fast right onto West Merritt. The tires squealed, and once more, the Corvette kept up with me. The final intersection put me back on 321. I made the fourth right onto the four-lane highway, putting us back where we started. A quick two blocks later, I pulled into an Exxon station and slammed on the brakes next to the gas pumps. The Corvette pulled up on our right and behind me. Quickly, I exited the Ford, drawing my Glock and stepped behind the cement column that separated two clusters of pumps.

I braced my gun against the concrete barrier. "Both of you," I yelled, "out of the car! Hands on your heads!"

The driver of the Corvette didn't shut off the ignition, and no one moved.

"Out of the car now!" I upped my volume even more. "Do it!"

The driver of a pickup in the next aisle took cover behind his truck. Two people came out of the station's convenience store and joined him. Both stared at me wide-eyed. One man held a cell phone.

"Police!" I yelled. "You people stay where you are!"

The driver's side window of the Corvette began to lower. I placed my sight picture square in the middle of the window.

"Take it easy, Madman. We're friendlies."

As the window disappeared into the car door, I saw Fred Mazzio's smiling face. I let out a long breath and holstered my gun.

"For chrissakes." I pulled my badge from my pants pocket and held it where the spectators could see. "Police officer. No problem here," I called out. "Just a training exercise. Everything's okay. Go about your business."

The driver of the pickup peeked over the hood. I waved to him. The man with the cell phone didn't look convinced and began tapping a number. I walked toward him.

"Police officer, sir. There's no problem here."

I kept the big badge held high for him to get a clear look. Finally, he nodded and clipped the phone back on his belt.

"Thanks for your concern," I said.

He and the other man returned to the store. The guy with the pickup jumped into the cab and moved out briskly. I walked back toward the Corvette and noticed the Florida Vietnam Veteran's plate on the back. That accounted for no front plate. Like Tennessee, Florida doesn't issue them.

From the open passenger's window, Mike Rodriguez said, "I believe you would have shot us."

I shook my head. "You two don't believe in coordinating our efforts?"

Fred leaned over and spoke out the passenger's window. "I told Mikey we should have called you, but he didn't want to."

"What?" Mike gasped.

If in doubt, I always blame Mazzio.

"I thought you owned a black Corvette," I said.

"Sold it," he said, still grinning, "and bought this newer edition. I like the style of the grill they started using in '05. We in the know call it a C6."

"Fascinating. I'll bet Mary could have sold it for a profit if I killed you."

"You're always so serious. Lighten up."

"Bullshit. Pull over to the far side of the lot. I'll be right there."

"You got it, sahib."

I jumped into the Ford and let out a long breath. Kate didn't give me a chance to get in the first word.

"What was that all about?"

I smiled to ease the tension. I'm not sure how much it helped. "Two of the lads decided to provide extra security, but didn't tell me. I'll talk to them now."

I tapped the shifter into Drive and moved toward Mazzio who had backed the Corvette into a spot away from any other cars. He and Mike had gotten out and were leaning against the driver's side fender, both grinning like bad little boys. I got out of the Ford.

"You scared the ladies."

Mike smiled and waved at Kate and Dixie.

"Seemed like you were a bit keyed up yourself, fearless leader," Mazzio said, his arms folded over his chest.

"And now I'm disappointed. I can't add two notches to the grip of my shootin' iron for capping two wise guys."

"You'd feel bad if you shot me by mistake," Mazzio said.

"In your dreams. I'd have your head stuffed and hang it on my wall."

"That's a scary thought," Mike said.

Fred looked at him. "Backstabber."

"Shut up, Freddie. You almost got me killed."

"Hey, guys, slug it out later," I said. "What was going on here?"

"We finished eating early," Fred said, "and wanted to keep you safe."

"He didn't want to help with the dishes," Mike added.

"Ya see what I have to put up with, boss?" Fred tried to sound frustrated.

"How did you know where we were?" I asked.

"Your wife mentioned the restaurant," Mike said.

"And I remembered the place from my last visit." Mazzio added.

"You should have called," I said.

"Yeah, yeah, yeah," Mazzio said.

"Doesn't seem like anyone's in any big hurry to punch your ticket, boss," Mike said. "You really think Dixie is in danger?"

"Probably not."

"Wanna say why?" Mazzio asked.

"Just a hunch."

"How long are we gonna keep this up?" Fred asked.

"Dixie wants to leave for New York on Friday. After that, we'll make different arrangements. Those who want to stay around can work on the murder investigation."

"Cool." Mazzio looked happy. "You'll need us to clear this big stuff."

"So, you don't think Dixie's a target for these goombahs?" Mike asked.

I thought about that for a long moment. "I doubt it. I'll ask Dank to follow her part of the way home, and I'll arrange for a couple of DA's investigators to meet her and escort her back safely."

"And what about you?" Fred asked.

"Beats the hell outta me. I've got the FBI involved now. Maybe they'll help out afterhours. Then you guys can lend your talents to the homicide."

"Like those Korean murders I solved for you." Frederick sounded overly proud of himself.

"Yeah, right. More pipe dreams," I said. "You solved them all alone, my ass."

"I did."

"You gotta tell me about this, Freddie," Rodriguez said.

"I'll tell you about Sam's girlfriend, too." Mazzio shifted his arrogant stare to me. "Where is she, by the way?"

"Not a girlfriend, you nitwit. Just a good friend." I didn't give him a chance to stick in another snide remark. "She's in Chicago. Got a new job."

"I'll bet you're heartbroken."

"Mike, is it too late for me to kill him and get away with it?"

Mike shrugged. "I don't want to get involved, boss."

"See how defensive he gets when I mention her?" Mazzio snickered. "Her name is Rachel. Really good-looking, but young enough to be his daughter."

I had had enough. "Good night, Mikey. Frederick, kiss my ass."

Chapter Twenty-Two

At seven a.m., I walked downstairs to find Wally Danko in the kitchen pouring himself a cup of coffee.

"I just made a fresh pot," he said. "You interested?"

"Sure. Kate will be down in a few minutes. Dixie does her shower thing in the morning. She'll be later. Want some breakfast?"

"What are you having?"

I shrugged. Breakfasts had been getting boring. I didn't look overly enthused. "Cereal and toast, I guess."

"Cereal?" Wally made a face and looked like he just sucked on a rancid lemon. "I'll make me and the fat man some sausage and eggs when we get back to the cabin."

I raised my eyebrows. "You growing boys gotta keep up those cholesterol levels."

"Gimme a break."

"I'll go outside and get Frederick Junior," I said. "He probably needs some coffee."

"Bastard's probably asleep."

"Sleeping on guard duty is a capital crime."

"Yeah, like he cares."

I opened the laundry room door to the garage and slapped the button that opens the overhead door. I walked outside and found Fred Mazzio sitting in the driver's seat of my Crown Vic tapping the steering wheel in time to music I couldn't hear.

He rolled down the window. Mick Jagger was screaming, "I cain't get no sa-tis-faction."

"You're awake," I said.

He turned down the volume. "Of course I'm awake. You think I'd

126

sleep while I'm on an OP?"

"I told Dank you wouldn't."

"Screw him. You know what they say about navy men."

I smiled as Phlash Phelps took a call from someone calling the *60s on 6* satellite station.

"Wally made coffee. Let's go."

Fred turned off the ignition and opened the door. "Hang on a second, fearless leader."

I did an about face.

"Your girlfriend up yet?" he asked.

"Dixie?"

"I know you've got a bunch, but yeah."

"She's taking a shower." I shrugged. "Then she'll be doing her hair and makeup and... You get the idea."

"Yeah, but before we go in, I gotta ask you."

"What?"

"You really think somebody's gonna sneak up and attack your compound here?"

I blew out a long puff of air. "Beats the hell outta me."

"I was awake all night and didn't see or hear a goddamn thing except the bugs and frogs and shit. It's like you live in a jungle."

"I think Florida is more jungle-like."

"Bullshit. I got houses all around me. You got...critters and woods and shit."

"At least there were no killers."

"Yeah, right. Hey look, Madman, I'll hang out here as long as you want, but it just don't seem like anyone is knocking down your door to cap you or Dixie."

"I hope so."

"You're a different story, but you think someone would take out a contract on her? She's not into much weird stuff, is she?"

"Hardly."

"See what I mean?"

"I do."

"You know, when we were working a case and couldn't find shit, you'd always say, 'When going straight at something fails, try the back door.'"

"I was quite the philosopher."

"Yeah, but it's a good idea." Mazzio leaned his back against the Ford and crossed his arms over his chest. "You think the guy who snuffed Buggarelli—and I kinda agree with Frank the Fool, it's no great loss—is gonna stick around and do you? Come on, he's in the wind, and a new guy or new pair is here or on the way. Those guindaloons won't assault your home. They'll wait and pop you on the street…some place where you can't dig in. Nobody's a hundred percent safe out there."

"I hear you."

He nodded several times

"Come on," I said. "You want breakfast?"

"Not the stuff you eat. The Pollock will scramble up some *swa-seege* and eggs when we get back to the cabin. He eats the same stuff every day."

* * * *

Fifteen minutes after I arrived at work, I called Pat Herlihy to remind him of the favor he promised.

"Sam, I'm sorry," he said. "We've been swamped here. I meant to call, but recently MS13 has moved in along with Haitian organized crime and the Albanians or Bulgarians or some other Balkan assholes."

"No sweat, Pat. Did you get anything for me?"

"Yeah, hang on a minute while I pull out some notes I made."

I heard rummaging for a few seconds before he came back on the line.

"When you worked the 5th did you know a PO named Hank Burkhardt? He drove 508 with a guy named Tony Morris."

"Sure, I knew Hank. He got killed chasing a burglar over a rooftop. And Tony had more time on the job than me. Must be long retired."

"Morris is retired, but Burkhardt's kid is working the same sector now. He inherited his old man's shield and Hank's love of breaking balls at the Shore Manor. He remembers stopping Greg Buggarelli, who tinned him and claimed to be working undercover."

"Hmmm. Only Greg's boss says he had no cases on the Shore Manor. And what cop working undercover tells a patrolman he doesn't know that he's working undercover?"

"Exactly. And this Teddy Burkhardt and his partner saw Buggarelli's car there on numerous occasions."

"Interesting."

"Yeah. And young Burkhardt got a couple more precinct cops to call me. They, too, had occasion to stop Buggarelli and got the same story. Now half the world knows Greg is on a secret mission."

"So, Greg was either a serious card player or working for Patsy LoScalzo as security at the game."

"Or both."

"Yes. Or both. I remember Greg was super competitive, but I never knew him as a star poker player. Maybe he was a big loser."

"And a big borrower."

"Who, if in a big hole, was offered a job in lieu of paying back the principal and vig."

"You're still pretty sharp for an old guy."

"Thanks. I'm flattered."

"You should be. And thankful, 'cause I called Tom Woods, the 1st Squad dick handling the gun shop burglary. A couple more guns have surfaced, but none of the subjects arrested for possession are willing to give up their seller. Seems universal that they would rather cop a plea and do some time than rat out the top dog and chance getting whacked for helping the cops."

"Not a bad hourly wage if you put a big price on your life."

"Exactly."

"Why am I so lucky?"

"Hey, like my wife tells me, you're too old to still be doing this. Retire…again."

"And do what? I used to spend too much time in my garden. Based on my old hourly wage, I calculated that every lousy tomato cost me $39.95."

"You always had a great line of bullshit. Write books about your old cases."

"Yeah, sure. I'll be the next Joe Wambaugh."

"Why not?"

"Pat, thanks for the help. I love you to death."

"Now I'm flattered. Take it easy, buddy."

* * * *

With my disturbing news, I walked out to the lobby wanting to tell Bettye. What I now knew was damning, but Greg Buggarelli was already dead and not someone to prosecute. It wouldn't hurt anything, but his memory. It all confirmed what we had suspected, but it put me no closer to his killer nor the one who killed Carly Nickels. I thought, perhaps, Bettye might see a few revelations in my new knowledge.

I had just gotten comfortable in the chair next to her desk when I heard the back door open and close. But that wasn't all I heard.

"You know, John, you've always driven like some retarded teenager," Frank said. "On the gas, off the gas. Never one constant speed. You take off from a stop sign like you're in a drag race and wait for the last moment to use the brakes. You could drive anyone crazy."

"Frank, you're just a candy-ass. Everybody used to say that."

"Screw you, Gallagher."

Then the pair of ace investigators appeared in the lobby.

John showed us his famous village idiot smile. "Hi, Boss. Hi, Sarge."

Frank threw the paperwork he had been carrying on John's desk. "Hello. Boss, you owe me for working with that fool."

"You two have a tough day?" I asked.

"Don't ask," Frank said. "I hate him. Always have."

John smiled again, like a numbskull on steroids. "You know, Boss, he's never changed. Frankie was a wimp back then, and he's a wimp now."

"How's it gonna feel, bean belly, when a wimp rips your head off?"

Bettye looked at me with what I took as genuine concern. "Are they serious?"

I shrugged. "They're both nuts. I've never been able to squash their quibbling. They're like two old married people."

"I'd never marry him, "John said. "He's an asshole. Oops, sorry, Sarge."

Bettye smiled for John.

Frank was about to speak when I broke in. "Time out, guys. I was just about to tell Bettye what I learned today. Cool off, sit down, and don't kill each other before we discuss this."

Frank dropped into the chair in front of John's desk. "You're asking a lot, boss."

"Francis, stop," I said, sounding like a frustrated father.

Frank nodded. "I still think John is a gold-plated shit head."

John screwed up his nose and used a falsetto voice. "Yeah, Francis, stop."

Once again, I had had enough. "Shut up, John. Don't make me kill you."

He feigned a serious frown. "Okay, Boss, I'll be good."

"Everybody, please listen."

John sat in his swivel chair. Bettye and Frank looked at me as I explained what Pat Herlihy told me.

"I told you Buggarelli was a backstabbing bastard," Frank said.

"I know you never liked him."

"Not just me, Sam," Frank said. "He was nobody's favorite."

I raised my eyebrows.

"I know you two were friends once, but he was never much of a talent, more of a big wind. And he wanted the bosses to think he was hot stuff. He kissed a lot of ass."

I shrugged.

"You disagree?" Frank asked, challenging me.

"No. Greg and I had our problems. I've never forgotten one thing, but who besides you and I would want to kill him?"

"There might be a waiting list."

John picked up the conversation. "You know, Boss, Greg told everyone how he used to work a patrol car in Wyandanch like he was in a combat zone. Truth was, he only worked there for about six months. Then he went to Communications until some rabbi got him a gold shield. You think he was a good detective?"

"Not the best."

"This doesn't surprise me," Frank said.

"Okay, maybe a bunch of people didn't like Greg. Guys who voluntarily go to Internal Affairs don't get many birthday cards from the troops. But where does this new information get us? Worst case scenario: He came here and killed Carly DeCenzo. Then he drove or flew back to New York and hopped into Dixie's car heading back here to kill me. How do we prove it?"

"Do we need to?" Bettye asked.

I shrugged again. "We're not taking him to court, but I'd like to close Bo Stallins' case with reasonable certainty. Then we need to find Greg's killer. That little rat bastard at the sheriff's office accused me of both murders."

"Are you sure Greg shot DeCenzo?" Bettye asked.

"No, not yet. I'm still waiting for Holmes or Barry to send ballistics information to Bill Werner. If Greg's Glock doesn't match the bullets in Carly, we're back to the starting line."

We all took a turn looking at each other.

Bettye broke the silence. "Darlin', I don't know what to say."

I nodded. "I hate to admit this, but I'm baffled."

* * * *

Baffled or not, I had work to do and work to delegate. I asked John to contact Dave Barry, whom I had asked to take custody of Greg Buggarelli's Glock 19, have his firearms examiner test fire the gun and send the TBI firearms section images of the test bullet. I needed those results to determine if Greg killed Carlo DeCenzo. I also wanted Barry to question Greg's widow and establish a timeline for him just prior to his trip to Tennessee. Knowing those things might narrow down my investigation a little. And he could toss in the use of two investigators to meet and escort Dixie home to New York.

While John was working on that, I'd nudge Gino Musucci and see what his moon-faced son had to say about his plans for me. I'd phone first, but a personal visit would be better. But before I could start anything, Ralph Oliveri called.

"I hate to tell you some of this, pal," he said, "but somebody out there doesn't like you."

"Tell me something I don't already know."

"Okay, how about this? And before we get started, I want you to know that lots and I mean lots of work went into getting you this 4-1-1. The Melville SAC suggested I mention that you owe us big time for this."

"Ralphie, sometimes I think you Feds are as bad as the crooks and conmen we deal with."

"I don't *have* to tell you this, you know."

"You're not a sociopath, Ralph. You have a conscience. Of course you *have* to tell me."

He took an exaggerated and audible breath. "I hate it when you're right. Okay, they went a long ways back listening to wiretap recordings. They had Buggarelli on tape numerous times, most often with Patsy LoScalzo Jr., but a few times with a hump named Jimmy Navarone, who works for Patsy."

"What's Navarone's story?"

"Started out as hired muscle, but because he's not just another pretty face or a complete idiot, he advanced and became a trusty scout for Patsy. Not exactly a consigliore, but an important guy who makes things happen."

"What was the gist of Buggarelli's conversations?"

"Most of the calls were about your pal Greg owing money and not being prompt in settling his debts. But they obtained more from an informant which puts some of the chatter in context."

"I thought so. How do things get clearer?"

"According to their stool, who's a regular in the game, Buggarelli lost lots and borrowed even more. Then lo and behold, he taps Musucci's shylock for twenty-five large to make a down payment on a house in Florida. The snitch can't figure out how he can be delinquent for around thirty grand plus vigorish and have the juice to score another twenty-five."

"Isn't fifty grand the going rate to kill a cop?"

"Smart boy."

"Anything on the wire taps suggest Buggarelli and one of the goombahs were talking strategy?"

"No. Most everything was typically cryptic. These mooks must assume we're eavesdropping. But the most recent call sounded like Bugarelli's pre-mission pep talk."

"Specifically?"

"Let me read you the transcript lines." Ralph cleared his throat. "Patsy LoScalzo: 'Have a nice time. Everything goes good for you and we're totally square. Understand what I'm sayin'?' Buggarelli: 'Totally?' Patsy: 'Totally.' Bugarelli: 'I'll call you.' Patsy: 'I know.' End of call."

"Melville's informant say any more?"

"He confirms Buggarelli's gambling losses and his business with

Franco Provanzano, the loan shark. He assumes that when Provanzano was not reimbursed fully in the stipulated time, Anthony Musucci was notified, and Musucci in turn told LoScalzo to get his player in line. He saw Buggarelli have private conversations with LoScalzo and Navarone. He saw Navarone, who's supposed to be a big guy, brace Buggarelli once or twice. All this is circumstantial, but about as much as you'll get without Buggarelli confessing the plans. And as we know, that ain't gonna happen now."

"Uh-huh. Anything after Buggarelli's murder that would suggest that they were responsible?"

"Just the opposite," Ralph said. "An unknown male caller using an untraceable cell phone spoke with Navarone. I'll quote again. Caller: 'Your man had an accident.' Navarone: 'How serious?' Caller: 'The worst.' Navarone: 'How?' Caller: 'Don't know.' Navarone: 'All right. Call me back in an hour.' End of call.

"One hour later, Navarone receives another call. The voice sounds the same as before. Very limited conversation again. Other party: 'It's me.' Navarone: 'Can you pick up that item for me?' Other party: 'Sure.' Navarone: 'Need anything?' Other party: 'Nah, I'm good.' Navarone: 'Can you send me something soon?' Other party: 'Sure." Navarone: 'I need this *present* soon—for an occasion. Know what I'm sayin'?' Other party: 'Yeah. No problem. I'll call ya.' Navarone: 'Good.' End of call."

"Aha," I said. "The baton has been passed."

"So to speak."

"And Melville has no idea who the mystery caller is?"

"No."

"Where did the phone come from?"

"Impossible to tell. Probably one of the million coming out of Manhattan."

"Too bad FBI technology can't get me a number."

"What would you do then?"

"Call and say hello."

"Watch your ass, Sam."

"Always do."

"I'm serious here. You want me to ask Carl to send you a backup team?"

"Not right now. I've got some help, but maybe soon. Let me see what Gino Musucci can tell me."

He sent a little stream of air through the phone. "Gino Musucci is your snitch? M'donna mi!" Ralph sounded like a little kid who learned that Willie Mays was my best buddy.

"I told you. Gino would like to live peacefully and prosper in beautiful downtown Prospect. So far he's cooperative and would like to make me happy. He's decided to go a little further than just a cooperative witness."

"Holy shit. You getting anything good?"

"I'll call and find out."

Chapter Twenty-Three

Gino Musucci answered my call on the second ring.

"Got a couple minutes to chat?" I asked.

"I'm talkin' with my general contractor right now. I'll call ya back."

"Hang on. Assuming your house will go over budget like everyone else's, this guy is looking at a cost-plus percentage on about a million bucks. I think he'll wait. I'm pressed for time right now."

He paused before answering. "Yeah, yeah, I understand. Gimme a minute."

In the background, Gino spoke to someone. "I gotta take this. It's personal. Be right back."

A chair moved a short distance across a hard floor. Footsteps on the same surface made it sound like Gino was leaving the room.

Moments later: "Okay," he said. "I'm back. Whaddaya need?"

"You want to do this on the phone? I could drive there."

"Yeah, phone's okay. Let's get it over with." He sounded a little impatient.

"Okay. What did Anthony tell you?"

"I spoke to him about what you learned from Alphonse and about Carlo's murder. He said he liked them both. He used Carly's machines in his place, saw him on a regular basis, but hadn't seen Alphonse in years. Only heard about what happened through the grapevine."

"Hmmm. Did he have any kind words about me?"

"Not exactly."

"Does he want to kill me?"

"He said you were crazy. He doesn't like you, but doesn't think about you. You're past history, but when next we spoke, I should tell you to shit in your hat."

I chuckled. "Okay, you told me. Do you believe what he said?"

Gino didn't answer immediately. "I don't know."

"That's comforting. You're leaving your options open. Good. What would Anthony gain from me being dead, aside from settling an old score which could backfire on him?"

"I'd have ta get back to ya on that one."

"Wouldn't your son want you to enjoy your retirement?"

"He'd better."

"It's doubtful some new redneck police chief would be as agreeable to your presence in Prospect as me."

"And I appreciate that. Ya know what I'm sayin'?"

"I do, but listen for a few more minutes. Word among New York cops in the know confirms the suspicions you voiced to me when we spoke in my office. They say Anthony is pleased that you're stepping down, but if you didn't, he could be a nasty customer."

"Yeah, so?"

"So maybe Anthony would like to see his mom live on the peaceful side of the Smokies and enjoy her golden years, but he's less concerned for your physical or mental wellbeing. A strong former leader is never totally out of the picture in any organization. With you *totally* gone, he could sit back, relax and never worry about someone second-guessing his style of management. Getting rid of your new friend the police chief, and, if I do say so myself, one hell of a homicide investigator, would almost insure his further tranquility."

"He's my son, for chrissakes. Whaddaya sayin'? Whaddaya askin'?"

"I'm not saying kill your son. I'm suggesting his intentions may not be in our best interest. I'm going to give you information which may prompt you to infer that Anthony is a liar."

"Like what?"

"Like reliable people say Greg Buggarelli, the guy murdered in the Foothills View Motel, was under suspicion. Buggarelli used to socialize with Patsy LoScalzo Jr. Greg's a known gambler with a losing problem, yet he keeps playing and borrowing from Franco Provanzano. Only he's not famous for paying his debts in a timely fashion. People say Buggarelli was thirty large in the hole. As you know, Provanzano's operating money actually comes from Anthony. Prior to his leaving New York, Buggarelli put ten percent down on a 250K home in Florida after borrowing that down payment from Frankie Pro. That makes fifty-five grand out of your son's pocket with a slide on the vig."

"Okay, okay, I hear ya. I know what you're gettin' at."

"I can further besmirch Buggarelli's reputation by saying that he's been stopped by precinct cops leaving Patsy's card game. He lied to the cops, saying he was working the game undercover. Only Greg's bosses say that wasn't true. He was carrying a gun stolen from a dealer in Farmingdale. The dick handling that case strongly believes people you may have known gave Buggarelli the gun. For what? No cop would procure a throwaway like that. Most recently, he's been seen palling around with Jimmy Navarone. I could go on."

"Little Jimmy Navarone?"

"I heard he's a big boy."

"Yeah. Little Jimmy is euphemistic. Ya understand what I'm sayin'?"

"I know the word."

"Jimmy is a *big* boy. Think Vito on steroids."

"Yikes."

"Yeah, and he's fuckin' nuts. If this Buggarelli was in with Navarone, that's not good."

"Everyone concerned now believes that Buggarelli was sent here to punch my ticket. His gambling debt plus the cash he put down on the house makes a generous fifty-five thousand for the hit. Sound about right?"

"Jesus Christ. Your own guy."

"Yes, I know the feeling. Now backtrack with me so we can lock in that theory. Buggarelli borrows from Frankie Pro and experiences technical difficulty repaying the nut. Then he gets chummy with Jimmy Navarone, a guy known to arrange convenient *disappearances* and is miraculously approved by Frankie for a new credit line of an additional twenty-five grand. Perhaps Anthony proposed a package deal to settle Greg's debt and rid him of the troublesome Jenkins."

"I still don't see Anthony wanting revenge after all this time. It's not like you're the only cop who broke his balls."

"Maybe his new associates have renewed his interest in me?"

"Like how?"

"Let's start with who he visits in Rhode Island and Boston."

"Okay, I found out who he's lookin' ta deal with."

"And the winners are?"

"'Ey, I feel like I'm rattin' out my kid. Could I ask ya ta tone down the comedy?"

That idea caused my attitude to crank up a notch. "Sure, as long as you see things from my viewpoint. Someone—probably your son—wants to put me on ice."

"Okay, point taken. Don't get hot under the collar." A brief moment later he continued. "Rhode Island: You know him as Arthur Carelli. And his stepson Stuart Solomon, who's a big part of that outfit now."

"Stuart Solomon?"

"Yeah, Blaze married a younger woman, a Jew."

"You're losing me. Who's Blaze?"

"Arthur's middle name is Biaggio. In English, that's Blaise. He uses the middle name with a little different spelling."

"He likes to play with matches?"

"He's a dandy. Likes to socialize with the ladies. Acts like a celebrity. Ya ask me, I think he looks like a fruit in the clothes he wears. Wouldn't be surprised if he didn't bat from both sides of the plate."

I shook my head. *What a world I live in.* "How about Stuart the stepson? What's he into?"

"Stuart is probably the guy Anthony is gonna deal with. Arthur is no kid. He'd rather not get his hands dirty. Stuie is inta designer drugs—the kiddy stuff—chemicals, pills…all that crap. But it's big money."

"Okay, I never had any dealings with Blaze or Stuie. How about Boston?"

"Two old time Micks—Gabe Corcoran and Aiden Hayho. What the hell kinda name is Hayho anyways?"

"Aha. One you don't forget. What are those two into?"

"Little of this. Little of that. But mostly they want to expand their arms business."

"What do you mean arms? More than street guns? Big stuff?"

"Yeah. So I hear. Those bogtrotters started out breaking legs and selling protection. Now they're big time. With the IRA calming down, they wannna cultivate a new market with those fuckin' Arab terrorists."

"Muslims."

"What?"

"They're not all Arabs."

He cut me short before I could show off my knowledge of the Middle East. "Whatever—terrorists. And my stupid kid wants a piece o' that. Wants ta drum up customers in New York and Jersey. He didn't ask, but if he had, I woulda told him ta forgettaboutit. Look, it's hard enough dealing with that RICO bullshit. You start palling around with terrorists, the Feds pull out their Patriot Act, and you disappear. A one-way ticket to Guantanamo or some fuckin' place. No lawyer, no nuthin'."

"Sounds like good advice."

"He don't listen. Never did. But he makes his bed, he can lie in it. My mother used ta say that."

"Tell me about this guy Hayho."

"I think he's originally from New York, but moved to Boston a long time ago. Far as I know, he's just another Irish hood."

I thought back a long time before asking, "He have a son named Patrick?"

"I don't know."

"Okay, I'll look into that. Can you confirm all this business I told you about Buggarelli and maybe the name of a pinch-hitting button man Navarone might hire to do me now that his first choice is out of the picture?"

"That's not the kind of stuff I can get you in an hour."

"How about overnight express?"

"Jeez. I can make some phone calls. And my brother-in-law, Sal, is here from Florida. I'll ask him ta do the same."

"Good. Thank you. I appreciate it."

"Yeah, right. I'm probably puttin' my kid in jail."

"Your son is on his own in a business he's making new and different. He knows the risks. I'm not going to sit back and take a round in the head for him. With or without your help, someone will learn the truth. But I'll repeat myself. I appreciate your help."

"I'll call ya."

* * * *

I decided to get a little fresh air and use my cell phone from the

140

parking lot to call Oliveri at the FBI field office. The sunny morning had turned overcast. High cumulous clouds, the color of a Russian Blue cat, covered the sky. One brave weather forecaster stuck out his neck that morning and predicted rain, but the air smelled like snow. It was a bit early for that, but stranger things have happened.

The phone rang three times before he picked up.

"Ralph, I hate to bother you, but I need another favor."

"Sure, buddy. I have a vested interest in keeping you alive. If you get whacked, no one will ever pay back all you owe me."

"Your sentiments are endearing."

"Your sarcasm is legendary. What do you need?"

"You've got to call Boston. That's most important. I need everything they know about an Irish hood named Aiden Hayho."

"Hay who?"

"Don't get wise. If he's the guy I knew years ago, I'm guessing he's in his late sixties. Find out if he has a son named Patrick and any past addresses in New York."

"What's he into now?"

"I hear he's one of a few people who Sonny Musucci is cultivating as new business associates. Hayho and another Irishman named Gabriel Corcoran are supposedly up and coming arms dealers looking for jihadists who need weaponry. And I'm not talking Saturday night specials."

"And what's your former connection?"

"If Hayho is the guy I remember, I've found the Irish animosity my friends at the Rackets Bureau mentioned."

"Tell me."

"Okay, get comfortable. I was a very young detective, first month in the squad actually. I caught a case of gang rape at a Friday night party held in one of the local high schools."

Ralph interrupted. "This sounds like a long story. Do I need to get a coffee?"

"If I elaborate on the gory details, you're going to need a martini."

"Oh, jeez."

"Anyway, a sixteen-year-old girl was raped by six jocks feeling their oats and liquor. The short version is she met one kid, liked the looks of him and they started hanging out. They danced, socialized and because this kid and his buddies had smuggled plenty of vodka into the gym, they drank. Once the girl was feeling no pain, the kid started copping a feel or two. She didn't object too much to the cuddling as much as him doing it in public, so she cooled off. To heat her up a little, this punk suggests a little mood enhancer and gives her a Quaalude or two."

"Jeez, Quaaludes are ancient."

"Yep. Methaqualone, Canadian blues, lulus, choice of veterinarians to tranquilize things as big as Clydesdales. But, since this girl only weighed a hundred-and-ten, one or two 'Ludes sent her into orbit. After that, our Don Juan lured her into a van and took off most of her clothes. She wasn't happy about the arrangement, but also wasn't in a position to do much strenuous complaining. Then, after her new friend finished, she happened to notice five more leering faces looking into the van. Her world turned to shit when each of the other young skells took a turn, sometimes two at a time, making her do things the Marquis de Sade would have condemned."

"Good Christ."

"Yeah. After the six mutts finished, they zipped up, had a good laugh, kicked the victim out of the van and drove away. An undetermined amount of time later, a couple leaving the dance heard moans coming from the shrubbery where the rapists tossed the girl. They flagged down a couple more kids who got a chaperone who called 9-1-1."

"And you got the jocks."

"Wasn't too difficult since she knew the boy who gave her the 'Ludes. He turned out to be the weak link and rolled on the other five who included a cop's kid, the son of an ADA, a local doctor's boy, another prominent and wealthy youngster, whose name I can't remember, and one Patrick Hayho, son of Aiden and Fiona."

"Uh-oh."

"Since I was new to the squad, an old-timer gave me a hand. Eddie Kroger was a big guy with curly blond hair and a winning smile. Good cop. Really knew his onions. But Eddie kinda lost it with these kids. If you saw the girl, you might, too. She was a pathetic sight. The ER nurses said they had never seen a rape victim so messed up and still alive. And these kids thought it was a joke. Those six filled the precinct cells and wouldn't shut up—acted like their pre-arraignment incarceration was a party. So,

Eddie and the desk sergeant got together. The sergeant opened the windows in the cell block. Eddie took the hose that the car man kept out by the gas pump to wash down any spills and stretched it back to the building. He hosed down the kids and left the windows open all night. They thought that was funny, too, until it dipped down into the lower forties, and they damn near froze."

"Your partner get jammed up?" Ralph asked.

"Not exactly. Nothing more than a halfhearted scolding by the lieutenant. But Aiden Hayho complained. He was a real hotheaded Irishman. He demanded to know why his son wasn't released to him and his wife. I said *tough shit,* and the precinct CO backed me up. All the rapists were over seventeen, destined for adult criminal court, not juvenile offender preferred treatment. The rape one and a few sundry charges meant no bail before arraignment. Then, a tough judge set big bucks on each kid. A couple made bail, but Patrick Hayho was one who didn't."

I took a deep breath.

"They all got convicted after a short trial. At first, nobody wanted to plead out, and I wouldn't agree to lesser charges to save time and taxpayer money. All the while, these kids thought it was still funny. Until they heard the verdict and sentences.

"After that, Eddie, a vindictive guy when provoked, dropped a dime on a state corrections officer he knew asking for the guards to suggest to selected inmates that these young lovers get paid back in kind for their treatment of the girl. Young Patrick got raped so many times, it's doubtful his head will ever get straight."

"And Daddy Hayho blames you?"

"Yeah, he did. And I guess I'm still not one of his favorite people."

"He sorta discounts what his kid and his friends did to the girl?"

"They never consider stuff like that."

"You go the extra mile to break his balls?"

"When they finally saw the handwriting on the wall, Hayho's lawyer and some others wanted to cop a plea. I opposed all of that."

"Yeah?"

"Yeah. We had those kids cold. Sooner or later everyone asked for deals, but because one kid belonged to a cop and another to an ADA, they started asking for probation for a plea to sexual abuse or sexual

143

misconduct—class A misdemeanors."

"That sucks. What did your prosecuting ADA say?"

"I told him I'd agree to rape two with a maximum of fifteen years, minimum of seven before anyone considered parole."

"How'd they handle that?"

"Nobody jumped for joy."

"So what happened?"

"The DA himself called and tried to intimidate me."

"And?"

"And I stuck to my guns. I said screw them. I had a good—no, great—case, and if they didn't like my idea, let them go to trial and face rape one with a twenty-five-year sentence and parole at twelve-and-a-half."

"You sure know how to make friends."

"Right again. And he reminded me about professional courtesy for two of the fathers. I asked him for some empathy for the victim. I suggested that if anyone pressed the issue, I'd get every woman's right's group and every parent of every girl in the high school to picket the district court."

"Has anyone ever told you you're nuts?"

"More than once."

"Come on, come on. What happened?"

"Everyone took the deal. No one would see daylight for seven years."

"And now Hayho, a hood with all kinds of juice, wants a pound of your flesh."

"I guess. And he's got a friend in Moonface Musucci."

"Lucky you."

"Maybe I should play the lottery."

"So Hayho and Musucci put their heads together and decide how to handle payback time."

"That's my guess."

"Gino told you this?"

"Gino says he'll try and confirm my suspicions."

"He name the new shooter?"

"Doesn't know."

"And you believe him because?

Chapter Twenty-Four

I felt damn near mentally and physically exhausted from all the phone calls I'd made and the information I'd gotten. I was gasping for a large whisky and a few moments of tranquility when John Gallagher walked into my office.

"Okay, Boss, we're done. Got everything you needed. How are you makin' out?"

"You first, John."

"Sure. Okay. Where do I start?"

I took that as rhetorical and waited. Ten seconds passed. "Whenever you're ready."

He took a breath and shrugged his shoulders. "Right. Dave Barry got someone to visit Mrs. Buggarelli. Joann is her name. Did you know that?"

"Yes, John. I know her name. Good work."

"She insists that Greg was home before he left on the trip. She claims he had to repair a couple of gutters. The weather was good, and he wanted to get things fixed before any snow started and before he moved out. That puts him in Smithtown at the time Carlo got killed."

"Sounds reasonable," I said. "Greg was a real prince."

"And she said it was her idea for the divorce. Said he was putting in too much time with the DA's office and had no intention of cutting back. My guess is he was spending that time at the card game. Anyways, she thought after he retired from the PD, they would be spending more time together, going places and so forth. Only that didn't happen. Also said that for years they'd just grown apart."

"Also reasonable. Joann mention if she suspected Greg of having a goomah on the side?"

"No, but then again, a woman scorned might not admit she lost her man to another."

"That was almost poetic, John."

"Yeah?"

"Yeah. How about the Florida house?"

"Since it was new to them and they didn't have any equity into it except the ten percent down and a couple months payments, the lawyers were going to take that money off Greg's half of everything. He was gonna move to Florida and said he'd take care of payments."

"And leave the DA's office?"

"Can't commute."

"No." I really wanted that whisky and some peace and quiet. "Did he give Holmes notice?"

"Not yet."

"Aha. I wonder if he had plans for other than being a full-time Florida resident?"

"We may never know."

"Did they pick up Greg's Glock?" I asked.

"Yeah. And the lab up there did a test fire and faxed the images to Bill Werner at TBI, who immediately did a microscopic comparison."

He stopped there and smiled.

"John, if you don't tell me the results quickly, I may expire from anticipation."

"Calm down, Boss. I'm gettin' there."

"Thanks."

"Not a match."

"Rats!"

"I know. Now we gotta keep lookin'."

"Bo Stallins has to keep looking. That's his murder."

"Right you are, Boss. But you can't kid me…you'll keep lookin'."

I sighed. "You're right. Got anything else before I tell you what I know?"

"Yeah. Frank woke up Wally Danko and asked about escorting Dixie back home. He's cool with that. Says he'll take her all the way if you want."

"Didn't Barry agree to send a couple of guys down?"

"I forgot to ask."

I wanted to make my whisky a triple.

"Then maybe you should call back," I suggested. "Save Wally the gas and time."

"Okay, Boss."

"Call Steven Holmes. He's the honcho. You'll make him feel important."

"Good idea. See, Boss, not asking Barry was a good thing."

"Sure, John. Perfect."

* * * *

At quarter after two, Fred Mazzio walked into my office.

"What are you doing here?" I asked.

"Couldn't sleep. I woke up a couple hours ago. Even with the room doors closed, Danko sounded like a diesel bulldozer with a broken muffler. So, I got up, and here I am."

"Have you eaten?"

"Stopped at Howell's for a sandwich."

"Good choice."

"Forget food for a minute," he said. "I got an idea."

"Good. I could use one."

"So far you're lookin' at Buggarelli's killer as a hit man, right?"

"Maybe."

He shrugged and pushed his hands out to the sides of his body. "So maybe there's another angle. Maybe him being sent here to cap you has nothing to do with him getting whacked. Maybe his wife or somebody else not involved with the mob wanted him dead."

"Could be, but they would have to have known where he'd be."

"Not the most difficult thing to find out. Think about it."

"You're right."

"Exactly. And if you're sending Dixie home on Friday guarded by Wally and then the DA's people, and we're in agreement that if and when someone tries to croak you, it'll be other than during the night. How about me, Mikey and Margaret work on this new theory while you and the two fools continue to march?"

"You want to hang around?"

"Yeah, I want to hang around. I get off on this shit—it's real police work."

"Okay. Make sure Mike and Maggie agree. John and Frank can continue on with a possible OC killing and you three look at the wife or whomever."

"Whomever? Man, you're hot shit."

Chapter Twenty-Five

I called Ralph Oliveri and told him about Dixie returning to Long Island, the new angle I wanted to pursue using my unofficial investigators, and how I'd love him to death if he could arrange for a couple of agents to work a few midnight tours at Casa Jenkins. I still worried about the unlikely event of Kate getting caught in a crossfire.

"I know I mentioned something about that." Ralph sounded a bit reluctant to commit. "But that was before we got involved in a joint investigation that's taken eight people to Chattanooga. Right now, we're strapped for personnel, buddy. I know what Carl would say if I asked."

"Hmmm," I said. "I'd feel safe sleeping in one of our cells, but I doubt my wife would like that."

"Oh, jeez, you're gonna dump this on me, aren't you?"

"I had hoped for a little help, Ralphie."

He let out an exaggerated sigh. "Maybe I could get one or two people from the Marshall's Service. They'd do it for witness security. They might do it for you."

"Might, huh? I feel so important."

"Look, I can't promise anything, and it may take a day or two, but—"

"I know. Lemme know how you make out."

* * * *

At 5:20, I pulled into the driveway and parked next to Mike Rodriguez's white GMC Envoy. The setting sun had added orange and purple layers to the powder blue sky. Birds were frantically buzzing about doing what birds do when they sense bedtime encroaching. The air was

149

almost cool and smelled clean, with just a hint of someone far away burning leaves. A world-class autumn day.

Inside, I found Kate and Maggie in the dining room playing Scrabble while Mike and Dixie watched the local news in the living room.

Everyone greeted me, but nobody jumped for joy at my arrival. After tossing my sport jacket on one of the wingback chairs, I made Manhattans for Kate and Maggie, got Mike a beer and refilled Dixie's scotch and soda. She looked a little sleepy, so I assumed I wasn't composing her second drink of the afternoon. The tension of our situation seemed to be getting to her.

I briefly spoke about the happenings of the day, mostly informing Dixie about the logistics of her Friday departure. Mike and Maggie mentioned their conversation with Fred Mazzio and how they looked forward to working a case and scrapping the bodyguard detail. After that, I began thinking about dinner.

I asked Kate, "You do anything about food?"

"No, sweetie, I didn't. Sorry, but…I guess hanging around so much has made me a bit lethargic."

I took a sip of Glenfiddich and shrugged. "No sweat. I'll have the matter in hand in scant moments." Then to the Mike and Maggie I said, "I've got a slab of Alaskan sockeye salmon big enough to choke Sarah Palin's pet moose. You guys staying for dinner?"

Maggie answered. "Freddie wanted to take us to your favorite barbeque place. He said everybody but John agreed. I guess his wife is afraid we'll lead him astray."

"He went there for lunch. Mazzio must be hooked on Howell's."

"Freddie would eat a whole pig if you held the head," Mike said.

"Is he paying?" I asked.

"You kiddin'?" Mike said.

"Okay. We'll miss your company, but the ladies and I will gobble up the salmon and wish you a good night."

After Kate won the Scrabble game and Mike and Maggie finished their drinks I said, "Thanks again, guys. See you tomorrow."

While I prepared the fish for baking and started cooking a pot full of cous cous pilaf, Kate steamed a bunch of fresh green beans.

With all that done and the dinner waiting for us, I popped the cork on a bottle of chardonnay, and we settled into a scrumptious repast.

Netflix provided the entertainment for the remainder of the evening. Just after Kate and Dixie wandered upstairs toward the bedrooms, Fred Mazzio and Wally Danko showed up a little early.

"You took everybody to Howell's for barbeque?" I asked Mazzio.

"Yeah, I love that place, but I'm surprised you go there. They don't sweep the floors that often."

"The food is good. What's a little dirt underfoot?"

"Great bunch of tap beers," Wally said.

I nodded. "Yeah. The English bartender is a whiz at mixing black and tans."

"Anything going on that we should know about?" Fred asked.

I shook my head. "Nothing new."

"Okay, boss," Wally said. "We got you covered."

"Should be another quiet night," Fred said.

I went upstairs, took a shower and once in bed, resumed reading an old Jonathan Valin novel.

At 11:30, the phone rang three times. Wally picked it up downstairs. Fifteen seconds later, the front door slammed. That didn't sound good.

I jumped up, pulled on a pair of jeans, shoes and a sweatshirt and grabbed my Glock from the night table draw. I flew down the stairs and once on the first floor, decided to exit the house through the basement. Without turning on the lights, I felt my way downstairs and left the house via the door on the chimney side. Cautiously, I worked my way clockwise to the corner of the elevated deck and jogged up the incline staying close to the lattice enclosure and then the garage. From there, I peeked out toward the driveway where Fred and Wally stood on the gravel. I walked over.

Once my foot hit the driveway, I said, "What's going on?"

Mazzio turned in my direction, pointing the CAR 15 at me.

"Whoa, partner," I said.

He relaxed. "You scared the shit outta me. Might wanna make a little noise before you sneak up on a man with a big gun."

Danko was smiling.

"I scare you, too?"

151

He tapped his chest. "Nerves of steel."

I nodded. "Same question. What's going on?"

Mazzio answered. "A white Caddy pulled into the driveway, paused for a couple seconds on top of the rise and then crept toward the house."

"No kidding?"

"Yeah, I'm making this up." The CAR dangled from his right hand.

"Don't get testy, Frederick."

He nodded, but didn't address my comment. "So, before they got past me, I got outta the car and took cover behind the right fender. As soon as I yelled, 'stop the car,' the driver hit the brakes and immediately put it in reverse."

"Just made a run for it?" I asked.

"Yeah. No hesitation. No dialogue at all. Did a turn up by the barn and took off."

"Know any more than it was a Caddy?"

"Looked like a Florida plate. The white one with the orange in the middle. And I thought I saw two heads, but it's tough to be sure with the tall headrests."

"And then you called Wally."

"Yeah and called 9-1-1. Told the locals to check the roads for a white CTS heading who knows where."

"Good job."

"Thanks."

"Any ideas," Danko asked.

I poked a thumb at Mazzio. "He's the only guy who owns a white Caddy with Florida plates. And I assume it wasn't his wife checking up on him."

"Florida was where Alphonse the Torch got whacked," Wally said.

"Don't remind me," I said.

When we returned to the house, Kate and Dixie were waiting for us in the living room with their assigned handguns close by.

"Hey look, two women armed and dangerous," Wally said and made the girls smile.

Mazzio explained what happened while I called the county duty officer to see if any of the patrol cars had found a trace of the white Cadillac. No one had.

Kate made coffee for Fred and Wally. I dug out the scotch for the girls and me. No one seemed overjoyed with the recent event.

Chapter Twenty-Six

At exactly two minutes after nine Thursday morning, Gino Musucci called me at Prospect PD.

"I been tryin' ta get a hold o' you."

"I'm not hiding."

"Yeah, right. I made those calls you wanted. You wanna know what I know?"

"More than I want a date with Sophia Loren."

"Cheez, always the wise guy."

"That term applies to more of your other acquaintances than me."

He snorted. "You wanna hear this or what?"

"Yes, Gino, I want to hear what you know."

"Okay then." A little more attitude showed through.

"I'm listening."

"Not on the phone. Take a ride over here. This is some sensitive stuff. Important stuff. Ya understand what I'm sayin'?"

"Is there a problem?"

"I don't know. Not on the phone."

"You want to do this now?"

"Yeah, now's good."

"Alright. Give me thirty minutes."

I walked out to the lobby. Bettye was sitting at her desk reading something official looking. John Gallagher and Frank O'Brien were looking over crime scene photos and reports at John's desk and making lists of something.

"Gino Musucci just told me he's got important information," I said. "It might be something good. He sounds impatient."

154

"You're going now?" Bettye asked. She looked a little concerned.

"He's got ants in his pants."

"You want some backup?" Frank asked.

I waited a long moment before answering. Actually, I did, but I didn't think it was the best thing to do if I wanted lots of the truth. "So far Gino's been pretty standup with me. I don't think he'd like too many ears listening to what he says."

Bettye gave me a cold hard stare. I shrugged.

"Okay, Boss," John said, "me and the Fool will hang around the phone in case you need something quick."

"Who are you calling a fool, you Irish degenerate?"

"See what I have to put up with, Boss?" John said. "If he stays around much longer, you owe me a raise."

"The both of you, knock it off. But thanks. Stick around. I might want you to follow up on something."

Bettye had to stick in her two cents. "You keep that cell phone on, Sam Jenkins."

"Yes, ma'am."

I jumped into the Crown Vic and wondered what new, thrilling, and exciting things I might learn from Gino Musucci on such a fine autumn day. The leaves had finally achieved the appropriate colors to qualify as being at their peak—long after their usual time. The air was again crisp and clean, and a big yellow-orange sun shared the clear blue sky with a scattering of puffy bleached white cumulous clouds. What could go wrong?

* * * *

My Ford rolled over the private bridge and up the long driveway toward Gino's rented home. The wide tires crunched over the pea gravel, and I came to a stop thirty feet from the front door.

I pressed the bell button, and melodious chimes pealed inside the house. Twenty seconds later, Vito answered the door.

I nodded. "How's it going?"

"Yeah. Howz it goin'?" he answered.

Typical New York greeting. Questions asked, but not answered.

155

"Gino's in the back room," he said.

"Lead the way."

We walked through the outer rooms and finally into the place that could be called a lounge or family room or opulent atrium…the room with a carpet as deep as the Marianas Trench.

Gino stood looking out the glass wall toward the mountains and initially paid me no attention until Vito left, and I cleared my throat.

Finally, he turned around. "Oh, hey, whaddaya say?"

"Morning," I said with my most diplomatic smile.

Gino was holding a highball glass filled with what I thought might be scotch and soda.

"Want a drink?" he asked.

I looked at my watch. "It's 9:35. I gotta wait for my Cheerios to digest."

He shrugged. "Suit yourself. Have a seat."

The lack of his usual smile and the wrinkles across his forehead weren't the only things that made me think that Gino was in a gray mood. Light gray slacks and a charcoal polo shirt under a three color gray Argyle cardigan, topped off a pair of gray patent leather loafers with tassels.

I sat. He sat. I spoke. "You've got some answers to what we last discussed?"

Gino took a long pull on his scotch. "Yeah. In a roundabout way, you were pretty well on target."

A long moment passed.

I looked at him carefully and wondered why he had all of a sudden turned shy about elaborating on my situation.

"You mean Anthony and the Boston Micks are looking to kill me?"

He raised his eyebrows and swirled the cubes around in his glass. "You might say that."

"Care to explain?"

Before he could, footsteps from beyond the archway leading into the room drew our attention. Vito stepped in and stood less than a dozen feet from Gino and me. He wasn't smiling, and I didn't like the black semi-automatic dangling at his side.

"I gotta do this now, Gino." He spoke as if announcing his intentions of taking the pet bulldog for a walk.

I took a quick look at Gino—no response and no expression. Finally he stood, still holding his glass of scotch and soda.

I stood and turned to face Vito full front. "Do what, Vito? What's your hurry?"

He raised the gun to about my chest level. Any cop would have recognized it as a Glock nine-millimeter pistol.

"That doesn't look like a Smith & Wesson," I said. "Shame on you for carrying an undocumented handgun."

"Come outside with me." He pointed toward the atrium door with his chin and waved the muzzle end of the Glock in the same direction.

"For what? Gonna show me your roses?"

Vito shook his head and grinned. "Always the smartass. You believe him, boss?"

"Gimme a minute, Vito," Gino said and then looked me in the eye. "Do this the easy way. Take a walk outside."

I was having a little difficulty assimilating my dilemma, but immediately remembered that I've always said, 'I'll be damned if I'd make my killer's job easy for him.'

"Screw you guys. If you're gonna shoot me, you'll have to do it here and buy all new carpet."

To say Gino's face showed a look of concern would have been an understatement. "Don't make this more difficult."

I couldn't stifle a laugh. "For you or me? If I'm not mistaken, that's a Glock 17 your pet gorilla is holding. Five will get you ten it's the gun that killed poor Carly Nickels. But then you knew that, didn't you, Gino?"

Gino didn't answer. He took a small sip from the glass of scotch he held as steady as a boulder. I switched my look from him back to Vito and watched two additional witnesses quietly step into the family room. One was pointing what looked like a 1911 Colt .45 in our general direction.

"Your call, Gino," Vito said. "You want the mess in here, or should I drag his ass outside?"

I didn't let Gino answer because I saw a slight distraction as my only chance to either save myself or at least give me the opportunity make a valiant effort to grab Vito's pistol.

"Before you flex your muscles, Vito, maybe you should ask the guy standing behind you if he intends to shoot me or you."

"Nice try, asshole." Vito fixed his look on me and raised his gun hand forward. I expected to feel the bullet before I heard the shot.

I was wrong. The blast from the big .45 echoed off the glass walls and reverberated in my ears with almost a pain.

Vito's hand dropped quickly, but with only five pounds of pressure needed on a Glock's trigger to trip the sear, his finger involuntarily squeezed off a round into the floor.

I didn't hear Gino say, 'There goes the carpet,' but Vito collapsed face down into the luxurious nap and in only seconds would be bleeding all over.

I drew my gun and crouched next to one of the oversized and overstuffed easy chairs. My eyes darted between Gino and the other two men.

"What's going on?" I spoke loud enough to hear myself as I assumed the others also suffered from a temporary hearing impairment.

"Put your gun away," Gino said. "You got nuthin' ta worry about." He drained the whisky from his glass, turned and took two steps to his rear and placed the empty tumbler on the wet bar.

I stood cautiously, still holding my gun on the man who had already lowered his Colt automatic. I used my foot to move the Glock a couple feet from Vito's hand.

"Nicky," I said, "What the hell are you doing here?"

Nick Cutrone answered, "In due time, Sam. In due time."

I focused on the other man, a short gray-haired dandy wearing a burgundy *Member's Only* jacket and black slacks. "I know you."

Gino answered for him. "My brother-in-law, Sal Polizzi."

"Put the gun on the coffee table, Sal."

He hesitated and switched his eyes to Gino for direction.

In a two-hand grip, I raised my gun to shoulder level and squinted down the barrel. "Do it now, Sal."

I assumed that Gino gave him a nod. "No problem, no problem," Sal said. "I'm cool." With his left hand extended to the side, he slowly bent forward and placed the Colt on the glass-topped coffee table with his right.

"Gino," I said, "join your friends over there. Make a nice small group."

When they were standing together, I holstered my gun, crouched down next to Vito and used two fingers to look for a carotid pulse. "He's still alive. You three go into the next room. Call 9-1-1. Tell them a cop's already here, and you want an ambulance. And put a rush on it." They didn't move quickly enough. "Come on, get outta here."

Once they were out of earshot, I began to turn Vito over onto his back. It was about as easy as bulldogging a rhinoceros.

I placed one of the couch pillows under his head, and he opened his eyes.

"Hurts like a bastard," he said.

"An ambulance is on the way."

He managed a smirk. "Who you kiddin'? Stick that ambulance up your ass."

Pink foam showed at the corners of his mouth. Vito had taken a .45 in the lung.

I shook my head. "You don't look too good. Take this opportunity to set the record straight. You kill Carlo DeCenzo?"

"You'll find out when you test the gun, so, yeah. I did Carly. So what?"

"Who ordered that?"

Another smirk and more foam, a little more red now. "Screw you."

"You were the number two shooter to come after me. Why did you kill Greg Buggarelli?"

He blinked a few times, and pain showed on his face. "Not me. Why would I kill him?"

"You wanted the job. Your goombah Jimmy Navaronne gave it to someone else, and you were pissed."

Vito grimaced in pain. "Keep dreamin'. Wasn't me. Now leave me alone."

Seconds later, Vito died.

On the way into the next room, I dropped a nickel on the spot where I saw Sal Polizzi standing when he fired the killing shot. At least the evidence technicians could reconstruct an accurate scene.

The three men stood together near a sliding glass door. They turned when I got close.

I shook my head. "Won't need the ambulance. The shot hit him just to the left of the spine and punctured a lung. Sorry about the wall-to-wall, Gino."

"Yeah, you look shattered."

I ignored that, assuming he needed time to grieve. Looking at Sal Polizzi, I asked, "You the brother-in-law from Florida?"

"Right."

"Where'd you get the .45?"

"It's my gun," Nick said.

"Yeah?" I must have sounded skeptical.

"Yeah. I've had it for years. It's on paper."

"Okay. Good. Now, excuse me while I make a few phone calls. I've got to call in a bunch of pesky policemen to deal with this." I pulled the cell phone out of my jacket pocket. "By the way, don't even think about going into that room."

I started out with a call to Bettye.

Chapter Twenty-Seven

Sergeant Lambert in turn sent John and Frank for assistance and moral support, dispatched one Prospect patrolman to keep an eye on what happened outside Gino Musucci's home, and she promised to track down Stan Rose and get him to work early and keep an eye on beautiful downtown Prospect while I muddled through the shooting of Vito Cinquemani.

My next call went to Ralph Oliveri.

"I'm glad you're in the office a lot. I'm going to make your day."

"You sound like Dirty Harry," he said.

"Wrong movie. As Woody Allen said in *Broadway Danny Rose*, 'What we have here, Lou, is a situation.'"

"Most of the time I have no idea what you're talking about."

"Ralph, you're a New Yorker and not a Woody Allen fan—shame on you. But listen, you're going to want to take a drive down to Kinzel Springs—like now."

"What's going on?"

"Well, I'm not dead, but Vito Cinquemani, the guy who wanted to kill me, is. And I didn't do it. Gino Musucci's brother-in-law did. Now, we're all standing around waiting for a few friendly G-men with a vested interest to join the party."

"Why do I know Vito's name?"

"Gino Musucci's *personal assistant*."

"Ming! Who's the brother-in-law?"

"Sal Polizzi of the Florida Polizzis."

"Jesus Christ. I think Carl will want to be there. Are these people talking?"

"I haven't asked yet, but they're the ones who kept Vito from

161

Wayne Zurl

punching my ticket."

"Holy Christ." There was a moment of silence. "Lemme get back to you. I'm on the way."

"I'll leave the light on for ya."

Since Kinzel Springs is within the county sheriff's jurisdiction, the shooting would be the responsibility of his Criminal Investigation Division. Since Vito had killed Carlo DeCenzo, the subject of Bo Stallins's open homicide and person of interest to Captain Rodney Burchfield, I called Bo directly.

"What would you say if I told you I just cleared your DeCenzo murder case?" I asked.

"Most of the time, I'm afraid to say anything when I speak ta you, but I'm listenin'."

"Remember me asking you to check on the carry permit of one Vito Cinquemani?"

"How could I forget that name?"

"Well, I've got a Glock 17 that you can ID as the murder weapon which was in the possession of Mr. Cinquemani, who is currently within your jurisdiction."

"I'll be derned."

"The catch is…Vito is quite dead."

"Who killed him?"

"Not I. But the person who did is waiting with me. Ready to copy an address?"

"Why do I think I don't want ta be anywhere near this?"

"That's not a bad thought, but you have no choice. And you'll have company. The FBI have a great interest in the case. They should be here shortly."

"I hate dealing with the FBI."

"They'll be nice to you, but I recommend leaving little Rodney Burchfield back in the office. I doubt anyone will get along with him."

Bo sighed. "I'm gonna have ta tell him."

"I understand, but keep him away, or I might make him the second corpse on the floor."

"Oh, Jesus have mercy. Don't get me inta the middle o' this."

I snickered. "Bring a few crime scene investigators and call the ME.

We'uns will be a'waitin' on ya."

Bettye had called off the responding ambulance crew, but the unmistakable high-pitched scream of a Prospect PD sector car in the distance told me that the first of my troops would be arriving shortly. I slapped my flip-phone together and dropped it into my jacket pocket.

"Sounds like the cavalry is coming," I informed Gino and company. "Half the cops in the county will be here soon as will a compliment of Feds from Knoxville. Everybody is going to want statements from you. If you want lawyers present, call them now."

"We didn't do nuthin' wrong," Gino said. "You want us to call in the lawyers?"

"I didn't say that. And I agree. The shooting was justified, but the question remains, especially for Sal, do you want a lawyer?"

Gino sounded frustrated when he said, "You were right here. We're good, right?"

"I think you were wonderful. Sal saved my life. You all get my approval. If you're happy with just me in your corner, I'm happy."

"Okay, then," Gino said. "You okay, Sal?"

Sal said, "I'm okay."

"I'll be giving my own statement," I said, "but when this dog and pony show is all over, the four of us have to talk—everything off the record. Agreed?"

"Yeah, agreed," Gino said. The other two nodded.

"Nicky," I said, "Let's do that like gentlemen. How about tomorrow lunchtime? Can you arrange for us to use table 35? Have something to eat and discuss things in private?"

He nodded and pulled a cell phone out of his pocket. "You got it."

A siren faded to silence as the Prospect PD car pulled to a stop outside the house. Right behind PO Jamey Hawkins, John Gallagher and Frank O'Brien pulled up in John's electric blue Saturn. I met them outside.

"Boss, what the hell's goin' on?" Jamey asked. "Bettye said someone got shot."

"Long story, kid. I'll get to you as soon as possible. For now, I need you to handle the outside for me. The county will be in charge here, but the FBI will be showing up, too. And for all I know, a Delta Team may parachute in. Keep a log of who shows up. If a county supervisor gives you any shit, find me. I'll take care of him."

Jamey nodded.

"That's about it," I said. "Can do?"

"Piece of cake, boss."

Jamey moved his car out of the way while I spoke to John and Frank.

"Go inside, and secure the back room. You'll know it's the scene by the very large dead body on the floor."

"Who's dead?" Frank asked.

"Vito Cinquemani, Gino's batman."

"You kill'im, boss?" John asked.

"Gino's brother-in-law did. Vito intended to kill me, but between Gino, Sal Polizzi and Nick Cutrone, they squashed Vito's plans."

"Nick is involved in this?" John sounded like I just said Superman came to my rescue.

"Don't ask. I'll explain later."

"This is some horror show," Frank said.

"You ain't seen nothin' yet. Wait till the county and Feds get here and start bumping heads."

Chapter Twenty-Eight

Being closer, the county arrived first. Bo Stallins pulled up in a black unmarked Ford. I began grinding my teeth when Rodney Burchfield bounded out of the passenger's side like an excited child on his first visit to the zoo.

I was standing near the front entrance as they approached. I looked Bo in the eye and silently growled. He understood and shrugged apologetically.

Burchfield, the take-charge guy, spoke first. "What's a Prospect car doing here? This is not your jurisdiction. For that matter, what are you doing here?"

I ignored Rodney and spoke to Bo. "Put a choke chain on this idiot." Then I walked past them toward the county crime scene van that just came to a stop near Jamey Hawkins' patrol car. I heard Burchfield say something, but paid no attention. Jackie Shuman and David Sparks stepped out of the white van.

"There's a dead body in the room all the way through the house. John Gallagher and another guy on my unofficial payroll are guarding the scene. The Glock on the floor is the property of the dead man. The GI .45 on the coffee table is what killed the guy on the floor."

"Okay," Jackie said.

"Try and keep little Rodney from contaminating the scene, but since the only possible defendant is already dead, it won't matter much."

Jackie shook his head. "Do we need ta know more of a story for this one?"

"Just that nickel on the carpet is where the shooter stood, and the guy renting this place is a recently retired organized crime boss from New Jersey who was instrumental in saving my life."

"Lord have mercy," David said.

Jackie threw his hands in the air. "I got nuthin' ta say."

I smiled and slapped him on the back. "You're two fine Americans. Go do your thing."

I was working hard on resisting the urge to go back into the family room and pour myself a glass of Gino's scotch when Ralph Oliveri's silver Crown Victoria pulled into the driveway. Special Agent in Charge Carl Harmon was riding shotgun and Ralph's sometime partner, Special Agent Bonnie Rowatt, sat in the back.

We completed the appropriate greetings and handshakes common to professional comrades and were about to step into the house when John Gallagher's voice caught our attention.

"Hey, don't touch that gun, and get your foot away from that spent shell."

That was followed by, "Do you know who I am?"

To that Frank O'Brien said, "We don't care who you are, Shorty. Don't touch the evidence."

I looked at Carl and half shrugged. "Sounds like my old-timers are trying to teach a county supervisor with no experience the finer points of crime scene investigation."

"Who are we talking about?"

"Captain Rodney Burchfield, Jr. from the sheriff's IAB."

Carl ran a hand through his short gray hair. "For chrissakes, what's he doing here?"

I shrugged again. "He thinks I've killed several people."

Carl repeated himself. "Oh, for chrissakes."

We walked toward the shooting scene, but paused as we encountered Gino, Sal and Nicky. Gino was standing against a wall with his arms folded across his chest and a look on his face that could only mean Gino was not a happy cappo. Sal Polizzi and Nick Cutrone were sitting on a sofa practicing their looks of disgust.

"What's going on?" I asked, looking at Gino.

"Who's the sawed-off little fuck who just came in here throwing his weight around?" Gino asked.

Carl Harmon rolled his eyes and sighed. "You talk to these gentlemen. I'll handle the other room."

Ralph Oliveri stayed with me while Bonnie Rowatt followed her boss.

I thought introductions were in order. Pointing to each of the players in turn, I said, "Gino Musucci. Sal Polizzi. And I know you remember Nick Cutrone from the Villa Napoli. Gentlemen, Special Agent Ralph Oliveri, FBI, Knoxville, formerly of South Ozone Park."

Gino said, "Howzitgoin?"

"Gino," Ralph said and shook his hand.

"No shit," Sal said, "I got a cousin lives in South Ozone Park."

"Son of a gun," Ralph said, and they shook hands.

"Whaddayasay, Ralph," Nick said.

"Hiya, Nicky. It's been a while." One more handshake.

I interrupted the snappy dialogue. "Back to my question. Why are you all looking so happy?"

Gino acted as spokesman. "That little blond fuck walked in, looked at us and started in. 'I want your statements, and they'd better be the whole truth,' he says. I gotta take that shit from some little prick I never met?"

I took a quick look at Ralph, who frowned and shook his head.

"The little guy is a county captain who works Internal Affairs," I said. "The tall guy's the detective. He'll be handling the case. If that runt bothers you again, just use the magic word. It will shut him up and piss him off."

"Whaddaya talkin' about?" Gino said.

"Lawyer."

"Oh, for chrissakes."

"Look, I won't apologize for Captain Burchfield. He's an asshole and doesn't work for me. But I can promise you that his involvement in this matter is almost over."

"Good," Gino said. "Little shithead."

I blew out a long breath. "Hang in there, guys. I've got to give a statement, too. Little Rodney thinks I killed Carly DeCenzo and would like to pin Greg Buggarelli on me as well."

"Jesus fuckin' Christ," Gino said. "And someone made him a cop? Jesus Christ!"

"Not me," I assured Gino. "Ralph, would you mind getting these gentlemen started on their statements, mindful that they are witnesses and not suspects in anything."

"Sure. I love taking statements." No one seemed to pick up on Ralph's subtle sarcasm. "Everybody okay doing this here and now? Anyone want a lawyer present?"

Gino renewed his thoughts of before. "We didn't do nuthin' wrong. For chrissakes, Sal saved his life." He pointed at me. "Whadda we need a lawyer for? Jesus Christ!"

"Sal, I appreciate what you did," I said. "Gino…Nick…Ralph will take care of you. I'll see how Carl's doing with Little Rodney. If you hear a shot, figure I killed him."

Ralph rolled his eyes. Nick grinned. Sal didn't know me well enough to comment, and Gino said, "Do it. Kill the little prick."

I found John and Frank standing with their backs against the wet bar. John's face was crimson, and if looks could kill, Frank would have been responsible for Burchfield's death. Knowing Frank, I was sure he was experiencing as much of a problem as me in not raiding Gino's liquor cabinet.

Carl and Bonnie were conversing with little Rodney while Bo Stallins and the two evidence technicians were working the shooting scene.

Burchfield took two steps toward the archway into the next room when he turned to face Carl Harmon.

"I want copies of those statements. I have a case to prepare."

Carl's shoulders dropped two inches, and he sighed in frustration. "Captain, close out your case with what information you've got. This is no longer an Internal Affairs matter. Let the detective and the evidence team work the scene. The assistant US attorney and I will also be dealing with this."

Rodney just couldn't leave it alone. "We'll see what the sheriff says about that."

But Carl would have the last word. He upped his volume considerably. "No, Captain, your involvement is over. If you press the issue, I'll have the US Attorney General call the sheriff and the Blount County DA. If you don't disenfranchise yourself, I'll consider bringing Federal charges against you for interfering in our investigation."

Burchfield turned and stormed out.

I looked at Carl. "Disenfranchise?"

He shook his head. "What an asshole."

I glanced at Bonnie, a good-looking redhead, a day or two over thirty. She winked. I smiled.

Carl and his agents might have eventually returned to Knoxville, but I would still have Rodney to deal with.

Chapter Twenty-Nine

Ralph acted as proctor while the paisanos wrote their statements. John and Frank followed me out of the house to get a breath of fresh air.

Deputy medical examiner Doctor Morris Rappaport and his assistant Earl W. Ogle had arrived a few minutes ago, and as we walked out were busy giving Vito a once over prior to his journey to the morgue. Having no desire to be around when Mo stuck his liver probe into the decedent, I suggested a change of scenery.

As soon as I stepped onto the pea gravel, my cell phone sounded off with the 1966 version of *Paint It Black*. I answered immediately and spoke to Fred Mazzio.

"Hey, Madman, it's me. What's goin' on? I hear you got into a shooting."

"How did you hear that?"

"I called Bettye to see what's up."

"Couldn't sleep again and decided to bother my desk sergeant?"

"Why are you so hostile? I wanna help."

He sounded sincere.

"Nothing for us to do. The county and FBI are here. We're just in the way. And if I stick around much longer, I may get collared for assaulting that little nitwit from IAB."

Mazzio laughed. "Maintain your cool, General Patton."

"Where are you?"

"In your office."

"Okay. Stick around. The fools and I will be back soon. Where's Wally?"

"Sleeping, I guess. Last I heard he was snoring like a wounded warthog."

"You want lunch?"

"Yeah. How about Howell's?"

"You've been there twice in two days."

"I like that place."

"You like the waitress who wears a T-shirt and no bra."

"Yeah, well, you got a point."

"We'll meet you at the PD."

It wasn't two minutes after I hung up on Mazzio before my phone rang again.

"Sammy, darlin'," Bettye said, "I hate to bother you, but the mayor called. He'd like to see you."

I closed my eyes and tossed my head back like a man about to collapse. "Grrrr."

"Did you just growl?" she asked.

"How did Ronnie find out about this?"

"I don't know, but you're right. He seems to know."

"Tell him I'm with the FBI. They're in charge, and I can't leave just yet."

"The FBI is in charge?"

"Not really, but he doesn't know that. I'll see him as soon as possible."

"Sammy, don't let him get you riled up."

"Riled up?"

"Don't you start with me, city boy."

"Bye, Betts."

I dropped the phone into my pocket and let out a huge volume of air.

"What's up?" Frank asked.

"The mayor wants to see me. Seems he already knows what happened."

"Think that IAB shitbird made a complaint about us?" John asked.

"I'll bet Rodney called the sheriff. The Sheriff called Ronnie, and now, as we speak, Darnell the dipstick is spraying gasoline on the fire."

* * * *

Before sitting down with our fearless mayor and his politically motivated and mentally challenged deputy, I wanted to sprinkle a little

171

lighter fluid over my own fire. I walked back into the house and waved for Ralph Oliveri to join me in private.

"Sorry to bother you again, but I just got a call and learned that the little fellow who Carl had words with is kicking up a fuss."

"Like how?"

"I'll get a full rundown for you after I get called in on the mayor's carpet. But thanks to the Prospect rumor mill, Captain Lightfoot here called his sheriff who called the mayor. That little worm is still pushing me as his number one suspect for two murders. And since you and Carl seem to be on my side, he's thinking FBI complicity and a major cover-up...for some unknown reason."

"You gotta be shittin' me. Let me get Carl in here."

"I've gotta get going. His Highness has already called twice. He's getting impatient. But, hey, just a quick tip for you. Our deputy mayor and Rodney Burchfield are in cahoots. I have no doubt that everything Rodney learns will be spoon fed to Darnell Means as soon as he can dial the number."

Ralph pulled a small spiral notebook and pen from his inside jacket pocket. "Gimme the deputy's name again."

"Darnell Means. A former law clerk from Maryville."

"Okay, I'll talk to Carl about this. But call me with whatever you learn."

"Will do."

Ralph walked back inside.

"Where'd you get all that info, Boss," John asked.

Frank broke out a big grin. "Did you hear him get that much on the phone, stupid?"

"I'm askin', Fool."

"Guys," I said, "I'm just having a little fun here at someone else's expense. Maybe Carl Harmon will get mad at Rodney and call his people, and those people will call other people. And indirectly we can stick it to Rodney and Darnell all at one time."

* * * *

Darnell and I sat in the pair of matching green leather chairs in front of Ronnie's massive mahogany desk, Darnell wearing a three piece medium gray suit and me in shirt sleeves so my holstered Glock, two extra seventeen round magazines and a pair of shiny nickel-plated handcuffs showed prominently. A show of superior firepower always gives a guy the psychological advantage.

"What happened today, Sam?" the mayor asked. "We heard there's another killin'."

I smiled cordially to keep Ronnie on my side. "Another killin' might be oversimplified. A man named Vito Cinquemani was hired to kill me. Now he's dead."

Ronnie's look of shock and abject fear interrupted my narrative, but after allowing only a moment for him to gain his composure, I continued.

"I don't want to sound overly dramatic." Actually, I did. "But I was just a short trigger pull away from death when a gentleman named Salvatore Polizzi, armed with a legal handgun, shot and killed Cinquemani before he could finish his job."

"Lord have mercy," Ronnie said. "And why were you where this Cinquie, Cinqua-whatever was?"

I refused to include Darnell in the conversation and directed my comments at the mayor. "As you know, Ronnie, the FBI and various other police agencies have joined me in investigating Gregory Buggarelli's murder. Gino Musucci, the man who is renting the Kinzel Springs home where this recent shooting took place, employed Vito Cinquemani as a personal assistant. Mr. Musucci was unaware of Vito's intentions until recently. When he learned about Vito's plan, he took precautions to prevent any harm coming to me. I went to Musucci's home to get information about people in New York, Rhode Island and Boston who figure prominently in this investigation."

Ronnie shook his lacquered head vigorously. As a testament to his hairspray, not a follicle moved out of place.

"And why did this man wanna kill you?"

"That's a long story, and since I believe that Captain Burchfield from the sheriff's office still intends to pursue a case against me with an eye on charging me with one or more murders, I decline to elaborate on any details without my attorney present." I punctuated the thought with a smile.

"Do what?" Ronnie said. It came out as almost a gasp.

Darnell decided to make himself heard. "You have to tell us what your actions were."

I looked at him with my street cop's evil eye. "I'll provide the mayor with an official statement prefaced, of course, with the clause detailing how I am making the report for administrative purposes only. I will not waive my rights against self-incrimination, to legal counsel, and I do not forfeit any of the guarantees granted under Miranda vs the US."

Ronnie jumped in quickly. "Now, Sam, don't get all excited. We're not pushin' ya here. Darnell jest meant we wanted ta know what happened."

"Excuse me, Ronnie, but as far as Darnell is concerned, that's bullshit. He's acting in concert with Burchfield. His intentions are not in my best interest. If you want more information, you'll get it only after my attorney approves my statement."

Darnell couldn't let my aspersion go unanswered. "We could suspend you pending an investigation, you know."

"No, no, no—" Ronnie began, but I interrupted.

"Go ahead, and if your little Rodney Burchfield interferes with this investigation, the FBI will prosecute him *and you* under Federal statutes. SAC Carl Harmon has already told that unprofessional, incompetent, petulant, miniature ignoramus as much. If you want to jump on board in an impotent attempt to break my balls, do it. I dare you."

Ronnie jumped in again before Darnell could shout another inflammatory remark or I could spring out of my chair and strangle the pasty-faced moron.

"Sam, Sam, Sam. Nobody's tryin' ta cause ya any trouble here. But ya have ta unnerstand our position. We need ta know why y'all are investigatin' a county case."

"That's the first easy question you've asked, Ronnie. I cleared the open murder of Carlo DeCenzo because I knew it was linked to our murder of Greg Buggarelli at the Foothills View Motel."

"Is that right?" Ronnie sounded astonished.

"Exactly," I said. Vito Cinquemani made a dying declaration to me admitting that he not only killed DeCenzo, but he copped to killing Buggarelli as well."

"Lord have mercy," Ronnie said. "Two people. What kind o' man was he?"

"A contract killer for the mob…among other things."

"Who overheard this dying declaration?" Darnell asked.

I shrugged. "Just me. But I've got the gun that will prove Vito killed DeCenzo. With a little more work, we'll link those who paid Vito to the murder of Carlo's father in Martin County, Florida and the conspiracy to kill me. Federal and local wire taps in New York tend to link Vito with several organized crime figures who wanted me dead. Originally, Buggarelli, a bad cop, had been hired to take me out, but my theory is that Vito wanted the money and killed Buggarelli to ultimately get the job. Fifty thousand balloons is a nice piece of change for a couple minutes work. So, as you should see, Captain Burchfield is way out of his depth and had better pull his nose out of this affair or get it bitten off."

"This is still only your word," Darnell insisted.

I wanted to smack the paunchy young bastard. "Prove differently. I'm not on trial here. If you and your tiny friend think I'm a killer, prove it. Arrest me without probable cause and I'll have your ass and everything you own."

"Sam, don't," Ronnie interjected.

"*Don't* my ass, Ronnie. Your deputy mayor obviously has an agenda here. I repeat my challenge. Prove it, or shut up."

Before Ronnie could comment further, his phone rang.

"Yes, Trudy. Uh-huh. Okay, put him through."

A few moments went by without a comment from Ronnie. He listened and nodded. Each time he heard a new message, his left eye twitched, his forehead wrinkled, and his mouth quivered. "Uh-huh. Yes, sir. Uh-huh. Yes, sir, I unnerstand. Yes, sir, I'll take care of that. Yes, sir, no problem. Yes, sir. We're good here. Yes, sir. Thank ya fer callin'."

He hung up, and I locked eyes with him.

Ronnie slumped low in his oversized swivel chair. He looked like a little kid who just walked out of the principal's office.

I glanced at Darnell and then back at Ronnie. The mayor let out an exaggerated breath, and his shoulders dropped two inches. He closed his eyes and shook his head.

"That was the chief assistant US attorney for the southeast region callin'. He told me, Sam, that you were part of a joint investigation providing the gubmint with information on organized crime activity and several homo-cides in various jurisdictions. He ordered me to leave you alone and said he's spoken to Sheriff Joe Don Hartung and the Blount County DA about this. He's subpoenaed Captain Burchfield and Darnell to Knoxville to answer questions in front of Justice Department investigators."

When Ronnie paused, I stuck in my two cents. "Sounds like Darnell might be in hot water." Then I grinned like a snake eyeing up a mouse.

"Lord have mercy, Sam. What is happenin' here?"

Good old Carl.

"I guess we'll have to wait and see."

* * * *

My foot had yet to cross the Prospect PD threshold before Bettye tossed a question at me. "What happened up there?"

I dragged one of the guest chairs from against the wall and placed it among the assembled multitude. Bettye was sitting in her normal spot. John Gallagher relaxed behind his desk with Frank O'Brien on a chair in front of him. Fred Mazzio had taken a seat next to Bettye and sat there leering at her. Wally Danko, obviously no longer snoring in his temporary bedroom, had pulled an armchair between the two desks and spun it around to face me.

"The mayor and Darnell Do Right tried to give me the third degree," I said. "That dipstick even tried to side with Rodney Rat Squad and insinuate that I might be in cahoots with the mobsters, and we've got some kind of criminal conspiracy going."

"You gotta be kidding me!" Frank threw one of John's purloined motel pens onto the desktop with a little too much enthusiasm for his partner.

"Hey, Fool, I'm sittin' here."

"Shut up, John. I'm having trouble processing this shit."

"Bottom line it for us, big guy," Mazzio said. "Are they throwing you to the wolves at IAB?"

"I think Darnell would have experienced an orgasm if that happened, but I was saved by the bell—telephone bell, that is." I ended my sentence with a smirk.

"You always do that," Wally said. "You say something and know we want to know more. Come on, out with it."

I let my smirk widen into a big-assed grin. "I guess it helps when I've got the chief AUSA of the southern district in my corner. He interrupted our conversation by letting the local politicos know that I'm part of a joint investigation, and everyone must stop breaking my shoes. Oh, yeah, before he hung up, he summoned Darnell the Dipshit to the Knoxville office of the Justice Department to answer questions. He also said Rodney the Rodent had a similar appointment. He wants them to show cause why I'm being pursued as a suspect."

"Hot damn," Mazzio said. "You might be old, bwana, but you can still bring smoke."

"Thank you, Frederick. You're too kind."

Bettye shook her head and gave me a worried look. "I don't want to throw a wet blanket on this, Sammy, but are you sure these people will be leaving you alone now?"

John Gallagher needed to be heard. "Yeah, Boss. You got enough horsepower with your friend at the Justice Department to squash these local boys?"

"Bettye," I said, "I hope so. I think so. And John, it's not my friend. Carl Harmon made the call, not me. Apparently little Rodney Rats annoyed him so much he wanted revenge. And a few well-placed words from me about our lovely deputy mayor led Carl to believe they were acting in concert."

"I wanted to ring that little bastard's neck," Frank said.

"Me too, Boss," John added.

"Well, darlin'," Bettye said, "I hope this business is over, and no more politicians or gangsters are gonna give you trouble."

"Thank you, Betts. That reminds me of something I've got to do—something that might make one of the gangsters think twice before causing me more grief." I stood up, intending to use the phone in my office.

"Whoa. Hang on, Madman," Mazzio said. "The Polish prince and I weren't with you at the scene of the shooting. Don't go nowhere before you tell us all the gory details."

I quickly elaborated for Fred and Wally and filled in a few gaps for Bettye, although Frank and John had already given her a pretty fair rundown.

When I finished, Mazzio commented. "Jeez, that was close. You musta been ready to poop in your shorts."

"It's difficult to relax while you're watching a monster looking down the sights of a Glock and you're only a dozen feet in front of the muzzle end."

"Mighta ended up in a fast draw contest, huh, Boss?" Gallagher said.

"John, I don't even want to think about it. Listen, I've got to make a quick call. It's important."

Chapter Thirty

I placed that call to my friend and former partner retired Detective Byron Thomas who lived in the quiet little community of Manorville on the east end of Long Island. He picked up on the third ring.

"Hey, Byron, Whaddaya doin'? Or should I say who are you doin'?"

"Hey, buddy, howzit goin'? I haven't talked to you since last Christmas. You doin' okay down there in sunny Appalachia?"

"Oh, just another day on the peaceful side of the Smokies. This morning a mook named Vito tried to kill me. But, as you can surmise, I'm still alive and kicking. Vito, however, bought the pomadori farm."

"You smoked somebody?"

"Not me. A good Samaritan named Sal Polizzi."

"Why do I know that name?"

"Remember a connected shithead called Moonface Musucci?"

"Who could forget that skell?"

"Sal is his uncle."

"Wait, wait, wait." Byron sounded like I had just told him J. Edgar Hoover came back from the dead. "That moon-faced prick hated you. Now you're tellin' me he sent his uncle to kill a guy who's lookin' to put out your lights?"

"It's a long story. You got a minute? Where are you?"

"I'm sittin' on my horse in the middle of Southaven Park. Yeah, I got time. It'll take me an hour to get back to my horse trailer, and it's your dime."

"Okay, cowboy, relax and listen. When I'm finished, I'll ask you to do me a favor."

"Yeah, sure, whatever you need. I only wish I had a beer or two. I like to drink while I'm listening to your drama."

I told Byron the complete story.

"Jesus Christ! What a hoot. I thought the worst you had down there were a few shoplifters and jaywalkers."

"We don't have any shoplifters."

"But you got mutts like Vito the button man."

"Makes life interesting."

"I'll bet. What kind of favor do you need?"

"Can you get a good camera with a telephoto lens?"

"Yeah. I think so. You remember Doug McGovern from the ID section?"

"Sure."

"When he retired, he opened up a photography studio. He's a pro—takes portraits and wedding pictures and all that shit. I hired him to take a portrait of my grandson. He's got any kind of camera you need."

"Good. Say hello for me. Now, here's what I need—easy job for you."

I gave Byron the particulars and asked him to fax me the results—something I wanted as an insurance policy.

* * * *

I looked at my watch and almost fainted. 2:35 and I hadn't eaten lunch. I walked out to the lobby to see if anyone else had eaten.

"We've been waitin' for you, Madman," Mazzio said.

"Sorry, guys. I lost track of time. How about you, Betts?"

"Been waitin', too."

"You guys were heading to Howell's. Go. I'll watch the desk while Bettye is out."

"You sure, Boss?" John asked.

"Yeah, go. I ate an adrenalin sandwich earlier. I'm good."

"Want us to bring something back?" Frank asked.

I figured that by the time I received my sandwich it would be close to dinnertime. "No, thanks. I'll take the girls out tonight." Then something dawned on me. "Shit. I forgot to call Kate. I hope she didn't watch the twelve o'clock news."

"If she did," Wally said, "she would have called here."

"Probably right. But, Frederick, I hold you personally responsible for not reminding me."

He looked shocked. He's so easy. "Me? Gallagher is your personal shoeshine boy. Isn't that his job?"

I gave him the gunman's salute. "Gotcha."

The other three stooges laughed.

"I'll get you for that, sahib."

"Yeah, in your dreams. Now go, so I can answer the phones and dispatch the cars in peace."

They turned and walked through the front doors. John said something to Fred, who took a swing at John, but missed because my middle-aged child ran away into the lobby.

I looked at Bettye and shrugged. "Children."

She smiled. "You started it."

I shook my head. "You're learning from them."

"No, sugar, I learn from you."

I shrugged again. "Go ahead, take your lunch hour. I'll hold down the fort. Sorry I made you wait."

She gave me one of those motherly looks designed to make naughty little boys think they'd been offensive.

"I'm not leavin' you, Sam Jenkins. Don't you remember what almost happened to you today?"

"Yeah. And I thought I would have crashed by now. But I wasn't kidding about the adrenalin. I'm still cranked. Maybe I should make a drink. Want one?"

She frowned. "Maybe not. Maybe you should talk."

I blinked a few times and attempted to look confused. "About what? I told you what happened."

"And you call those men fools."

"Hey."

"Hey, your own self. Someone almost shot you this mornin'."

"Pfui. *Almost* don't count 'cept in horseshoes and hand grenades."

"You are impossible."

"No, I'm not. For a few minutes there things looked bleak, and the only plan I could come up with reminded me of the Alamo."

"Oh, Lord have mercy. Sammy, I am so sorry."

"Thanks, but everything came out in the wash. And thanks to Sal Polizzi, in the future, I'll refute the old adage, 'There is no honor among thieves.'"

* * * *

Over sushi, Tom Yum soup and assorted Thai curries at the Lemon Grass restaurant in Maryville, I told Kate and Dixie all about my adventure.

"Sweetie, that's about as close a call as I'd like you to have between now and when you retire. How long until your contract is up?"

"July, Katherine. Why do you ask?"

"Because then you can retire—again—and be a fulltime fisherman or gardener or whatever you'd like to be."

"Yeah, right. And who will solve the unsolvable? Who will avenge the downtrodden? Who will—?"

She didn't let me finish. "Oh, pa-leeze. Stop."

"Hey, I cleared two murders today. Don't *pa-leeze* me."

Dixie set down her glass of wine and touched her lips with a cloth napkin. "Two murders?"

"Sure. As he was dying, Vito copped to killing Carlo DeCenzo. That one was easy. The gun he was carrying was the murder weapon. And then in a dying declaration, I got him to admit to Greg's murder. Quite a finale if I do say so myself."

Dixie nearly choked on her last sip of wine. "Why would he kill Greg?"

I shrugged. "Never heard why. Vito expired on me."

"So, this is totally over," Kate said. "Good. The tension of these last few days made me think about how people on the Gaza Strip must feel."

"Why do you think this man killed Greg?" Dixie asked again.

"Just conjecture," I said. "Probably a number of reasons."

"And other people heard his dying declaration?"

I smiled. "No, just me."

"That's not solid for court," she said. "You need more corroboration."

"Hey, Dix, you're not checking over some junior detective's case here. I'm not prosecuting Vito. Someone is going to bury him."

"Don't you want your closeout to be solid?"

"Anyone who doesn't believe me can prove otherwise."

"Who?" Dixie still looked as if she couldn't believe what I was telling her.

"Who indeed? I'm the man. I say Vito murdered Greg. It fits. These wise guys kill people like we change our socks. Case closed. Can I taste that massaman curry you're got?"

Dixie made a face, but pushed her plate toward me. I took a forkful mixed with a little rice.

"Thanks," I said. "Very good, isn't it? Solving murders makes me hungry."

Kate touched my forearm and smiled. Dixie took another sip of Riesling. I saw light at the end of my tunnel.

Chapter Thirty-one

Just before 7 a.m. the next morning, Dixie and I prepared to leave. I had stowed her luggage in the trunk of the Crown Vic, Kate had made coffee, and I rustled up a little breakfast. Kate chose a small container of flavored yogurt. Dixie ate half a slice of toast, and I wolfed down some bread, cheese and sliced ham.

Before we walked out, Dixie thanked Kate for her kindness and hospitality.

"It was good to see you," Kate said. "Safe trip home. Everything's okay now." She gave Dixie a hug.

I looked at Dixie. "Ready to saddle up, partner?"

She nodded.

I ended our parting scene. "See ya later, Kats."

Even with dark polarized lenses, I squinted and half closed my eyes as we drove due east on US 321. The bright autumn sun had just peeked over Elejoy Mountain and sent a piercing brightness through the windshield. Our only relief came from the low-lying clouds that hugged the roadway inside Walland Gap.

"Thanks for the shade, Mother Nature," I said.

"That was bright, wasn't it?" Dixie said.

"Mmm."

"The colors on those mountains are beautiful," She said.

"Not bad, but we've seen better. I think it has to do with how much rain we get in September. You know, with everything going on, I didn't take much time to notice this year."

"I can see why you moved here. Every day is like a drive through the park."

"The hills were a big change for a kid from flat old Long Island. I see it every day, but try not to take things for granted."

"I can't imagine you would."

Dixie reached over and ran her hand through the hair at the back of my neck. That was something she often used to do. It always got the same reaction from me.

"Oh, Sam, do you ever think what it would have been like if—?" She didn't finish and didn't need to.

I nodded. "I often wonder, but have no answer."

I looked away from the road momentarily. Dixie gently bit a tiny section of her bottom lip. That was also something she often did. I always thought it looked incredibly feminine. Then she moved to her right and repositioned herself in the passenger's seat to look directly at me.

"Big cars with consoles and bucket seats are inconvenient, aren't they?" I didn't mean it as a question.

Dixie sighed and turned to look straight ahead as I swung the car over the Old Walland Highway Bridge and crossed the Little River. Once I had the car on a straightaway, I continued her pre-mission briefing.

"You have each other's cell phone numbers on speed dial. Communicate with Wally if you need to stop for any reason. He'll do the same."

Dixie blinked a couple of times and nodded. "Okay."

"You'll be in the lead most of the way, so check your rearview mirror often. Make sure he's still behind you. Set your cruise control at five over the speed limit. That's fast enough, and no trooper will bother you."

She smiled. "Okay, boss. Sounds like you're sending me out on a special operation."

"Hey, wise guy, I'm worried about you and want you home safely."

"I know. Thanks. But like you told me, this is over. Remember? I'm just driving home."

"Yeah, right, but humor me."

Dixie reached out and touched my hand. "I will."

I smiled. "Good. Now I'm happy."

We drove in silence for the next few minutes. Dixie looked at the scenery as we passed the city park on McTeer's Station Pike.

As I entered the town square, she said, "Such a pretty town. You're

Wayne Zurl

so lucky."

"It's not all roses, but for the most part I'm happy and think I really stepped in it."

She showed me a sad smile as I pulled into the lot of the municipal building and took the parking spot reserved for the police chief.

I tapped my four-digit code into the keypad at the back door.

"Wally said he'd be here at 7:30." I looked at my watch. "We've got time before we meet him at the garage. Then I'll open up, and you can jump into your fast little car and head home."

Dixie's eyes are very expressive. I remembered how most often they sparkled and showed an inner happiness that couldn't have been explained better with words. That morning her eyes suggested a burden within her, somewhere between guilt and sorrow.

"Can we sit in your office for a while?"

"Sure."

I led the way down the dimly lit hallway. When we reached the lobby, I switched on a couple of overhead lights and then the lights in my office. Dixie and I sat in two of the saddle-tan guest chairs and stared at each other.

"You doing okay?" I asked.

"I guess."

She didn't look very happy.

"I've got to ask you something."

Her face changed. Her eyes narrowed, and her forehead wrinkled. She looked terribly frightened.

I took a small plastic bag from my pocket and dumped a little gold object into my palm.

"Give me your hand," I said.

Dixie held out hers. I took it into mine, felt a tremble and dropped a tiny Chinese good luck charm into her palm.

"Do you have the chain that goes with this?"

Her face blanched and her hand shook more. "You knew?"

I nodded. "Where's the chain?"

"I threw it away."

"Where?"

186

"In some river along the Interstate between here and Crossville."

"The Tennessee River."

"I don't know."

"Do you still have the butterfly?"

Tears ran down her cheeks and she sniffed. "Yes, I'd never. I couldn't. You gave that to me."

"Good. What happened to the old blackjack I gave you years ago after that guy attacked you in the parking lot?"

"Oh, my God."

I felt her body shiver.

"Dixie?"

"In the river."

"Did anyone see you?"

"I don't think so. There was no traffic. I just stopped for a moment and threw them into the water."

"Uh-huh."

She squeezed my hand. "And you knew."

"Yes. I can't read much Chinese, but I recognized the symbol for luck. They attach one of those charms to every chain sold by the Lucky Jewelry Company in Chinatown. That's where I bought your butterfly."

"What are you going to do?" A touch of fear tainted her voice.

I didn't pause for dramatic effect, but I took a long moment to respond. "Nothing." I shrugged. "Well, I'm going to kiss you goodbye and wish you a safe journey. Go home, Dixie. This is over."

"Oh, Sam, I have to explain."

I shook my head. "Not to me. I don't care."

"Please. I have to."

I nodded. "Okay."

She dropped her eyes and squeezed my hands with a force I didn't think her capable of. "At first I told Greg I didn't want any dinner, but after I went to my room and unpacked, I thought I wanted at least a drink and maybe something small. So, I walked next door. His window was open, and I heard him on the phone. I didn't know who he was talking to, but he said something like, 'I know we were friends. I understand that, but I need that money. Where else am I going to get that kind of cash? Besides, we've had a problem for years. I'm not his friend any more. You want him

Wayne Zurl

dead. I'll kill him. End of story.'" She looked up and into my eyes. Tears rolled over her high cheekbones.

"You knew he meant me?"

She shook her head. "I suspected, but wasn't sure. I knocked on the door, and he let me in. And I asked. At first, he denied he meant you. I didn't believe him. Then he finally admitted it, and I said, 'For God's sake, Greg. Sam used to be a good friend.' Greg laughed and said you were always the one who scored, the one who made it big and even though you were married, I liked you best. He said those things as if he hated you."

"Maybe he did. Who knows what goes on in someone else's head?"

"Then he said he couldn't let me tell you. That scared the hell out of me. When he reached for my throat, we struggled briefly, and he tore the chain off my neck. I reached into my purse, grabbed the blackjack and hit him. When he went down, I hit him again."

I nodded. "I understand. You had to defend yourself. And thank you. You did all of that for me. I can't imagine how difficult it's been for you."

She began sobbing, tears cascaded down her cheeks. Her eye makeup ran in little rivulets of black. I handed her my handkerchief, and she wiped her face.

"Oh, Sam, I can't even say his name without it tearing me apart. He was going to kill you. And for what?"

"Money? A better life as he saw it? He was a gambler and hit the bottom of the barrel."

Dixie wiped her nose and sniffed. "And you're just going to let me go?"

"No. After you kiss me goodbye, you're going to promise you'll drive carefully on the way home, and then be happy in your life. That work for you, kiddo?"

"Oh, Sam."

She stood, and I followed. Dixie put her arms around my neck and kissed me passionately.

When we parted I said, "Wow."

Dixie blinked a few times. "Yeah, wow. I always said you were the best kisser I'd ever met."

I offered her a half smile. "Something to put on my tombstone."

She almost smiled. "So that's it? Will I ever see you again?"

At times like this, I refuse to get maudlin.

I sighed. "That depends on you. I'm here and will probably be the same guy."

Dixie nodded. "Always you."

"Yeah, the one and only."

"You're taking a big risk for me."

I shook my head. "It's time for me to play judge and jury. I say you acted in self-defense. I'm satisfied, and no one else on my side of the fence matters. I've got you covered. Forget this. I know that's easy for me to say, but if you can't get your head around things, ask someone for help—just make sure that someone is bound by confidentiality and keeps their mouth shut."

"Do you know what you're doing?"

I gave her one of my theatrical smiles. "I'm the police chief. I know everything."

She managed a small grin, touched my cheek with one hand and held out her other, palm up. "Should I throw away this little charm?"

"No. Give it to me. It's on the evidence inventory. When this is all over and forgotten, we destroy everything but the paperwork and photos." I shrugged. "It's all I have to remember you by. I'll fasten it to the chain with my Army dog tags. No one will ever know what it is. Just be sure to hang on to that jade and gold butterfly."

"Always."

I needed to take the coward's way out or shed a tear and risk losing my stoic hero status in Dixie's eyes.

"I'm guessing Wally is waiting for us outside."

Dixie nodded and again wiped her eyes with the handkerchief.

It only took us two minutes to walk across the parking lot to the garage. Wally Danko parked his metallic brown F-150 in front of the garage office with the motor running and windows down. His chin rested on his chest with his eyes closed—totally at peace. I tapped on the passenger side door.

He slowly opened his eyes and looked to his right. "Hey, boss."

"Been here long?"

"Couple minutes."

"Gassed up, and ready to go?"

"You kiddin' me?"

I chuckled. "I'll get Dixie's car."

"Okay."

I carried her two bags to the overhead door and used my key to start the automatic opener. Dixie opened the car's trunk and I dropped in her luggage. When I turned, she didn't move, but stared at me. A lump in my throat began to swell. I didn't want to leave her looking like anything other than the tough guy she had known for years.

"Let's crank it up," I said.

She nodded, slid into the driver's seat and rolled down the window. I bent over to look at her and say a few final words. A single tear ran down her left cheek.

"Goodbye, Sam."

Somehow, I knew she meant it was for the last time, and I couldn't make the same words come out, but finally I managed, "Take care of yourself, Dix."

A second tear joined the first on her cheek.

I needed to change the subject. "I gave Wally directions for a shortcut GPS doesn't know about. That will save you twenty minutes. Follow him to the Interstate. When you get to I-40, pass him. He'll follow you all the way to Chambersburg. The DA's guys will meet you at the motel. Wally will wait while you check them out. Call Steven Holmes, no one else. Make sure they are who they should be."

She nodded. "I'll remember."

"Okay. Have a safe trip home."

She nodded again. "I love you, Sam."

I touched her cheek and couldn't force out any words. I straightened, and she rolled up her window and backed out.

As I stepped up to Wally's truck, I tapped twice on the fender. "All yours, old man, and thanks."

He nodded. "No sweat. Gotcha covered. I'll call when she's in PA."

I watched as they drove off.

Chapter Thirty-Two

Before I left home that morning, I told Kate she probably wouldn't hear from me until I picked her up and headed to our farewell dinner with the remainder of my unofficial investigative team. After Dixie left Prospect, I opened up the PD and met Bettye when she arrived a few minutes before eight.

"You're in early," she said.

I nodded. "Uh-huh."

She dropped a laundry-bag sized purse into a desk draw and hung her jacket on the coat rack standing between her desk and John's. "What's the occasion?"

"I opened up the garage. Dixie Foster needed her car to drive home."

Bettye nodded. "She's safe now. I guess she's relieved."

"Yeah, everything's over. Life is back to normal."

She shot me a look, and for some reason the *pricklies* ran up my spine.

"You two had something special going on, didn't you?"

The question sounded accusatory, and I wasn't going to listen to that. "I've known her for almost forty years. We worked together a few times. For a long time, she occupied the same position in my life where you are today. I like Dixie. She's a good person. Neither she nor I ever did anything inappropriate."

Bettye sensed the tension in my voice. "I didn't mean to imply—"

I interrupted. "I know. And I didn't mean to sound testy. It's just that, uh…I'm probably never going to see her again. This is a rerun of saying goodbye to the old friend I left eighteen years ago. I feel just like I did when you told me you had to resign. I don't like loss."

She looked sad and a little guilty. "I'm sorry. I didn't want—"

I held up a hand. "Don't. We're okay."

She looked down slightly and then turned her hazel eyes upward. "You sure?"

I gave her a big grin. "Totally convinced."

Bettye's smile lit up the entire lobby. "Good. Now, I expect you want me to make us some coffee."

"I *expect* nothing of the sort. But if you do, I'll walk across the square and bang on the back door of Tillie's Tea House. It's too early for them to be open, but maybe something just came out of the oven."

"Okey dokey, darlin'. Just not somethin' too gooey. I don't want my hips growin' and stretchin' my britches too much."

"Roger that, Sergeant. Pastries sans goo. You got it."

I returned fifteen minutes later carrying two cheese Danish without the intended gooey lemon topping. Bettye had brewed up a pot of two-thirds Columbian dark roast and one-third cherry-flavored coffee I had picked up from a roaster on Michigan's Leelanau Peninsula. My second breakfast rated a *spectacular* on my scale of cuisine.

At 9:30, Bettye stepped into my office holding two sheets of paper.

"Sammy, this just came over the fax for you." She handed me the pages. "And just what are you going to do with those?"

"Don't ask."

"Oh, Lord have mercy. You are goin' ta drive me ta drink."

"I already have."

* * * *

At ten to one, I pulled into the parking lot of the Villa Napoli and parked two spots away from Gino Musucci's Black Mercedes S-500.

Nick Cutrone's daughter, wearing a black pantsuit and crisp white blouse, met me at the hostess' station.

She offered an appropriate femme maître d' smile while holding several menu folders. "Hello, Sam. Daddy and a few others are at his table. Would you like me to take you up?"

"No thanks, Rosie. I know the way."

Nick sat in his usual chair in front of a door leading to the kitchen. Gino was sitting under the Pagliacci poster with his back to the wall. A chair next to his remained empty—my seat. I'd have the operatic clown

192

on the poster looking over my shoulder. Sal Polizzi occupied the seat across from Gino and next to a young man I'd yet to meet. All four were, like me, wearing sport jackets with open collar shirts. The three other tables on the raised platform were conspicuously unoccupied.

I wondered if anyone had cleaned and oiled the sub-machinegun strapped under the table—just kidding.

"Gentlemen," I said. "Happy lunchtime."

Nick stood first. "Sammy, whaddaya say?"

We shook hands.

Gino followed suit as I stepped toward the empty chair. "Howzit goin', kid?"

Handshake number two.

"Better than yesterday, thanks. You alright?"

He waved away my question dismissively and looked a little down in the mouth. "Yeah, yeah, I'm fine."

I reached diagonally across the table. "Hello, Sal."

He half rose and extended his hand. "Yeah, howzit goin'?"

Then Gino picked up the dialogue. "Sam, this is Teddy Aragone, my sister Angela's kid. Teddy, Chief Sam Jenkins."

I guessed Teddy to be in his early thirties. He had conservatively cut dark hair, an olive complexion and an overall polished look. He stood before Gino finished his introduction.

"How do you do, sir?"

After the final handshake, I answered Teddy. "I'm feeling pretty chipper today. This your first time in Tennessee?"

Before Teddy could respond, Gino stepped in. "Teddy will be working for me now. He's, uh, takin' Vito's spot."

"Aha."

The kid's sharp appearance and intelligent face suggested MBA, not up-and-coming mobster. Maybe he was both.

"You might remember Teddy's father, my brother-in-law, Pete Aragone."

I didn't have to stretch my memory too far. Peter 'Shiny Shoes' Aragone was the husband of Gino's youngest sister and the best dressed garbage man in Nassau County. Actually, Pete was owner of Gold Coast Carting and a lieutenant in the Musucci family business with more juice than anyone else in the organization I'd ever met.

"Sure, Pete and I met once."

Actually, I sat in on an interview where detectives questioned Pete about the intimidation of homeowners who attempted to cancel their garbage pickup.

Gino took a sip from a highball glass full of ice and what I assumed was scotch and more soda than I'd care for. "Pete's name will come up in conversation today. Something important."

I nodded just as Nick's grandson, Vinnie the bartender, stepped up to the table.

"Get ya a drink, Mr. Jenkins?"

"Yeah, Vinnie, thanks. Single-malt with a splash."

"I just got in a bottle of Oban. Wanna try it?"

"Sounds good."

Nick made a sweeping gesture with his hand. "And bring us another round, Vincent."

Vinnie smiled. "Will do, Pop."

Apparently, Vinnie didn't move quickly enough for grandpa. "Go on, Vincent. Get outta here. And send Millie up."

The kid gave Nick a conciliatory look and retreated down the steps and toward the bar.

"Our waitress will be here in a minute," Nick said. "We'll order and then talk. But no hurry. Lunch will be a while. Tommy knows we gotta finish our drinks."

I picked up the menu lying in front of me.

"Whaddaya doin' wit' that menu?" Gino asked. "You told me you wanted scungill'. I had Nicky get it special. He had it flown in this mornin', for chrissakes."

I smiled. "Yeah. Good. Scungill' it is. I can't remember when I had it last—probably at Southside in Lindenhurst."

Nick jumped all over me for that. "Hey, Tommy can do better than that place. You wait."

"Fra diavolo, right?" Gino asked. "But not too spicy."

"Yeah, fra diavolo," Nick said. "But never too spicy. Whaddaya think we are…Mexicans or somethin'?"

Everyone laughed. I smiled again. Gino and Sal drained their glasses.

Nicky nodded, looking like the proud father of a world-class Italian-American chef. Teddy took a sip from a glass still half full of red wine.

Vinnie returned with a tray of drinks. After everyone received a fresh glass filled with their hooch of choice, he asked a logistical question. "Has everyone decided on a wine to go with your lunches?"

Nick answered for everyone. "There are two bottles of Chianti classico in my office, Vincent—the stuff that's not on the wine list. Pop the corks now, and give them a little air."

Vinnie nodded. "Sounds good." And not to incur the wrath of granddad, he promptly departed.

Gino raised his glass. "Salute."

Following Italian tradition, four more glasses came up, and we each returned the sentiment.

Gino set his glass down and sighed. "Sam, I wanna apologize again for what Vito tried ta pull off. I swear to ya, on my mother's grave, I didn't know about it until Sal told me what he found out."

Millie, the waitress with no familial relationship to the Cutrones, appeared, order book in hand. When she got ten feet from the table, Nick shot her an icy look and held up a hand. She stopped in her tracks. Nick raised his forefinger and shooed her away. Millie retreated down the four steps, but stayed in visual contact with her commander.

"Not necessary," I said, feeling overly magnanimous. "I need to thank you, Sal and Nicky, for dealing with the situation so efficiently." I looked at each participant as I mentioned their names. Gino nodded. Sal looked at me and except for a slight movement of his mouth, he remained impassive. Nick lowered his eyes and appeared a little sheepish.

"Okay. It's over. Forgotten." A big grin crossed Gino's face. "Except that fuckin' carpet. Ya shouldda gone outside when I said. Now, I gotta have the whole damn thing ripped up."

I tossed a hand up about shoulder height. "Come on, I know you've got renter's insurance."

Sal and Nick laughed. So did Gino and I, but Teddy only smiled politely, as if he hadn't seen the humor in Uncle Gino's remark.

A long moment passed as everyone took a hit on their drinks.

"So," Gino said, "you cleared Carlo's murder. That's good. Marie will feel some closure. Best she can, anyways. What about this Buggarelli guy?

Whaddaya know?"

"Vito went for it," I said. "Almost his last words."

"You gotta be kiddin' me. That don't sound like Vito."

I shrugged. "What can I tell you? Hard not to believe a dying declaration."

"He say why?"

I shook my head. "Passed over to that big pizzeria in the sky before he could."

"Still and all," Gino said. "I find it hard to believe. Sappin' a guy to death wasn't his style."

Nick asked, "You think he was coverin' for somebody?"

I turned my palms up. "Who? Any of you gentlemen sitting on an idea?"

Gino and Nick shook their heads. Teddy said and did nothing.

"I ain't heard nothin' about that," Sal said. "You say this guy, Buggarelli, was sent here by Jimmy Navarone?"

"Yeah, in a roundabout way. You may have already heard that the FBI will be speaking with Anthony, Patsy LoScalzo and Navarone about this. The Feds say they've collected bits of evidence and chatter, but you'll have to ask them what they can prove. The agents at the Melville office are handling that, and they wouldn't tell a local Tennessee cop Shinola."

"Yeah, I heard," Gino said. "They didn't waste any time. And that brings me to something I'm almost ashamed to say."

I could hardly wait. I had anticipated hearing something that would tickle me, but so far, that was only my conjecture.

Gino took a long drink of his scotch and soda. He set the glass on the table and sighed. "It's no secret my son was involved in this. Stupido! I told you before, a very foolish move on his part. First, for gettin' together with those hotheaded Micks and then for arranging to orchestrate…you know. I'm embarrassed that I had his man, Vito, right under my nose. I never saw it. Believe me, Anthony will not forget his indiscretion. And this pisses me off. You don't know how much."

I could guess.

Gino took a breath, sipped his scotch and set it down again. No one wanted to interject a thought while he was on a roll.

"Doin' somethin' like this—which made no fuckin' sense—tells me that Anthony is not fit to lead a troop of Girl Scouts, much less my business."

Gino was beginning to flush. He picked up his glass, but placed it down without drinking.

"Sam, I'm talkin' to you as a friend now and not a cop. Ya understand what I'm sayin'?"

I nodded, crossing my fingers under the table. "Sure, Gino. I understand. I respect that."

Wise guys love when you use the word *respect*.

He nodded and grabbed his glass again. "Good. Yeah, good."

He took a long drink. "Anthony is out. Out. Let him run his restaurant on the Island. He can make a good buck. He's got a family. Let him spend time with his kids and grandchildren. He's out."

I thought that was a good choice by the organization. Like the Republicans giving Michelle Bachmann the heave-ho.

I said, "Uh-huh." Everyone else remained silent.

"Teddy's father will be taking my spot. Petey is smart. He's not motivated by anger or stupidity. Something like this will not happen again. We do things, we do them for a reason. Not because of some thirty-year-old hard-on. And as you know, Sam, we got an understanding with the cops. An unwritten thing. We have respect for you. You have respect for us. You know what I'm sayin'?"

I nodded. "Yeah, Gino, I know."

He rattled the cubes in his glass, took one last drink and slammed the tumbler down. "I'd hate people ta think we were like those Russkies or the fuckin' Albanians. Bunch o' fuckin' animals. They got no honor. No class."

"Gino, just to clarify, what we say here, stays here," I said, just to say something and sound like I belonged.

"Yeah, yeah, thanks, but it's not like this will be a secret for long. For chrissakes, the Feds will know about everything by tomorrow."

I doubted it would take that long.

I thought changing the subject might stimulate conversation before the salads arrived.

"It didn't happen here, and I'm only indirectly involved, but there's little doubt that Alphonse DeCenzo's uh, death might be linked to all this.

197

Sal, will the FBI in Florida be poking their noses into people we're speaking of today?"

Polizzi had been staring at his bourbon. He shot Gino an inquiring look before answering.

"Don't ask," Gino said. "That's another reason we're making some additional...personnel changes."

"Uh-huh."

"Yeah, those involved will have to let the chips fall where they may. I'll take care of this situation. You'll be satisfied. Don't worry about it." He shifted in his chair, looking terribly uncomfortable. "We'll see if those guys at the FBI can prove anything."

A momentary silence descended on the table. Nick took the lull as his cue. He raised a hand and snapped his fingers. Millie trotted up the steps and took a place next to her boss.

"All ready, Mr. Cutrone?"

"Yeah, Millie, start here." He pointed at Gino.

"Me and him," Gino poked a thumb at me, "are havin' the scungill' that Tommy is makin' special." He looked at me. "Over what? Penne okay with you?"

"Sure. Who wants to twirl capellini around in red sauce when he's wearing a white shirt?"

Gino shook his head. "Jeez, always with the jokes. Okay, Millie, two o' those."

"Make it three," Nick said. "And Caesar salads for everybody. Wit' anchovies."

Millie nodded. "Very good, Mr. C."

Sal wanted lasagna Bolognese, and Teddy asked for chicken saltimbocca. Good choice by the kid. I might get to like him—unless someone sent him to pick up on my case where Vito left off.

Chapter Thirty-Three

Everyone had finished lunch and declined Nick's offer of an aperitif when Millie appeared with a bill in hand, but didn't seem to know what to do with it. When Nick didn't come to her rescue with a quick answer, schlep that I am, the guy who owed my three goombahs a sizable debt, spoke up.

"I'll take that, Millie."

She began to circumnavigate the table in my direction when Gino said something to me.

"I thought we had an agreement? I said I'd get lunch. Gimme the tab, sweetheart."

Millie's eyes shot back and forth in confusion, from me to Gino and finally rested on Nick, looking for guidance. He poked his chin toward Gino. Millie retraced her steps and handed the little black leather folder to him.

"I know what we agreed to, Gino," I said, "but after yesterday, buying lunch is the least I can do."

"'Ey, forgetaboutit," he said.

Before he could elaborate on his statement, Nick waved Millie off.

"You wouldn'ta been in that position if it wasn't for Vito and my schooch of a son. I got this. Come back here, Millie."

"'Ey, gentlemen, don't fight," Nick said. "Let this one be on the house."

"No way, Nicky," Gino said. "Don't get involved here. Sam and I had an agreement."

Nick shrugged.

"And our agreement stipulated I'd buy the wine. So, add that and the drinks to my bill and I'll go away happy. Capiche?"

Gino laughed. "You're hot shit. Yeah, capisco."

When Millie returned with two amended bills, I looked at mine, felt a sharp pain in my wallet and handed a credit card to the young lady.

After Gino and I added twenty percent tips and signed on the dotted line, everyone stood. There were more handshakes. Gino hugged Nick, slapped him on the back like he was an old cousin, and we all prepared to leave. But I still had unfinished business.

"Gino, can I see you for a minute?"

"Yeah, sure. Whaddaya need?"

"Let's go to the bar. I'll buy you a drink."

He gave me a look half way between apprehension and distrust. "I'll follah you."

We took two seats at the far corner of the long mahogany bar facing outward. Teddy Aragone remained standing to our right. Vinnie began walking over.

"Teddy," I said, "would you give us a minute?"

Teddy looked at Gino before answering. He received a quick nod.

To Gino, he said. "I'll use the men's room and then meet you in the car."

Gino told Vinnie to bring him a shot of sambuca, and I ordered a Rob Roy on the rocks.

Vinnie walked away, and Gino asked, "What's that you ordered?"

"Scotch and red vermouth."

"Kinda sweet?"

"Not especially."

"Any good?"

"Sure, I'm not a masochist."

"Maybe I'll try one some time."

I nodded, but remained silent for a long moment.

"It's your dime," Gino said.

"Uh-huh." I continued to wait while Vinnie dropped off our drinks. When he left, I said, "Am I going to have to worry about Anthony or his Irish buddy for the rest of my life, or is this really finished?"

Gino took a tiny sip of the clear liqueur and sighed deeply. "I told Anthony to lay off. He will. I can't answer for those Micks."

"I think you have more influence over the Irish than you think. I'd appreciate it if you telephoned whoever is in overall command in Boston and square this."

He nodded. "Yeah, okay. I'll make the call. Don't sweat it."

"Then all we have to worry about is the—" I was about to say 'the kid' when I remembered that Sonny boy was pushing sixty. "Your son occasionally gets something in his head, and he won't let go. He may be out of the business, but he still has associates that can be bought."

"'Ey, look—"

"Let me finish. I don't want to be peering over my shoulder for the rest of my life. And I especially don't want to worry about the people I care for. Will you do something for me to seal this?"

"Whaddaya talkin' about?"

I took the two pages Byron Thomas had faxed to me out of my jacket pocket and unfolded them on the bar.

"They're both essentially the same, but since two were sent to me, I'll offer both to you. They show that my guy had plenty of time to do what I asked."

Figuratively, two shots.

Gino looked at the enlarged photocopied pictures of Anthony's grown-up daughter and young granddaughter, both with perfect circles drawn around their heads, representing the reticule of a riflescope. The crosshairs centered on their foreheads.

"What the hell is this? That's my granddaughter and her kid."

"I know that. Look, Gino, I'm not trying to scare you or promise you and your wife any grief. I know you love your grandchildren. So, show these to your idiot son. Tell him I've still got friends, but not much of a conscience. This worked once before, and the thought remained with Anthony for thirty years."

"Whadda you sayin'?"

I told him the old story, just as Kate made me tell Dixie.

"Jesus Christ," he said. "I believe you would. Everybody used to say you were crazy like a shithouse rat." He downed half the sambuca. "That son o' mine will drive me ta drink."

"You already drink. Smack him in the head, and tell him if he tries to screw me, he's screwing you and his mother. You do that, like you mean it, and there will never be another problem."

He drained his glass. I sipped my Rob Roy.

He slammed the glass onto the bar a little too forcefully. "Don't worry about it. I promise. You and yours are safe. I guarantee it. Don't ask me ta kill my stupid son. My wife couldn't handle that, but I'll take care of this."

"And you'll call the Irish hoods."

"Yeah, yeah, yeah. I'll take care of them, too. I said don't worry about it."

Gino was still shaking his head as I took a long sip of the Rob Roy. I thought changing the subject would be a good thing.

"So, how's the new house coming? Think you're going to like living in the mountains?"

"The new house? Contractors and builders? M'Donna mi. Bunch o' fuckin' prima donnas. You'd think I was talkin' to a room full o' brain surgeons."

* * * *

We pulled two tables end to end down the center of Howell's pub. Kate and I sat across from Fred Mazzio and Maggie McDermott.

"How come you're not eatin'?" Fred asked me. "A small sandwich and a small beer? You not feelin' good?"

"I ate a big plate of scungell' over pasta and a Caesar salad for lunch."

"Oh, poor Sam," Maggie said, hamming it up. "You're forced to do so much as the police chief."

"He's got a tough life," Kate said. "He's gobbling up a fancy Italian meal while his wife is home eating a small container of yogurt."

"Us civil servants make those sacrifices for you retired civilians," I said. "Oh, yeah, don't forget I had to suffer through a half bottle of the finest Chianti I've tasted in years. It cost Nick Cutrone thirty bucks a bottle, wholesale."

Fred asked, "So you ate with the goombahs?"

"Yeah, at the Villa Napoli. And I would have taken everyone there tonight. Why did you pick this place?"

"I love this place."

"Didn't you ask anyone else?"

"Why?"

"You're a piece of work, Frederick."

"Yeah, so what? Gimme the poop you got from those guindaloons."

I got everyone's attention and told them the gist of my lunchtime conversations.

"I remember Pete Aragone," Frank O'Brien said. "Short, dapper guy with an Errol Flynn mustache. Lived in Huntington or someplace on the north shore."

"That's the one," I said, just as my cell phone blasted off and filled the room with *Paint it Black*.

"Answer that, "Kate said. "Mick Jagger is trying to get out of your pocket."

I flipped open the phone to hear Dixie Foster's voice.

"Everything go okay?" I already knew the answer. Wally Danko had called while we were driving to Howell's.

"Fine," she said. "Wally just left, and two investigators met us at the motel. I never had to check on them. Steven Holmes sent Paul Greenberg and Mort Stark. I've known them for years."

"Good. In five hours, you'll be home. Thanks for calling."

I heard nothing for a long moment.

"Dixie?"

"Yes, I'm here. I just want to say thank you…again. Sam, I—"

"Stop. We'll talk when you're home. Don't worry about what's happening down here. I'll let you know what I learn from the FBI. They plan to make a fuss on the Island over all this. Let me know what you hear at the DA's office."

"Can you talk now?"

"No. I'll need a day or so."

"Okay. Call me at home. And I…Thank you, Sam."

"Be careful going over the bridges. Those New York drivers are crazy."

She laughed softly. "Bye, Sammy."

I snapped my phone shut. "Wally just left Dixie at the motel in Chambersburg. Two guys from the DA's office met her. Mission accomplished."

* * * *

Kate and I left Howell's after saying our goodbyes and offering thanks for everyone's time and efforts. Mike and Maggie shrugged them off while O'Brien and Mazzio assured me they'd never forget how much I owed them. But we all knew that anyone of the old bunch would only need to ask, and we'd all do the same for them.

I made the left turn onto US 321 heading home when Kate asked, "Are you sorry to see her go?"

I could have played coy and asked who, but there was no point. "Dixie?"

"Yes."

"Actually, quite the opposite. We all would have been better off if she had never planned her visit."

"Wow."

"Greg would have had no excuse to be here. If he showed up out of the blue, I certainly wouldn't have greeted him with open arms. His goombahs would have had to find a different way to get at me, and Dixie would never have been involved, and… And I don't know exactly what else."

"The bad guys would have sent someone else, sweetie. Or since Vito was already here, use him from the start. He did kill other people, right?"

"Right."

"And once again, you came out smelling like a rose."

I looked to my right for a long moment, and the car began to drift to the left.

"Hey, watch the road."

I steered Kate's Infiniti back to my side of the centerline.

"Why the dirty look?" Kate sounded surprised.

"Smelling like a rose?"

"I know you don't like me to get too serious or poetic about things like this, but *you* know that I'm proud and pleased that, once again, you worked your magic to resolve a nasty situation."

I glanced over at Kate and smiled. "Thanks." I gave her thigh a squeeze.

"Watch the road, please."

We were only half way home when I switched on the satellite radio. Chuck Berry had just finished telling us that he had *No Particular Place to Go,* and the Beatles started in with *Help.*

John Lennon's words hit home.

Help, I need somebody
Help, not just anybody
Help, you know I need somebody
Help!
When I was younger, so much younger than today
I never needed anybody's help in any way
But now these days are gone I'm not so self-assured...
Help me if you can. I'm feeling down
And I do appreciate you being 'round
Help me get my feet back on the ground
Won't you please, please help me?

Was that an omen? I had to admit I was getting too old for things like this. I didn't even want to count all the favors I'd called in. Help indeed.

* * * *

At 9:30 the next morning, Ralph Oliveri called me at home.

"Have you had your coffee yet?"

"Yeah, long time ago. I'm sitting here writing checks and paying a few bills."

"Well, drop everything. Have I got a story for you."

"Speak, Ralphie."

"Yesterday Carl gets called into the chief AUSA's office on the top floor, and he drags me and Bonnie with him. You're gonna love this."

"I'm gonna wet my pants if you don't get on with it."

"Yeah, yeah, okay. Well, your buddy Captain Burchfield is sitting in an interview room when we get there. The chief, his name's Dex Livingston. Some name, huh?"

I laughed and put on a theatrical voice. "Dex Livingston, All-American boy."

"Yeah. A real upward mobile superhero. Anyways, he briefs us on what he wants from Burchfield. Then Carl says Bonnie and I should take a first run at him and see what happens."

Ralph paused for a moment to chuckle.

"And?"

"And the little shit crumbled in about thirty seconds. I just gave him the evil eye, and Bonnie almost had him peeing in his pants."

"Good."

"Yeah. He gave up everything and everybody."

"Specifically?"

"First off, we learned that he gets his horsepower from his father and uncle who own B&B Trucking—big campaign contributors, to the party in general and to Sheriff Joe Don Hartung in particular."

"Sure, B&B operates a fleet of out-of-tune twenty-ton dump trucks that spew black diesel smoke into the atmosphere, ride on bald tires and I'd bet that each truck has at least a half-dozen equipment and safety violations a piece. But you never see a county cop writing them a summons." I snorted in disgust. "And people say contributions are not bribes."

"Aren't you cynical? But on target. B&B's contributions got little Rodney his job and promotions. Far as we can tell, he's not much of a cop, but, man, has he got clout."

"Until now?"

"Right you are. That boy squealed like a pig for a deal. He gave up a county commissioner who initially called Daddy. Daddy, in turn, called Rodney, who had a sit down with the commissioner, who introduced him to your old pal in Prospect, Deputy Mayor Darnell Means."

"So Means was Burchfield's handler."

"Right again. And Means took his orders from that commissioner...another old friend of yours, Micah Blevins."

"I thought so. He's Darnell's uncle. Can you pursue this?"

"Ugh! I'm hurt. Of course, we can. And we have. So far, for spilling his guts and putting everything in a statement, Rodney gets to keep his job, but not his assignment. He'll be moving from Internal Affairs to the jail as an admin officer."

"Good. He belongs in the slammer. Maybe an inmate will take him hostage some day."

"You're so bitter. But you're not alone. Sheriff Joe Don sounded outraged at Rodney's behavior."

"Like he didn't know."

"Of course, he disavowed any knowledge of this little witch hunt and promised to never let something like it happen again. Dex may have a funny name, but nobody laughs when he brings smoke down in the name of the US attorney general."

"Good for Dex. If he can get the AG to give me a pass for just one day, I'd put six in little Rodney's X-ring."

"Hold on to your hatred. You may want to use it on someone else."

"Okay, keep talking."

"After we finished with Rodney, we took a shot at Darnell. But, he acted like more of a tough guy than his comrade. Initially, he wouldn't go for spit with Bonnie and me. The arrogant prick kept playing the lawyer card, claiming to be one. So, Carl and Marty Saunders took a shot. And as you know, they too are lawyers—real ones, not just law school graduates who couldn't pass the Bar. I have to admit, they softened him enough that he gave up his uncle Micah. But he wouldn't put anything in writing."

"Bastard."

"Yeah. Without more to corroborate Burchfield's statement, we know what happened and who did what, but getting a conviction might not be so easy."

"But these pricks were willing to make their deals to crawl back into the woodpile?"

"Sure they were. Don't lose heart, bubbee, I'm not done yet. Carl and Dex the Wonder Boy worked deals that should satisfy you."

"Does it include the death penalty?"

"Don't be absurd. But you won't be going head to head with Darnell any longer. He's resigning as deputy mayor, effectively immediately. And after Dex Baby called the state party chairman threatening an embarrassing situation unequalled in this state since the Scopes trial, we got a callback confirming that Uncle Micah has submitted a letter of resignation as chairman of the county commission for health reasons."

I sighed, long and audibly. "You're right. I'm a realist, and this makes me happy."

"Good. So, may I put another one on my tab of things Sam owes me?"

"Why not? And give one to Bonnie. Thank Carl, too."

"Don't worry about Carl. I think he had an orgasm when he heard we cracked Rodney. Man, does he hate that guy."

"Any news about what your guys in Melville are up to? They making any progress?"

"I'll have to get back to you on that one."

"Thanks, Ralphie. I can't wait to wander upstairs on Monday and see how our mayor took the news. I hope it ruins his weekend. I just have to decide if I should act professional or gloat and shove everything up his political ass."

"Those two options are not necessarily mutually exclusive."

I laughed. "Good point. Thanks again, and let me know what happens in New York."

"Will do. I'll call you."

Chapter Thirty-Four

I'd been doing the cop thing for a long time. While it's not the general rule, there is often a lull after that big one—the case or incident that gets your adrenalin flowing and carries you through the aftermath like a personal supercharger. At times like those, lack of activity is rarely welcome—it only allows you to think about things better stored in the back of your psyche. A quiet Sunday did nothing to dissipate my uneasiness.

I was experiencing one of those days when I returned to work on Monday. Dixie Foster had pulled up to her home on Long Island around two Saturday afternoon and checked in to say she was okay. Of course, I knew she would be, but I still wanted to hear she had gotten home safely. I was beginning to think like my grandmother.

She promised to call again and fill me in on the happenings at the DA's office. But I had to content myself with waiting a day or two for that call.

I also wanted to hear a bottom line from Ralph Oliveri, about what the FBI did in New York—who got pinched and for what.

The local Feds had begun turning Blount County politics on its ear, and I wanted to hear what Mayor Ronnie Shields thought about losing his numbskull deputy, Darnell Means. But at 10:30, Ronnie had still not called down and summoned me for a chat.

I wanted to make sure the rental cabin that John Gallagher's neighbor had so graciously loaned to my crew of out-of-town helpers was left in shipshape condition, and that seemed to be the only thing I could personally control. I walked out to the lobby and confronted that topic.

* * * *

209

"John, did you check your buddy's cabin after the herd of ex-cops left?"

"Yeah, Boss. It's okay."

"You're sure? I want that place looking better than when we moved in."

"Yeah, I'm sure. Everybody cleaned up their own room, and everybody helped clean up the kitchen, dining room and living room. It looks good."

"Do I have to hire a crew of Merry Maids to go over that place? Am I going to get embarrassed when your neighbor starts screaming about us leaving his place a mess?"

"Calm down, Boss. The cabin is spotless. Maggie wouldn't let anyone go until she inspected everything. The cabin's clean. All I need is that bottle of scotch I promised Wilber."

"Your neighbor's name is Wilber?"

Bettye looked up from the report she'd been reading and smiled.

"Yeah," John said.

"Who the hell names a child Wilber anymore? How old is this guy?"

John sighed and tossed his hands in the air. I assumed I had frustrated him. "I don't know, Boss. He looks like forty-something. Wilber was his father's name. He's a junior."

Before I could bitch about parents saddling their children with socially unacceptable names, Bettye interrupted and held her phone at arm's length. "Sam, it's Ralph Oliveri. He says he's got information that will make you plotz—whatever that means."

"Thanks. I'll explain *plotz* later. Switch it to my phone?"

Bettye smiled, fluttered her eyelashes and shooed me toward my office.

I walked behind my desk and grabbed the phone after two rings.

"Good plotz or bad plotz?" I asked.

"I don't know. Good for you I suppose."

"What's that supposed to mean?"

"It means the shit hit the fan up north. You sittin' down?"

"Yeah, I'm in my high priced, overstuffed swivel chair. I'm leaning back now. Okay, I'm comfortable. Go ahead, speak."

"Has anyone called you sarcastic in the last few minutes?"

"Ralph!"

"Okay, okay. I've got a lot to tell you, but you may want it in person. I'm not comfortable doing it over this phone or in your office or mine. There's some very confidential stuff going on here."

"Jesus, what happened?"

"Can you take a drive up here?"

I looked at my watch. "It's quarter to eleven. I could meet you for lunch."

"Let's make this quick. How about a beer at the Crown and Goose?"

"Sure. I'll be there in thirty-five, forty minutes."

"See ya."

I drove north on Alcoa Highway, crossed the Buck Karnes Bridge, and merged onto I-40 eastbound. I got off at the Western Avenue exit and wound my way through the back streets of downtown Knoxville until I found the parking lot across from the Crown and Goose on Central Avenue Pike. I entered the restaurant/pub through the barroom door and found Ralph bellied up to the bar.

"Hey, sport," I said.

"Howzit goin'?" He picked up a three-quarters full pint of lager off the polished surface of the bar. "Let's grab a spot over there."

He pointed to a small round table in an otherwise unoccupied corner of the room.

"Okay, I'll meet you."

I waved to one of the bartenders and ordered a pint of Irish Ale. Ninety seconds later, I sat across from Ralph.

"What's with all the foreign intrigue?" I asked.

"You're not gonna believe this. Or probably you will. This is some shit."

I took a long sip of the dark ale and smacked my lips. It was really quite good. "My bladder ain't what it used to be. Tell me quick before I have to retreat to the men's room."

Ralph shook his head like someone amazed at recent happenings. "I spoke to a guy up in Melville. Yesterday they rounded up all the usual suspects and squeezed their balls in a vice."

After another sip I said, "Those goombahs are used to vices. Did your

211

buddy say they talked without their lawyers?"

"Yeah. Strange, huh? But our guys hit pay dirt."

"Yikes."

"Yeah, I'll say. You won't believe this was so easy, but Jimmy Navarone fell on his sword and flipped on a yet-to-be-disclosed bunch of associates for immunity and relocation to Wit Sec."

"Navarone did what?" Ale almost discharged through my nose. "He's taking responsibility for everything?"

"He admitted sending Vito Cinquemani after Carlo DeCenzo and you. Also for recruiting Buggarelli. It looks like Bugagelli's murder is on Vito, for reasons unknown to Navarone."

"Navarone's a soldier. On whose authority was he working?"

"That's where it gets fuzzy."

"Fuzzy?"

"Yeah. He won't give up LoScalzo Junior or Sonny Musucci. But he'll take all the heat. And help the AUSA up there clear six or eight high profile homicides and provide enough info for him to enhance a couple of big RICO cases they've got pending."

"Let me guess, the perps are not members of the Musucci organization."

"Probably not."

I shook my head in disgust, but with more than the average person's amount of understanding.

"Did he clear the Alphonse DeCenzo murder?"

"He's dancing around that one. Probably hasn't dreamt up a good enough reason for him to have personally wanted DeCenzo dead. And he won't commit to arranging it because that would do wonders to pinpoint who ordered it."

"And the one who ordered it doesn't have a deal with the Justice Department."

"Exactly, but in time anything can be negotiated."

"Sure, he might give up the shooters and *negotiate* not to name the client. The best probable case is that Navarone gives up the two goons that he hired, guys who never knew exactly who ordered the contract. Why not? Hit men are not exactly a dying breed. Two go to the slammer and two more step up for the next job."

Ralph shrugged. "Better than nothing." He sipped his beer.

"This doesn't make a lot of sense. Navarone hasn't explained the reasons for all the murders and the contract on me. Is this AUSA happy only getting Navarone for those things?"

"He'll close some major stuff with Navarone's help. In the end, his scorecard is what matters. You're still alive, and no one is overly concerned about three dead wise guys and a dirty cop."

"And Patsy Junior and Moonface both skate."

"For the time being."

"Don't be naive."

"I'm not. This is a good deal. And we've got a few new angles. We may get something on them in the future."

I couldn't have sounded enthused if I wanted. "Yeah, right. The major shitheads go untouched while Navarone collects his Musucci salary, probably with a bonus, and the Marshal's Service relocates him to a condo in Panama City Beach and protects him—from who? He's going to get all the protection he needs from the goombahs he works for."

"Whom."

"Don't get grammatically correct with me, Ralphie." I stopped to drink half my pint and lowered my voice. "Look, I'm sorry. I shouldn't yell. I just hate to see that moon-faced shitbag go away unscathed."

"Okay, I understand. But you haven't heard everything yet. This may cheer you up a little."

"Yeah?"

"Yeah. Musucci will go on—for now. But we don't know exactly what his future holds. Now here's more startling news."

I raised my eyebrows just to show Ralph I was interested.

"Anthony's new partner in crime, Aiden Hayho, will not be in a position to give you any trouble."

"Oh?"

"A Sergeant Belson at Boston PD homicide reported to our SAC up there that their harbor patrol found Mr. Hayho floating in the Charles River, somewhat weighed down by five rounds in strategic parts of his body—a full house, so to speak—three .45s and a pair of .38s."

"Ouch."

"Yeah. I feel his pain—well almost. Hayho's out of commission and so far, no clues. The slugs match nothing on file for other murders. They used clean guns. No suspects and there is nothing but a lot of conjecture about who ordered the hit."

I downed the remainder of my ale. "Jesus, Gino, why are you doing this to me?"

"Is that just a guess?"

"Yeah, but a damned good one."

"Your new pal is looking out for your welfare."

"And his own." I shook my head and slammed the empty pint glass on the little table.

"You want another of those?" Ralph asked.

"Yes. I'll spend the rest of the day in the men's room, but I want another drink."

Two minutes later, Ralph returned to the table with a pair of fresh pints.

He slid my glass to me and asked, "Can you find out if Gino ordered the hit on Hayho?"

"Sure. We'll sit down for a chat, and he'll confess. You think Gino might have trouble sleeping after this one, and he's just waiting to unburden his soul?"

"Sorry I asked."

"I'll bring up the subject with Gino, but if you guys organize an office pool and bet on possible answers, you'd better pick, 'I don't know what the hell you're talkin' about.' You'll be the big winner."

"I guess."

"This is too easy to understand and too tough to prove. Gino gets pissed at his moron son. He arranges for his old goombahs to step up and apply pressure where needed. He maps out a whole new table of organization for the family from which he wants to retire and makes sure his son knows he's no longer part of that free enterprise system. Then he gets in even more solid with me by ordering a hit on one of the loose cannons who wanted to kill me. He assumes I'll breathe easy and not object."

"Do you object?"

"Boston is not in my geographic area of employ, but I'll call this Belson and see what he can tell me."

"I hear you."

I gulped a sizable portion of my new pint. "And Gino swore to me he was out of the business."

"And you believed him because?"

Chapter Thirty-Five

I drove back to Prospect PD, trotted up the back steps, down the hall and crashed into Bettye's guest chair.

She said, "I'm afraid to ask."

I sighed deeply. "Go ahead."

"Okay, what happened?"

John Gallagher slid his chair closer. "You looked pissed, Boss. What's up?"

I told them everything I learned from Ralph.

Bettye said, "Lord have mercy."

"Holy shit," John added. "Hayho got whacked, too?"

"Yep. Guess who ordered that?"

"Our new neighbor?"

"Who else?"

John shrugged. "But I guess that's good for you. No more troubles."

I rolled my eyes.

Bettye asked, "What are you goin' to do, Sammy?"

"Not much to do. Gino is not going to confess. And if he said something off the record, he could recant the statement and claim everything was done to protect me, his new goombah." I shook my head. "I should find a police job in the Australian Outback."

"Look on the bright side, Boss. Life will now be leisurely."

"John...I don't know what to say."

"You're dumbfounded and flustered."

"Yes, I am. And while I'm trying to alleviate that condition, how about you call all our helpers and tell them how this fiasco played out."

"Okay, Boss, I'll handle it."

* * * *

216

While John did his telephone work, I planned to confront the mayor.

"Betts, I'm going upstairs and force a showdown with Ronnie. Christmas will come and go if I sit here and wait for him to invite me up."

"Oh, darlin' just what do you mean by a *showdown*?"

"Nothing drastic. I can't lose my job, and I won't take advantage of him. He's too easy. But he needs to know exactly how all this political backstabbing ended."

"Want me to call Trudy and say you're comin'?"

"No. He'd only run out the back door. I'll use the element of surprise."

I opened one of the big glass doors to Ronnie's outer office calmly and quietly. Ms. Connor typed away on her computer as I stepped into the room. I noticed that Darnell Means' chair was empty and the usual clutter removed from his desk. Trudy Connor tapped a key, adding a period to the last sentence, looked up at me and smiled.

"Hello, Mr. Jenkins. You doin' aw right today?"

"Hi, Trudy. Is anyone in with Ronnie?"

She didn't answer immediately. She's very protective. I tilted my head and gave her a fatherly look.

"Um, no sir. I don't guess there is."

"Good. I'd like to go in. If it makes you feel better, announce me. But I'd prefer you didn't. If you don't, and he asks, I'll say I didn't give you the option. I'll never let you hang out to dry."

She nodded slowly and gave me a knowing look. The feminine grapevine in the municipal building had been spreading the story about the demise of Darnell Means and the conjecture on the rest of the local political shenanigans from the very beginning to the end.

"I know you wouldn't, sir. You've been getting' a hard time lately. I don't want to add to your aggravation. Go ahead. I don't think he's doin' anythin' important."

"Thank you."

I found Mayor Ronnie Shields behind his immense mahogany desk, his chair turned to face the bay window overlooking the town square, feverishly manipulating his smart phone with both thumbs. I cleared my throat loudly to draw his attention. He spun around and looked up. Ronnie's embarrassed expression made me think I might have caught him sexting some clandestine girlfriend.

He forced a weak smile. "Oh, uh, Sam. I didn't hear ya come in. You doin' aw rot today?"

I nodded. "Hi, Ronnie. Am I interrupting something?"

"Uh, no. I's jest texting LaDonna. Figgered we might could go out ta eat t'night."

"Uh-huh. Got a minute to talk?"

"Uh, sure, sure. Jest lemme finish."

He thumbed in a few more letters, made an exaggerated gesture of pushing the transmit button and sent his message into the ether.

"There ya go." He flashed a big phony smile. "I figgered me and the li'l woman might like ta go ta the Longhorn Steakhouse over Alcoa way. Ya ever been?"

"No."

"Uh, well, yeah. It's good."

"Uh-huh. We need to have a serious conversation."

"I figgered."

He seemed to be *figgering* a lot that day. Ronnie slumped down a few inches in his burgundy leather throne. He wasn't wearing the jacket to his dark gray suit. His white shirt looked fresh and crisp. Gold nugget-shaped cuff links that matched an ostentatious pinkie ring held his French cuffs closed, and his pink and purple paisley tie might have cost as much as a good heart transplant.

"I've had an unreasonably lousy few days," I said. "And much of my trouble was generated by your *former* deputy mayor."

"I know. I know, Sam. And I'm sorry, jest as sorry as a man can be." He squeezed his shoulders together in an odd, contrite manner. He acted very young and vulnerable.

"Are you apologizing because you feel sorry for me or because you played a part in Darnell's plan?"

His eyes popped wide, and he struggled to sit up.

"Do whot? You think—?"

I cut him short. "No, Ronnie, I didn't think you took an active part in that half-assed plot to break my balls. But I find it difficult to believe you knew nothing about the absurd things those three assholes tried to pull off."

He spread his arms out to his sides and began blinking like a camera set on motor drive. "Sam, I assure you I—"

"Okay. Let's leave it at that. We know that Darnell is history in Prospect. And I assume you know what's happening with Rodney Burchfield and Micah Blevins."

He nodded.

"I need you to listen to something, and I suggest you think long and hard about what I say. You should take my advice seriously. Whether you implement my ideas into your professional life is up to you. It's your business, but I feel an obligation to offer an opinion that will be very important to your future." I hoped that sounded menacing enough.

Once again, he began sliding further into the tucked and buttoned seat of his chair. "Yessir, go ahead."

"You're good at your job, Ronnie. No one can argue that. I like you, and I believe you're a basically honest man—not something I'd say about most politicians. But with all due respect, Mr. Mayor, you'd better get your head out of your ass, or someday you're going to find yourself in a situation at least as embarrassing as the one now confronting the three imbeciles who tried to screw me or possibly in one with more serious criminal ramifications."

Ronnie sat there almost immobile, looking like a teenager getting thoroughly dressed down by a stern assistant principal. The more I talked the more he slumped into his chair. I wondered what I'd do if he disappeared beneath his desk.

"You do a fine job running this city. Your problems begin when you get involved with the petty and sometimes borderline illegal favors some nitwit politician calls for."

He dropped his eyes and began picking away at a hangnail on his left thumb.

"I know you don't speak much Latin, but I strongly suggest you forget the term Quid Pro Quo. You keep going to bed with these political shitheads, and someday I won't be able to protect you. You just may find your ass in jail."

"Sam, I—"

"You don't need to explain anything to me. But before you roll over for someone that wants a questionable favor and promises you something in the future, think about the value of what you're looking to get in return. Is it so extravagant that you'd risk losing your family, your reputation, your self-esteem and even your freedom to get it? For God's sake, man, learn to say no."

He looked up and opened his mouth. I held up a hand to keep him from speaking.

"I'm almost finished, and then I'll leave you alone. Here's a quick story about something I learned almost forty years ago, when you were only a little kid. New York was feeling the aftermath of a serious police corruption scandal. Every department in the metropolitan area needed to send home a message to their cops about the importance of professional ethics. But the old way of having a chaplain stand up in front of a recruit class and say, 'Son, don't tarnish the tin,' wasn't going to work. So, a smart cop devised a very simple exercise. He handed every cop who attended an in-service ethics workshop a sheet of paper with twenty values listed. He broke the class into small groups of five or six people each and told them to come to a consensus of the most important five and the least important five. *Five only*, top and bottom. And they had only one hour to accomplish that.

"I won't ask you to guess what happened. I'll tell you. Not one group could totally agree. They all got close—maybe seven or eight choices, but not five. People felt so strongly about their personal convictions that not one swinging ass would give in to his teammates. Heated arguments took place. There were some cops who wouldn't budge.

"I'll make this story as short as possible and tell you that every group in every class placed the same kinds of values on top and bottom. Everyone ranked family, love, peace of mind, freedom and respect highly. Things like money, power, prestige and peer acceptance were always on the bottom—with little or no spiritual value.

"So, ask yourself, what would you lose if you illegally or immorally took steps to gain money, power or prestige and got caught? And, thanks to our three stupid colleagues, you see how easy it is to get pinched. And do you really need these people to consider you one of the good ol' boys?"

He didn't comment. I shook my head.

"Thanks for your time, Ronnie."

I stepped toward his door, and he sighed deeply as I grabbed for the polished brass lever.

"Sam, don't leave yet."

I turned and glared at him.

"Come back. Sit down."

I moved back in front of his desk and looked him in the eye. He nodded slightly and held my gaze.

"Please, sit down," he said.

I dropped into a green guest chair and waited.

"Sam, I'm sorry about what happened to you over the last week—the things those gangsters wanted to do and the things Darnell and his people tried. I'm jest sorry as can be. Please believe that."

I nodded. "I do."

"What you said makes perfect sense, and I'm not makin' excuses. But I know you unnerstand how things have worked for so long."

"Of course I understand, but I'll never condone it." I relaxed my shoulders, let out a long breath and crossed my legs. "Look, Ronnie, I'm not naïve enough to think that favors don't make the world go around. Everybody does them and asks for them, me included. But they can be given and received, and you can still run your shop within the boundaries of morals and reason. And you should never forget that when there's a tossup on what to do, you always base your decision on what's best for the organization. You don't do something for personal profit or gain." I took another breath and shifted uncomfortably in the chair. "I'm lecturing again. I guess I'd better go downstairs and run the PD." I began to stand.

Ronnie shook his head. "Not yet, Sam, I've still got somethin' ta say."

I shrugged and once again settled into the green leather. "It's your dime, boss."

"Darnell is gone. I don't know what he'll do next, but I suppose someone, somewhere will give him a job. He's got politics in his blood, Sam, and his family is well-situated. But I promise you, he's finished in Prospect."

That was both a scary and sobering thought.

"Tomorrow is a new day, Sam. Let's start out fresh. Okay?"

He stood and extended a hand over the wide expanse of his desktop. I stood and shook his hand.

"Friends, Sam?" He flashed his campaign smile.

I wanted to smack him and drive home my points. I didn't.

"You bet, Ronnie."

I left the office with one thought in mind. What could I do to prevent Darnell Means from ever getting another job in the public sector?

Chapter Thirty-Six

My conversation with Ronnie Shields made me tired and disgusted with Blount County, Tennessee. I wanted a drink and wanted to sleep uninterrupted for ten hours. I had worked too many days in a row. Too many things crowded a small space in my mind. I needed a vacation. I wanted to sit on a boat on a big lake, catch fish and extricate Prospect from inside my head. I'm getting terribly selfish in my old age.

But I still felt compelled to do something and still craved a pound of flesh.

Billy Joe Elam was recently promoted to lieutenant at the sheriff's office—but he didn't work there. He was permanently assigned as the personal assistant, bodyguard and general all-around handyman for retired Sessions Court Judge Minas Tipton. I rang Elam's cell phone, exchanged pleasantries and got down to business.

"How's he been doing lately, Billy?"

He sighed before answering. "Mostly okay. He has a few bad days, but so far, nothing serious."

Minas Tipton was ninety-two years old and still one of the most powerful men in the county, perhaps the state.

"Has the doctor made him lay off the booze?"

"Tried to, but it don't do no good. Judge won't listen to nobody. On those bad days, he jest asks for an extra drink or two."

"At his age, why stop now?"

"Be my guess, too."

"Think he's up for a visitor? I don't want to aggravate him, but I need to discuss a little distasteful business."

"I think he'd like ta see ya, Chief. He talked about you jest the other

223

Goodbye!

day, what with the recent troubles in the county. He's wonderin' if ya might not be callin' on him, if fer nuthin' more than ta bitch about the yayhoos they pick ta run this county."

I chuckled. "Sounds like he's prepared. And since he's not on the wagon, I guess he'd appreciate a new supply of Gentleman Jack."

"You know he would. You comin' over now?"

"Now is good for me."

"He's already had lunch, but ya want me to ask Loretta ta fix us some cake or somethin'?"

"I'll let him set another date for a social call. Let's make this simple—a drink in the parlor would be fine."

"Yes, sir. You come when ya can. He's not doin' nothin' but watchin' that damn TV. He could use some company."

"You sound a little frustrated, Billy."

"I hate ta see him get lazy. Nobody pays him visits 'cept you and his granddaughter. He hasn't seen his daughter in months. They had a fallin' out. He needs somethin' ta do. The more he works, the sharper he seems. If you've got a job for him, he'll appreciate it." He paused for a long moment. "Every day I wonder how much more time he's got left." He sniffed. "I'm gonna miss him."

"Yeah, me too. I'll see you in half an hour."

Billy Joe had been a lot chattier than I'd ever heard before. I wondered if he was more worried than he let on, or was I the only one with whom he could voice his concerns for the Judge?

On the way to the Tipton homestead, I stopped at the liquor store in the Browns Creek shopping center on US 321 and picked up a bottle of Glenfiddich for John Gallagher's neighbor, Wilbur Junior, another fifth of Gentleman Jack Daniels for the Judge, and watched my credit card balance soar into the stratosphere. I attempted to tell myself it was only money, but my Scottish bloodline doesn't allow inane statements like that to compute.

That morning, we awoke to a slight drizzle, but when I started my drive to the Judge's home in Maryville, the drizzle increased to a typically gentle, but intense Smoky Mountain rain. I could almost hear Ronnie Milsap singing a song by the same name. The wipers slashed back and forth across the windshield of the Crown Vic as I drove past the elaborate entrance to Maryville College. I turned left on Court Street and made my way to Montvale, which took me to Sandy Springs and from there, I passed many new and old upscale homes until I reached the long private drive to the Georgian revival-style home Minas Tipton built in 1946 when he left the Army.

I parked under an ancient maple, void of leaves and offering little shelter from the rain.

"Nuts!" I said, after looking into the back seat and finding that I had given Kate the umbrella I usually keep there. I grabbed my scaly cap from the front seat and slapped it on. I hate hats, but I'd hate more looking like a half-drowned water rat from the downpour if I walked thirty yards to the front door uncovered.

A column-supported, gabled overhang sheltered me as I pounded the old hand-forged iron doorknocker three times to announce my presence. The noise could have woken the dead.

Less than sixty seconds later, an attractive gray-haired woman, probably a few years older than me, answered the door.

She smiled as she held open the door. "Why hello, Mr. Jenkins. It's been a while since we've seen you."

I pulled off the cap and began unbuttoning my trench coat. "Hi, Loretta. You're looking lovely on this miserable day."

I handed her my hat and coat, but didn't shake like a soaked dog.

"Why thank yew," she said. "It looks like the rain will never let up."

"They say we might get between two and three inches in the next forty-eight hours."

"Oh, Lord have mercy. I might need a canoe ta git home."

"Let's hope not."

Loretta smiled again. "Jest go on inta the parlor. I suspect the Judge will meet ya soon."

I returned the smile and walked through to a living room filled with genuine Federal Period antiques and enough framed political photographs to make Woodward and Bernstein gasp.

The Judge's home felt at least ten degrees warmer than I'd ever consider keeping my place. But, then again, I wasn't ninety-two years old. I hoped that my Right Guard wouldn't fail beneath my Harris Tweed sport jacket.

I didn't wait two minutes before Minas Tipton walked in from his office across the hall, followed by his faithful sidekick, Billy Joe Elam.

Tipton stopped a dozen feet from me, pointed his cane like a dueling pistol and smiled. "Sam Jenkins, you rogue. How you been, son?"

"Not too bad for an old man. How are you doing, Judge?"

He lowered the cane and used it for support as he stepped up to face me.

"Old man? Who are ya kiddin'? If I remember correctly, you're the same age as my daughter. If you're old, what the hell am I?"

We shook hands, he grasping mine with both of his after passing his cane to Billy Joe.

"You're looking pretty good, young feller," I said.

The Judge wore a Tattersall white and blue shirt and knitted navy tie beneath a charcoal gray cardigan and above light gray slacks. That was about as casual as the old cutthroat ever got.

"You are one lyin' Yankee, Sam. I got one foot in the grave, and you're tryin' ta snow me."

"If I had feelings, Your Honor, they'd be hurt." I looked over the old man's shoulder. "Hello, Billy Joe. Good to see you."

He fired off a half smile as he handed the cane back to the judge. "Chief, you doin' aw right t'day?"

Again, the question to which no one expected an answer.

Billy was a big guy, about six-two and heavy, but not fat. He shaved his head and sported a dark, neatly trimmed mustache. He always wore a suit—today a gray pinstripe.

"Grab a chair, Sam," the Judge said, "Come on now, sit down. Sit down."

Before sitting, I handed Billy Joe the bottle of Gentleman Jack and addressed the Judge. "I found an ol' boy named Jack Daniels hitchhiking down the road a'piece and brought him along."

Billy set the bottle on a walnut sideboard, and the Judge beamed.

"Thank ya, Sam. Thank ya indeed. Ya never forget me, do ya?"

"My mother always said, 'Never go visiting empty handed.'"

Tipton snorted and shook his cane at me. "That heathen doctor o' mine, a Hindu or somethin', has been tryin' ta get me ta stop drinkin'. I tell'im I'm too old for that ta make a difference. What else have I got left? Thanks ta Loretta, I eat healthy enough. Gave up cigars twenty years ago. That swarthy rascal expect me ta give up everything?"

I grinned at the old boy's rhetoric. "I don't pay them visits very often," I said and, for luck, knocked on the wooden lamp table next to the sofa where I sat, "but whenever a doctor tells me something I disagree with, I always say the same thing. I sign your checks. That makes me the boss. I appreciate your educated advice, but I'll do as I damn well please."

The Judge treated me to his signature canned laughter. "Ha, ha, ha, ha. No wonder so many people say you're a bastard. But I like ya, Sam—'cause you're honest. Lord knows I don't find many like you in the crowds I run with."

"Thanks for the compliment, but to hell with the people who call me a bastard."

"Ha, ha, ha, ha," he said again. "You still drinkin' scotch? Course ya are. Billy, get the Chief his usual. Can't understand it myself. Stuff tastes like iodine ta me. Billy, I'll have some o' that good Tennessee sippin' whiskey if ya please."

I sat on a red and white striped sofa across from the Judge who had dropped into a wing-backed chair. Billy Joe handed me a short glass with two cubes and an inch and a half of Famous Grouse scotch. The Judge hated the whisky, but loved the label. Tipton received roughly the same dose of Gentleman Jack.

The old man knocked back almost half the contents of his glass and smacked his lips. "Rainy days like this give me pains I wouldn't wish on a Democrat. Ha, ha, ha, ha."

"I know the feeling." I raised my glass to him and Billy Joe. "Cheers, gentlemen."

The Judge nodded and Billy took a sip from his glass.

"I wish ya would have called earlier, Sam. We could have had lunch. But Billy Joe here says you've got some bidness ya want ta discuss."

"I won't pussyfoot around, Judge, because I know you've heard about what Micah Blevins and his two pet chimps tried to do to me."

He didn't let me finish. "Never could abide those Blevins folk. The other two, I know by name only. What is it you want, Sam? That US attorney not punish them enough for ya?"

227

I shook my head. "It's not that. Micah is too old to make another run for public office and the Burchfield boy is a gutless little stink bug who'll count his blessings he's still got a job. If Joe Dee Hartung ever throws him out, he couldn't find work pumping gas. It's Darnell Means I worry about."

The judge took another drink, lowered his eyes and looked at me through snow-white eyebrows. "Your former deputy mayor."

I nodded. "I'm going to give you something, and you can do with it as you see fit. Maybe I'm projecting something for the future that will never happen, but I'll let you consider the possibilities—and the fallout that could be more than embarrassing."

I pulled a photocopy of one of Prospect PD's field interrogation reports from the inside pocket of my jacket and unfolded it.

"I know you're familiar with our UR-18s. This one should be of special interest." I held it up for him to see.

"Billy." The judge flicked a hand in my direction.

Lieutenant Elam stepped toward me. I stood and handed him the report.

"Officer Harlan Flatt happened to be on the outskirts of Townsend one night when he found someone parked in the rest area on the north side of US 321."

The judge raised his eyebrows as Billy Joe handed him the five-by-seven inch piece of paper. The old man put on a pair of reading glasses he snatched from the table to the left of his chair.

"I know Harley Flatt," he said. "Good policeman."

I nodded as he began reading.

"Subject here is Darnell Means," he said. "What was that boy doin' in *that* rest area at 12:30 at night?" He dropped the glasses back onto the table.

"That's the sixty-four-dollar question. As you know, that rest area is an infamous spot frequented by male prostitutes and an occasional female of the same ilk. It's gotten so much bad publicity that regular folks won't go near it after dark."

Tipton nodded. "I know all that, Sam. What did young Means have ta say for himself?"

"Just what Harley wrote down. He felt tired and stopped for a rest."

"Lord have mercy. Means jest lives down the road in Maryville with his wife. Sounds like hogwash ta me."

"Me, too. Now, here's the potential problem. Guys who patronize prostitutes won't stop. They have an abnormal need that never gets satisfied. And Means considers himself an up-and-coming politician. This recent episode of attempting to sandbag me cost him his job in Prospect, but he'll find a new mentor, someone other than Micah Blevins and start stuffing campaign envelopes and sucking up to the right people to get himself a future endorsement."

The Judge listened patiently and nodded in agreement.

"Someday," I said, "he'll be given a job in the public sector. And someday another cop will catch him in flagrante delicto with a paid man, woman or sheep to whom he's not married. You know better than I what embarrassment that will cause the political party with which he's affiliated."

Tipton shook his head vigorously. "I do. I do indeed. This is the Bible Belt, for God's sake. Average people will commit the same stupid acts, but those hypocrites won't tolerate that behavior in public servants. Means is a damn idiot. And you're right about a potential embarrassment. It's jest waitin' ta happen. You're right indeed." He shook his head several more times. "And why'd you sit on this, Sam?"

"Self preservation. Who wants a bucket of manure dumped in his living room? I talked to Darnell about this—told him to get his act together. That might have influenced him for a day or two at most, and then he got vindictive. The kid is a self-centered fool with a serious mean streak—along with his off-color propensities.

"For spite I could have dropped this on my friends in the media. But what would that have done? Prospect would have looked like Sodom and Gomorrah in the Smokies, and Ronnie Shields would have had a stroke. The city had enough embarrassment after the Buck Webbster scandal."

"Of course, of course. Thank you, Sam. I appreciate this." He waved the field interrogation card at me. "I assure you, I'll take care of this."

The Judge downed the remainder of his drink. I took a quick glance at Billy Joe who had been looking at me. He half smirked and raised his eyebrows.

Chapter Thirty-Seven

I didn't get the ten hours sleep I wanted, neither that night nor the next. I wasn't sure whether I should blame the recent events or simply remember that I haven't slept well for decades. A good night for me is five or six hours sleep. Better, is a night without the weird dreams that wake me up in a less than desirable state of mind.

My most recently featured nocturnal saga had me falling off a bulkheaded shoreline into a dark body of water. As I thrashed around like an idiot rather than swimming for a nearby boarding ladder, which I could have accomplished when I was five years old, I panicked when I noticed that the almost black water felt oily and smelled like death. I attempted to wipe the viscous liquid from my body just as an old Army "Mike" boat, specifically, an LCM-8; a flat-bottomed, square-nosed affair about seventy-five feet long and twenty feet wide charged straight for me. It was the Noah's Ark of johnboats—normally used to transport troops and tactical vehicles in amphibious operations.

I struggled to swim away using a combination dog paddle and drowning man stroke. As I flapped my arms like a madman, making no headway, the boat veered off sharply, away from the bulkhead. As it turned, I saw thousands of snelled fishhooks towed from the stern of the Mike boat on long leaders of monofilament swinging in my direction. Afraid that I'd get hooked and helplessly dragged in the roiling wake, I wrapped my hands around several dozen of the lines and let the boat tow me away from the land. I blinked and squinted as the water splashed on my face, and as I looked up toward the top of the transom, I saw Vito Cinquemani staring down at me, grinning like a malevolent clown.

I awoke abruptly and tried to shake off the nightmare. Once I cleared my head, I considered putting Dr. Freud on speed dial.

* * * *

Bad dreams notwithstanding, John Gallagher was correct; our world leveled off and, for at least forty-eight hours, became tranquil—until Bo Stallins called me.

I found myself back in the same spot where this chapter of my life began—Blount Memorial Hospital. I met Bo in the same place with him leaning against the wall near the triage station, across from the emergency room entrance. But this time he didn't escort me down to the morgue. Instead, we took an elevator up two floors to a private recovery room just down the hall from the ICU.

"Thought you'd wanna hear about this," Bo said.

"Why would you think I'd give a rat's ass about him?"

"Kinda saves you the trouble o' doin' it your own se'f."

"Gimme a break. I've got better things to do in life."

"Well, he was your former boss."

"Horseshit. He wasn't in my chain of command. He was a scrotum head who worked for the same employer."

"Lord have mercy, but ain't you soundin' angry."

Stallins was enjoying himself entirely too much.

"Back to my previous statement, gimme a break."

He laughed like a little kid who just saw his best friend wet his pants. "Wanna see him?"

"Not especially," I said. "But since you dragged me down here for some perverse reason, why not?"

I followed him into a room bleached out by fluorescent lighting. The hospital bed had been tilted part way up elevating the patient's head. Small machines, monitors and hanging plastic bags surrounded Darnell Means, each connected to him by tubes and wires. Thick layers of gauze bandages covered his wrists and extended up onto his forearms making him look like Popeye the Sailorman. His eyes were closed. The machine measuring his pulse, body temperature and heart rate peeped occasionally.

"What do the doctors say?" I whispered.

"Oh, he's gonna make it," Bo said softly. "Lost some blood, but not enough ta kill him."

"He cut his wrists." I didn't try to disguise the derision in my voice. "What kind of man cuts his wrists?"

Bo smiled.

"Men step in front of a speeding subway or eat a 12 gauge. He wanted someone to find him and save his miserable ass."

"Well, maybe you're right. But since we ain't got too many subways in Blount County and I guess he decided not to splatter his brains on the bathroom ceiling, he settled for cuttin' his wrists with a steak knife."

"Couldn't even get a suicide right. Asshole."

"Can you think of anyone who might have wanted to do this, makin' it look like a suicide?"

"Only anyone who met him and especially me. What's he say?"

"Says he ain't in the position to talk yet."

"I repeat. He's an asshole."

"Man, but ain't you bitter." He said that with an adolescent smile.

"Why are you gloating?"

"Me?" The smile intensified.

Before I could comment further, Darnell moaned. We looked at him. During that moment of silence, he opened his eyes and looked at me. I looked back.

In retrospect, I probably wanted to smirk, but even I couldn't kick that pathetic specimen while he was down that low.

"You should charge him with attempted suicide." I turned to face Stallins.

"Don't ya jest love our jobs?"

I poked Stallins in the shoulder. "We done here?"

"Be my guess."

In the hall, I said, "You're a sick man."

He laughed like a fool. "You got any idea why he'd do this? Doc said I could talk to him, but at the moment, he ain't sayin' much."

"I know exactly why he did it. But why should I tell you?"

"'Cause we'uns are best buddies?"

"And people say I'm a piece of work."

"Come on, what set ol' Darnell off?"

"Simple, his political party just handed him his walking papers and ruined the boy's dreams and aspirations for a life in politics."

"You're gonna have ta explain that in more detail."

"Okay, but let's go back to that same table at Howell's, order two more beers, and I'll give you all the gory details."

* * * *

The relative lack of activity at work over the last two days bothered me. There was really nothing wrong, but I began to get impatient waiting for Gino Musucci to mention something about the recent developments in New York that I knew he was aware of. So, when there's a lack of action in my life and my deficit of patience leaps to the forefront, I tend to stir any convenient pot to see what might float to the surface. I called Gino.

"We need to talk," I said.

"'Bout what?"

"Things. Recent things."

"Whaddaya talkin' about?"

"The last time we had lunch, you bought. It's my turn. You hungry?"

"Jeez. I got my lawyer here. We're goin' over the contract ta build my house."

"I thought you already signed a contract and the builder started breaking ground."

"Yeah, I did. And they did. But the lawyer said I shouldda waited for him. So, now he's here, and he's reading the contract."

"Is he looking for ways to screw the people building your house?"

"He's lookin' to keep me from gettin' screwed."

"I'll take your word for it. Look, attorneys have to eat just as you and I have to eat. Bring him. Unless you'd rather not have him listen to our conversation."

"What the hell are you talkin' about?"

"I'm talking about what's happened in New York. And more importantly what happened in Boston. Capiche?"

"Yeah, yeah, yeah, I hear ya. Okay, let's have lunch. Just you and me. What time?"

"I'm easy. When can you ditch the mouthpiece, and meet me at the Villa Napoli?"

He must have been looking at his Rolex or thinking because he didn't answer immediately. "How about one?"

"Good. I'll call Nicky. We need table 35."

* * * *

I arrived at ten to one, sat down and asked Rosie to send me a glass of wine and put in an order for two portions of fried calamari as our appetizers. In two minutes, Vinnie brought me a glass of Sangiovese. Gino arrived, stylishly late and alone, at 1:05.

We shook hands, he sat and told Rosie "Tell the kid ta bring me a scotch and soda with a lot o' ice."

Rosie smiled and headed toward the bar and her son Vincent.

"So what's got your shorts in a twist?" Gino asked.

"I thought you would have called me, considering what's been happening up north. I felt neglected."

He shook his head. "I'm tryin' ta build a house here. I got other things on my mind."

"Good. I wish you good luck and fair weather. I hope you get in ahead of schedule."

"Yeah, thanks."

"You're welcome." I took a sip of wine. "I assume you've heard that Jimmy Navarone is taking the fall for almost everything that happened?"

He nodded thoughtfully. "Yeah, Jimmy's a head case, but he's a standup guy."

I rolled my eyes. "Swell. But there's one item not accounted for."

"What's that?"

"Your son's Irish playmate, Aiden Hayho was killed and tossed into the Charles River."

Gino was about to address that issue when Vinnie showed up with his scotch.

"Thanks, kid," Gino said.

"Sure, Mr. Musucci. Would you like me to send a waitress over?"

"Give us ten minutes, Vinnie," I said, wanting to show Gino who was in control.

"You got it, Mr. Jenkins."

Vinnie disappeared, and I looked Gino in the eye. "We were about to discuss the demise of Mr. Hayho."

"Yeah, right." He shrugged. "Shame, he's got a family. But that's good for you, no?"

I nodded. "Yes. In the big scheme of things, Hayho's death eliminated one person who might continue to complicate my life. But I can't go around wishing people who don't like me to vanish, can I?"

Gino took a sip of scotch. "Where are you goin' with this?"

"I'd like to know who did it."

"You workin' cases in Boston now?"

"No, a cop named Frank Belson is, but like the numbskull who reads the *National Enquirer*, I've got an inquiring mind, and I need to know."

"And you think I had him capped?"

"Did you?"

"I oughta tell you to kiss my ass, but that wouldn't be neighborly."

He gulped his drink and looked annoyed.

I sighed. "Do you have an educated guess who might have killed him?"

"He was an asshole. From what I hear that bogtrotter pissed off a lot o' people. They say a couple o' spooks nailed him. He musta pissed off the one who runs all the whores in Boston, Tony Whatshisname."

"Tony Marcus. Maybe, but I don't believe in coincidence, do you?"

"'Ey, whattaya want from me?"

"Okay, Gino, simple English. You say you didn't put out a contract on Hayho. Fine, I believe you. I'm not wired, and I know what it takes to sustain a conviction. Even if you confessed over lunch, you could recant tomorrow, and I'd have squat. Nothing would happen except my curiosity would be satisfied. Okay, let's try a new tack. Did you speak to *anyone* about me and did you show *him* the photocopy I handed you?"

After another sip of scotch he answered. "I did."

"What did *he* say?"

"*He* called you a few choice names."

"I'm not surprised. Good. He thinks I'm serious."

"Yeah, he *knows* you're serious. He's stupid, but not that stupid."

"That's a relief. I'd hate to… You know what I'm saying. And you know I have no desire to bother your granddaughter and her little one. I merely wanted to capture Anthony's attention."

He nodded. "I know that. And you got his attention…again. He explained the past to me. He believes you. And I understand why you did what you did. So, okay, it's done. I told him that if *anyone* did something to you or someone you care about he'd be held responsible and pay the price. He believes me, too."

"Do you think that Anthony would have offed Hayho to keep that loose cannon from doing something that might put him and his family in jeopardy?"

Gino shrugged. "He might have thought about it, but between me and Petey Aragone, the word went out that no one, and I mean no one, was to take on any work from my son."

"Interesting."

"Yeah, very. Now look, I'm asking you as a gentleman, is everything we say here confidential or what?"

I took a long moment to give him the impression that I had to think about that. "Sure. No problem. This is just between us. Think of me as you do your priest."

I smiled. He didn't.

"Good."

"When you spoke to Anthony, were you two alone?"

"No, I wanted Carolyn there. I wanted her to understand the situation entirely. So, if Anthony got his stupid ass up in the air, she'd bring him down to earth. She's got a good head, that Jew. And she can handle my son. She's smart."

"Her maiden name was Baransky, right?"

"Yeah. Harry Baransky's daughter."

"Your accountant."

"Right."

"He still alive?"

"Passed away five, six years ago."

"Hmmm. What did Carolyn say when you relayed my message?"

"She had a few choice words for you, too. Said things I never heard from a woman before."

"Besides that."

"She told Anthony that if he tried anything funny and got you pissed, she'd cut his balls off."

"Ouch. Tough girl."

"You don't know the half of it."

"So, to make her life simple, she'd do anything to keep my people away from her family?"

"Whadda you think?"

"I think you and Pete Aragone can keep the boys from doing a job for Anthony. I'm sure you conveyed to them that Sonny no longer occupies a place on the organizational chart, and any contractual work which may, in the past, have been business as usual, is no longer fair game."

"You know, you sound like a fuckin' lawyer."

"I'm sure you meant that as a compliment, but please don't say anything like that in the future."

That got a smile from Gino as a waitress dropped off our appetizers.

"What's this?" Gino asked.

"Your appetizer. Fried calamari. The red stuff is marinara sauce."

Gino made a face. "I can see that."

"You said you liked squid."

"You remembered."

"I'm a police chief. I remember everything."

"Jesus Christ. I'm supposed ta believe that?"

I grinned.

The waitress asked, "Are you gentlemen ready to order?"

I looked up and smiled. "Haven't decided yet. Give us a few minutes, but in the meantime, would you bring my father a glass of wine? What would you like, Pop?"

"You're somethin' else," Gino said. "I'll have what he's drinkin'."

The waitress left. Gino spread out his napkin and dug in. I got back on topic.

"Did you or Pete tell the boys that Carolyn's wishes were also off limits? With Hayho out of the picture and her thumbs on Sonny's nuts, I'd be happy, and the kids would be perfectly safe."

He stopped with a forkful of calamari half way to his mouth and looked at me as if I just suggested Mother Theresa had gotten collared for solicitation.

I shrugged. "I'm just saying."

Gino set down his fork and gulped almost all his scotch. "Holy shit. Fuckin' broads. You might be right."

* * * *

I had one more job to finish before I could really put this caper to rest.

The sign above the storefront read:
The Brothers Fine—Diamonds and Other FINE Jewelry
Inside, I found a short, thin man of about seventy sitting on a stool behind the counter reading a newspaper. A New York Mets ball cap covered most of his short red hair.

"Hey, Bernie," I said. "How's it going?"

"Sam. Hello. How are ya? How ya doin'? How ya been?" All that came out with almost a singsong delivery.

I pointed at his copy of The Maryville Times. "You reading about all the dirty little secrets in Blount County?"

He pushed his wire-rimmed bifocals back on the bridge of his nose with the middle finger of his right hand. Where had I seen that before?

"Oy, it's no different here than in New York—only on a smaller scale."

I didn't exactly agree, but I let that one slide and inquired about his brother. "How's Irv doing? He's not working today?"

He waved both hands at me, a gesture only a New Yorker would use. "Don't ask. He's at the dentist again. His teet' he gets cleaned four times a year. That's too much."

"Hmmm. I guess he's got a reason."

"The reason is he's nuts. Mashugana. I can't deal wit' him."

So much for brotherly love.

I shrugged.

Bernie smiled. "What can I do for ya?"

"I need an eighteen inch gold chain. Something pretty thin so it can go through a jump ring."

"Sure. Anything for you. I got a tray right here."

Bernie jumped off the stool and scurried to his left behind the counter. A moment later, he reappeared with two black velvet lined trays.

"Here's some chains. These are plain to use wit' a pendant." He pointed to the tray on the right. "If that's what you want, 'cause these are more fancy." He pointed to the tray on the left.

"These," I pointed at the appropriate tray, "to use with a pendant."

"Pick what you want."

I chose a simple affair that looked like what Dixie once had holding her jade butterfly.

"This will do it," I said. "How much?"

"For you?"

"Who else?"

"Will that be cash?"

"Would you prefer cash?" Stupid question.

He shrugged. "Hey, cash is cash. You understand what I'm sayin'."

"Cash it is."

He gave me a number, and I started peeling off greenbacks.

When I got to the end, I said, "I'll toss in an extra ten. Can you send this to New York for me?"

I handed him a slip of paper with Dixie's name and address.

Bernie read my note. "Ah, that's on Long Island. Suffolk County, right?"

"Correct. Send the package insured, okay?"

"Always."

"Thanks."

"Hey, anytime. You're always a gentleman. And thank you. Thank you very much." He pushed his glasses up again.

* * * *

"You haven't mentioned it, but did you call Dixie?" Kate asked.

"No, she called me. Couple days ago."

"And?"

"She's home. The trip was uneventful. Typical delays at the GW and Throgs Neck Bridges. Construction on the Grand Central caused a traffic jam before she could merge onto the LIE. But after that, it was clear sailing eastbound."

"Nothing more?"

"No, she's back to work. Life is as it once was."

"Do you really believe that?"

"No, of course not. She went through a lot."

I began sprinkling spices on two filets of steelhead trout.

Kate stepped closer to me. "What are you putting on there?"

"Powdered garlic, kosher salt, lemon pepper, tarragon, and lemon slices."

"Go easy on the garlic."

"You like how I make fish. Mind your own business."

"You don't need so much garlic."

"Yeah, sure."

She stepped to my right further down the counter. "How would you like these potatoes?"

"Salt, pepper, some crushed garlic and then butter and half and half."

"Again, with the garlic. You're obsessed."

"I draw the line with oatmeal and corn flakes, but all other foods need garlic."

Kate took a sip of chardonnay and continued to dice a potato and drop the little cubes into a bowl of cold water. "Did you ever find out who killed that man up in Boston?"

"Just a guess, but I'd say Sonny Musucci's wife took out an unsanctioned contract. She was present when Gino conveyed my thoughts about leaving us alone and what I might do if he persisted with his half-assed revenge scheme. Also, Gino mentioned that word on the street is two black thugs killed Hayho. Those old-fashioned mob guys don't use black shooters. I figure Carolyn thought she could keep Sonny in line, but exercised no control over his partner from bean town. Hence, she eliminated her problem."

"Wow, don't mess with Carolyn."

"It's nature. What mother wouldn't kill to protect her offspring? Carolyn happens to be a lioness who knows how to hire a pair of hit men."

"Hmmm. Do I want to know what your thoughts were about being left alone?"

"Not really. I asked Byron Thomas to help in conveying a message. He established that I still have considerable influence in the Musucci neighborhood."

Kate shook her head. "Is life really back as it once was for us?"

"Certainly, unless you keep objecting to my use of garlic."

THE END

Look for Sam Jenkins and all the regular characters from
East Tennessee to appear again in
A BLEAK PROSPECT
coming next year from Melange Books, LLC.

About the Author

Wayne Zurl grew up on Long Island and retired after twenty years with the Suffolk County Police Department, one of the largest municipal law enforcement agencies in New York and the nation. For thirteen of those years he served as a section commander supervising investigators. He is a graduate of SUNY, Empire State College and served on active duty in the US Army during the Vietnam War and later in the reserves. Zurl left New York to live in the foothills of the Great Smoky Mountains of Tennessee with his wife, Barbara.

Zurl has won Eric Hoffer and Indie Book Awards, and was named a finalist for a Montaigne Medal and First Horizon Book Award. He has written seven novels and more than twenty novelettes in the Sam Jenkins mystery series.

Author Links:
Author website: http://www.waynezurlbooks.net
Twitter: http://www.twitter.com/#!/waynezurl
Facebook: http://www.facebook.com/waynezurl

Other books by the author at Melange

From New York to the Smokies
A Leprechaun's Lament
Heroes and Lovers
Pigeon River Blues
A Touch of Morning Calm
A Can of Worms
A New Prospect

www.ingramcontent.com/pod-product-compliance
Lightning Source LLC
Chambersburg PA
CBHW050509260626
47157CB00004B/1258